AURORA DAWN

Works by Herman Wouk

Aurora Dawn
City Boy
The Caine Mutiny
Marjorie Morningstar
Youngblood Hawke
Don't Stop the Carnival
The Winds of War
War and Remembrance
Inside, Outside

This Is My God (nonfiction)
The Caine Mutiny Court-Martial (play)

HERMAN WOUK

AURORA DAWN

or, The True History of Andrew Reale
Containing a Faithful Account of the
Great Riot, together with the Complete
Texts of Michael Wilde's Oration and
Father Stanfield's Sermon

With Drawings by Alajalov

LITTLE, BROWN AND COMPANY
Boston   Toronto   London

ISBN 0-316-95509-4

Library of Congress
Cataloging-in-Publication
information is available.

10 9 8 7 6 5 4 3 2 1

MV NY

*Published simultaneously in Canada
by Little, Brown & Company (Canada) Limited*

Printed in the United States of America

This story is dedicated to Irwin Edman

PREFACE TO THE ILLUSTRATED EDITION

IN THE DECADE since this novel was written, radio has given way to television.

Who would have dreamed, a mere ten years ago, that the money-crammed world of radio was a bubble about to burst?

Or who would dare to suggest today that commercial television —with its mammoth floods of cash, its huge studios, its racketing parlor games, its jigging advertisements, its solemn potentates— may someday be pricked by an electrician who will devise a more agreeable entertainment tool?

Meantime sponsors are still sponsors; glamor girls are glamor girls; cringing executives are cringing executives; and ulcers apparently are ulcers. In the halls of Radio City, between rounds of the unchanging hot fight for place and money, boys still chase girls. The little box that sold us things in our homes by giving us music, yarns, and jokes, gratis, has yielded to a larger box that does the same job with pictures added. Miracles of engineering; trifles of amusement; at the heart of it all, the peddler. *Plus ça change . . . !*

Television, like radio before it, is a revival of an old form of entertainment, the free show or come-on. The purpose of the come-on is only incidentally to please. The main idea is to catch attention, hold it, and then divert it to whatever the man is selling. The instability inherent in this amalgam of sketchy amusement and hard-eyed selling causes most of the abuses and follies

7

pictured in *Aurora Dawn*. None of that has changed. Aurora Dawn is a more rampant goddess than ever.

The American people have accepted their broadcast entertainment in the ancient form of the free show. Who are novelists that they should prescribe differently? To crusade against the come-on seems faintly ridiculous. But perhaps it may be useful to raise a laugh against some of its abuses, which are not so much monstrous or evil as just plain silly, and unworthy of an adult civilization.

H.W.

Fire Island,
August, 1956.

PREFACE TO THE FIRST EDITION

*T*HE WRITING *of this story was begun to relieve the tedium of military service at sea in wartime, which, as sailors will tell you, is even more monotonous than in peace, despite occasional interruptions of terror.* AURORA DAWN *was started aboard the* U.S.S. Zane *at Tulagi, Solomon Islands, in 1943. The first part was completed aboard the* U.S.S. Southard *at Okinawa in 1945; and the book was finished at Northport, Long Island, in May, 1946.*

This chronology is introduced because of the recent publication of more than one novel intended to expose the inner workings of the advertising industry, which this story may be said to resemble in setting and certain points of detail, though not, surely, in matter or manner. The coincidence, such as it is, cannot injure the other books, and will not greatly distract the readers of this one. Let me be forgiven, then, for publishing AURORA DAWN *unaltered in those points of similarity.*

"The artist's revenge" is a familiar flaw in satire. In so far as a grudge dictates the writing of any portion of a book, the work is marred; humor is one thing, lampoon another. The true distinction of humor is that it raises laughter against folly, not against individual fools. All this is self-evident. Yet, to go on in the pertinent words of LeSage, "There are some people in the world so mischievous as not to read a word without applying the vicious or ridiculous characters it may happen to contain to eminent or popular individuals. I protest publicly against the pretended discovery of any such likenesses. My purpose was to represent human life historically as it exists; God forbid I should hold myself out as a portrait painter."

THE AUTHOR

Northport, Long Island,
July, 1946.

9

CONTENTS

13

PART I

The Beautiful Brahmin–
The Faithful Shepherd–
Bezalel

CHAPTER 1

*Introducing us to Andrew Reale
and the Beautiful Brahmin.*

ONCE THERE was a bright and spirited young man named Andrew Reale, who came into the world in the second decade of the twentieth century and grew up in the third and fourth, and was thus convinced that the road to happiness lay in becoming very rich very quickly. To call this a conviction is not quite clear, because in the same way he was convinced that it was a good idea to breathe—that is, he did not expect either conviction to be challenged and could hardly have argued very successfully in their support. It was, rather, an axiom on which his life rested. This is enough of his background to explain most of his actions, at least in the early stages of his history, and we may proceed forthwith to the first moment in his life which merits the attention of the reader. He is on a train speeding south from New York, and is staring very hard at a strange young lady.

Walk through any express train on the Atlantic coast and you will probably chance upon a girl much like this one. Usually one, occasionally two, and sometimes a group of them, can be seen lounging in the parlor car. They are as easy to pick out as high-caste Brahmins, and can be recognized by the same tokens: their distinctive clothing, their pallid, abstracted air of human beings devoted to a difficult ideal, their unique and uniform way of wearing their hair, and the paint marks on their faces. They are known in journalists' jargon as "glamour debs," a sect of young females which adheres to its symbols with a fanaticism rare in these lax times. The girl who sat in the parlor chair opposite our hero, intent on a copy of *Harper's Bazaar*, was to the other members of her cult as the Dalai Lama is said to be to the monks of Tibet. Other girls painted their mouths into a vicious pout, according to the fashion; she had achieved a glaring red masterpiece of a pout. Something in the arrangement of her hair made the current mode, a rather disheveled, unsightly one to the detached view, suddenly seem as inevitable as the outcome of a tragedy. Her sweater was a triumph. There was a mathematically exact carelessness in the way the sleeves were pushed up above her elbows. There was an ineffable machine-tooled precision in the slovenly way it hung about her hips. Girls with a less happy touch labored for hours, all in vain, to achieve this uncannily correct, cut-crystal sloppiness.

This charmer was as responsive to Andrew Reale's presence as a compass needle is to the North Pole, but, unlike it (to the confusion of behaviorists, who say that human beings are soulless bundles of responses to external stimuli), she would not make the slightest movement in his direction. In fact, the magazine seemed increasingly to claim her attention until in her absorption she resembled a nun conning her breviary. Andrew's consciousness, on the other hand, was divided among three ideas in the following order of importance: the beautiful young stranger, the secret mission on which he was traveling, and, receding into the background, the sweet savor of his early-morning farewell to his sweetheart, Laura Beaton. This last, a photographer's model of extravagant attractiveness, had been renamed "Honey" by the agency which managed her fortunes, and it was by that name that Andrew thought of her. He loved Honey with his whole

—*Known in journalists' jargon as "glamour debs"*—

soul; she loved him no less in return, and their marriage and everlasting bliss awaited only what they both called "a good time for it." From this, and from the fact that she was now third in his thoughts while a strange female was first, the casual reader may instantly surmise that Andrew was a light and wicked philanderer, ignoring the simple truth that a young man is less likely to focus his thoughts on a girl who loves him unreservedly than on one whom he suspects of not loving him at all or of loving somebody else as much.

Admirable or no, our hero was becoming more and more contemplative of schemes having no more worthy goal than the opening of conversation with the young lady. He continued his uneasy glances, and she her impassive reading, until she was betrayed; for, like an animal with a will of its own, her hand crept softly up to her hair and bestowed an anxious, supervisory caress over her entire coiffure. Poor Andrew watched the hand with an eager eye that did not miss the delicacy of its form or the sweet grace of its little movements. It seemed to him that her fingers, as they curled around a roll of her hair, were like a half-opened white rose. Honey's hands were more beautiful; it cost an advertising agency a standard price of one hundred dollars to associate the charm of her hands with a brand of lotion or nail polish; but Honey's hands were in New York, and this hand was, at the moment, within a few inches of Andrew's nose. As the girl stirred her hair, a faint, delicious perfume came to his nostrils, which flared enthusiastically.

At this moment, both became aware of a sound which broke disagreeably on their pleasant silent duel. Starting as a low, vague rasp, it had risen in a few seconds to an assertive, slabbering, unmistakable human snore. Leaning back heavily in a chair behind the young lady, a stout, gray, sparse-haired man, to whom half-opened white roses were evidently objects of little concern, had given up the effort of maintaining his dignity as a human being on an early-morning train, and had subsided into the character of a large, breathing mound of flesh. The sound rose in volume. The fair one caught Andrew's eye, and she smiled. Andrew burst out laughing.

"He's happy," he observed, with a nod at the sleeper, from whose limp, fat fingers a dead cigar was just dropping to the floor.

"But I'm not," said the girl, putting her hands to her ears.

A colored steward in a very white coat came through the corridor announcing breakfast. Andrew was only twenty-five, but in his work he had already learned to seize the passing chance. He invited her to breakfast with the pleasantest smile he could muster, a smile implying that he was offering her, entirely impersonally, an escape from distress. Andrew smiled often, and most often when he was trying to gain a point. He had extremely white, perfectly even and well-shaped teeth. The girl's glance seemed to flutter for a fraction of a second to the teeth and away from them: it happened so quickly no one could be sure. In any case, with a slight, modest pause, she thanked him very much and accepted.

Let us leave them for a moment on their way to this breakfast, which is to be such a turning point in Andrew's life, leading him into an unexpected series of adventures, upsetting his career, and giving him an all-too-intimate knowledge of a lover's anguish, and let us consider the familiar irony of destiny as demonstrated anew at this instant by Andrew and his unknown young beauty. All they know is that they are about to breakfast in pleasurable company. Andrew is a-tingle with elation, and his beloved Honey, to whom he has never been unfaithful, is temporarily out of his mind. The difficult mission on which his train is whisking him through the winter brownness of Maryland is out of his mind, too. Such is the effect of a bud of seventeen on an ambitious young man, and so far is he from keeping in mind what long shadows such trivial events may throw across the green paths of the future; even as a young shoot can cast a shadow across the entire breadth of a park in the slant light of dawn.

And the young lady? Reader, I yield to the lady novelists, who insist that young ladies have minds and will describe their workings at length. Like the Ptolemaic celestial hypothesis, this approach is productive of believable results, within the limits of its first assumption. This historian is unable to report what the young lady was thinking and submits that perhaps it does not matter. Few people are governed by what young ladies think—least of all the young ladies themselves. This deep, but entirely wholesome truth, is one of the many that will be demonstrated in the course of this astonishing tale.

CHAPTER 2

Telling a little more about the Beautiful Brahmin
and bringing Andrew farther along his way.

I̵T DOES NOT OCCUR to city dwellers that American railroads are
capillaries of mechanized civilization threading through a wilder-
ness, until they come one day as Andrew Reale did to the end of
the line, and must eke out the rest of a journey over roads as
primitive as any in such backward countries as Afghanistan or
India. True, we usually climb aboard a bus instead of a yak or
oxcart to convey us the rest of the way, but if the superiority of
our culture is to rest on a showdown between the yak and the
country bus, we had better take pause. The yak is slow, fractious,
and not amenable to assembly on a conveyor belt; but does the
bus give milk, or answer to its name in the night, or bring out
new models each spring by simple association with other busses?
It is a nice dispute, but it borders on political economy, and the
reader will doubtless be pleased if it is left unresolved in order
that the narrative may gather speed.

Andrew clung to the dusty, cracked leather seat of the bus
which jolted from Providence, West Virginia, to the township
of Smithville (distance forty-one miles), over an asphalt road
sagging piteously here and there where a frugal contractor had

economized on asphalt and reaped the rewards of individual enterprise. He made an earnest effort to close his mind to the beauty of the sunset over the darkening hills and to arrange his thoughts for the accomplishment of the task ahead. It was the first major enterprise of its kind with which he had been entrusted; it called for daring, quick wit, ability to act singlehanded, and an unwillingness to be daunted, all of which qualities he had displayed to such a degree in the last two years that at last this mission had fallen into his hands. Pride and eagerness glowed within him when he thought of it. With the best will in the world he set about imagining the obstacles he was likely to encounter, and the measures he must take to win the day; but in whatever direction he set the current of his thoughts, it invariably meandered over an erratic, untraceable course until at last it found sea level in a troubled contemplation of his hours at breakfast and thereafter with the Beautiful Brahmin. A casual flirtation—the mere automatic response of a healthy young man—had led him into a startling experience.

There are many solid metaphysical arguments buttressing Bishop Berkeley's great philosophical doctrine that no reality exists outside the mind, but empirical evidence supporting it is thought to be rare; yet there is one phenomenon utterly Berkeleian in its nature and effect, and that is a cup of coffee in the morning. It sheds so dulcet a radiance on a world which twenty seconds before the ingestion of the brew usually seems stale and grisly, that we are forced to conclude the sudden change is not in the world but in the mental tone of the observer. Now—follow this philosophical thread carefully—if you admit the fact that the external world has actually remained unchanged while seeming to undergo a profound metamorphosis in the instance of coffee in the morning, are you not forced to go the rest of the way and admit that at all times, even if less obviously, the aspect of the world must depend on the mental state of the observer? And since aspect is all we can ever know (experience being only perceivable through the window of the brain), are you not thrust into the arms of Berkeley and compelled to the position that the world as we know it is a product of the mind? Leaving you to consider at leisure the staggering implications of the thesis, we return to our tale.

The coffee our hero shared at breakfast with the Beautiful Brahmin had its customary effect both on the external world and the internal Andrew. In its train of familiar miracles it brought the gift of tongues. Andrew commenced to talk with amazing vivacity and speed and—as he was now recalling with acute spasms of embarrassment as the bus jounced along the hilly road— he did not stop talking for hours.

The breakfast had begun awkwardly and silently enough. The girl kept her eyes either on the food, which she attacked with great vigor, or out the window during the intervals between dishes—which were brief, for they were the only people in the car and the steward, energized by a night's sleep, hovered over them and sprang panther-like on empty plates and glasses. Her persistent avoidance of his glance gave him the chance to scrutinize her. Aside from the very thick, very black hair and the alert brown eyes it was hard to select her distinguishing features. She had clothed, coiffed, and painted herself with such mannequin accuracy that she seemed an embodied fashion rather than a person: the Last Word made Flesh. Gradually, however, beneath the gilding he discerned a satisfying lily. He first noticed how young she was: her skin was firm and clear under the rouge and powder, and the curves in her cheeks had the roundness of true girlhood despite the shadows under her eyes which betokened late hours rather than advanced years. Her mouth was a full eighth of an inch smaller all around than her carmine artistry pretended, and in its natural state would have made a better match with her short and snub nose. Her hands continually drew his eyes; all their movements were tense, and in every action they fell into naturally graceful lines, like cats. They were too small and too

26

thin to be really beautiful, he supposed. Her body was shaped according to the Providential design for young ladies' bodies, and was most pleasing to the view of Andrew whose eyes deviated little from the Providential design for young men's eyes.

He would probably have been surprised to know that all this while the girl was also giving him a thorough if less direct scrutiny, that she had noted with approval the squareness of his shoulders, clearly a tribute to his bone structure and not to his tailor, as well as his curly, sandy hair, his handsome if rather long features, and above all his well-cut mouth and the flashing beauties it contained. He would surely have been astonished to know that she had given him a nickname within five minutes of the moment she had first noticed him, and that she thought of him as "Teeth."

Along came the coffee, and the silence was broken up, all too effectively for Andrew. It was bad enough that he told her the story of his life, from his origin in a Colorado schoolmaster's abode through his young manhood at Yale and his rapid rise since then into his present position (described at length, with names of important people studding the account like raisins in a bun); bad enough that he soared into a dithyramb on his plans for the future, omitting, as he now recalled with shame, any reference to his beloved Honey; but, worst of all, in an incredible fit of weak-mindedness, he disclosed to her the whole truth of his present enterprise. A tingle of remorse crawled up his spine as he recalled this. The girl had been a gratifying audience. It is in the nature of young ladies, under certain circumstances, to rise to great heights of prolonged and artistic listening. She fixed grave wide eyes on him when he was serious, sparkled with laughter at his least sally, filled his pauses with quick questions that spurred him on to fresh bursts of monologue, and, in fine, subtly conveyed to him that he was rather a wonderful fellow. This elevation of spirits lasted for several hours, as they moved back to the parlor car without a perceptible break in Andrew's epic narrative. Then, just when he was becoming a bit giddy with success (this was in the midst of spilling the beans about his current adventure), he thought he noticed a tinge of quiet amusement in the girl's expression at the wrong times. It was impossible to define, much less to challenge, but, illusion or no, it made him uneasy, and his cataract of eloquence suddenly lagged to a sluggish trickle, then vanished into the sands of silence.

The girl, after vainly roweling him with a few more questions, seemed satisfied that he was exhausted, and did a little talking herself. Said she:

"Well, I'm certainly glad I ran into you. This train kills me. I die every time I have to take it. If you knew how I hate to get up at three o'clock in the morning to catch a train—I don't as a rule, I just stay up all night, that's what I did last night, I rhumba'd until two-thirty, then went home, took a shower and changed my clothes. I probably look it. I loathe morning trains. I feel so filthy by ten o'clock I can't bear to touch myself. My face is like a cobblestone street this minute—" (it was like the blandest Bavarian cream, thought Andrew). "The only good thing about this train is that it gets me to Mother's six o'clock at night, so that all I do is eat dinner and fall into bed, and that's one day out of two killed. I visit my mother every now and then for a weekend—my parents are divorced. Mother isn't bad, but her husband is the most horrible goon."—(The word "goon," a main prop of young feminine conversation in that decade, meant a harmless, fumbling, shambling fellow. It was loosely used to refer to all males except the current object of a young lady's desire.)—"He writes books—novels and biographies and things that nobody ever buys. He just wrote a book about Thomas Chatterton—what a pancake! Not that he has to worry, the way Mother is fixed. He was her English instructor at Wellesley. Mother is a terrific aesthete, anyway. She had a sensational crush on him at college—that's nothing, I'm mad about my Fine Arts prof and I know he's a goon, but I can't help it, he's beautiful—but Mother never outgrew hers. Three and a half years after she married Dad she decided that old Literature A-4 was the big thing in her life, and she walked out on Dad, leaving me in the middle. I don't mind it except when I have to visit Mother and her husband is around. He's so polite I could die, and I know he despises me. He always wants to talk about school, and how my painting is coming, and—"

"Do you paint?" interrupted Andrew with some surprise.

"Yes. Oh, nothing good, yet—but I'll be good some day. I'm going to spend a year in Mexico as soon as I can talk Dad into it. He thinks I'll be raped by bandits."

The porter here put his head and one white, starched sleeve into the car and announced, "Washington, D.C., five minutes."

"I change here," said the girl, cutting off her disquisition abruptly and beginning to wriggle into a camel's hair coat as lethally casual as the rest of her array. Andrew sprang to her assistance and swung a heavy bag down from the rack overhead with an easy movement which the girl watched appreciatively. For more than an hour Andrew had been increasingly aware of a very awkward circumstance; they had, in this extravagant barter of confidences, somehow neglected the detail of exchanging names. They had passed so quickly from formality to the mushroom intimacy which springs up between wayfarers who have no intention of meeting again, that Andrew had never introduced himself. He suddenly felt that this was an impossible situation, that she must not be allowed to vanish into anonymity.

"It's a little late for this," said he with one of his pearliest smiles, "but anyway, my name's Andrew Reale."

"How do you do, Mr. Reale?" said the girl. "It's been fun talking to you." With this she relapsed into a prim silence, smoothed her coat once more, and folded her gloved little hands in her lap with feline grace.

Andrew, a little out of countenance, could not let it rest so. "And what's yours?" he inquired, with as much genial music as he could instill into the syllables.

The girl looked at him with the oddest expression, not unfriendly but quite unfathomable. "I don't feel like telling you," she said in a pleasant and definite tone.

Our hero felt as though he had driven a car at sixty miles an hour into a rock wall. The three minutes that elapsed before the train drew into the station were longer than the three hours which had preceded them. Not another word could Andrew dredge out of his reservoir of easy civilities. He sat in silence until the girl left the car with an airy "So long," which he barely acknowledged with a grated "Good-by."

As Andrew's recollections took this turn he groaned aloud. "Rough road if you ain't used to it," commented the bus driver, a gaunt gray man in blue denims, taking a bite from a large meat sandwich and resting it on the ledge in front of him.

"How much longer to Smithville?" asked Andrew, bracing himself on his bucking seat.

"We're right close," answered the driver out of that side of his mouth which was unoccupied, "but you got to change to another bus and it's a good twenty minutes from the depot to Father Stanfield's."

Andrew started. "Who said I was going to see Father Stanfield?"

"I been on this run a long time." The driver threw a brief, knowing look at Andrew. "You a tobacco man?"

"No," said Andrew, and with the bitter reflection that conversations with strangers did not lead him into felicity, he became silent. The bus joggled, bumped, and whined its way through the deepening twilight. Andrew forced himself to attempt a cool estimate of his indiscretion with the Beautiful Brahmin. After much shuffling of the ingredients of the situation, he decided that the girl would probably forget him and everything he had said the moment she resumed her devotional reading in *Harper's Bazaar;* also that she was an irritating child, and that some vestige of collegiate emotions was responsible for his passing interest. This palatable conclusion freed his thoughts for weightier matters during the rest of the journey.

In Smithville, a town so entirely composed of low clapboard structures that it seemed to have skipped the brick-baking stage of history, Andrew changed to a bus labeled "SPECIAL—FOLD." The coach was crowded with an oddly non-rural group of tourists, apparently in holiday spirits, well dressed for the most part and conversing noisily. As Andrew took his seat the driver dimmed the interior lights and started out along the asphalt highway, but soon swung off to a hard dirt road which climbed, descended, twisted, and wove like an Indian trail through thick overhanging trees that obscured the starlight. The forgotten scent of night dew on green leaves came agreeably to Andrew as the bus crushed past branches. Ten minutes of this plunge through forest darkness, and the bus came over a hill and around a bend and was suddenly out in the clear, rolling down a road that sloped into a wide valley. In the center of the valley floor Andrew could see a cluster of buildings, toward which the bus drove with increasing speed. The chatter of the tourists became more animated, and they began to put on their coats and pick up packages. Soon the bus turned through an illuminated archway of stone on which was fastened in white wooden letters the legend: "The Fold of the Faithful Shepherd." Rattling the pebbles of a wide gravel driveway, the vehicle slowed and stopped before a large, auditorium-like building with a wide, whitewashed porch brilliantly lit up.

"Tabernacle," said the driver. All the tourists descended and streamed eagerly up the steps of the porch—all except Andrew, who lingered behind and asked the driver, "Which one is the Old House?"

The driver, a wiry little man who looked strangely neat in a gray mail-order suit, eyed Andrew carefully; then he nodded his head at one of the shadowy buildings, "That's it." Andrew thanked him and picking up his bag walked off into the gloom.

Reader, the author is as anxious as you to follow him to the Old House, whatever that may be, and uncover the nature of this mission which is to bring him closer to the riches his young heart ardently desires. However, we can no longer delay acquainting you with the true heroine of this tale who even at this instant is engaged in an astonishing episode herself. She is none other than Laura, alias Honey, Beaton; but it would be as incongruous to meet her at the end of a chapter as it would be to see the dawn break in the west at the end of a wearying day.

CHAPTER 3

*Containing some very sound reflections
and introducing the heroine and other
important personages.*

*B*ULFINCH OPENS HIS GREAT "Mythology" with the poignant words, "The religions of ancient Greece and Rome are extinct. The so-called divinities of Olympus have not a single worshiper among living men." Since this is true one might think that the nine Muses who were minor deities in the Zeus heaven would have lost religious currency, too, but, mysteriously, they have survived Olympus, and are evoked by poets even unto this day. Indeed, there has been talk of a tenth, "American Muse," who presumably is to descend from the nonexistent Olympian heaven and sing of railroad trains, smoking factories, broad fields of waving alfalfa, the sweat of workers, and similar objects of the modern poetic phrensy. Now, present-day authors are technically hobbled by a definite religious tradition that limits their range of invocation to the divine or holy personages of the Scriptures if, indeed, they have any religion at all. Invocation is a sound, necessary practice in instances such as the present, when the author frankly requires supernatural aid to sing the praises of a heroine whose beauty and worth far exceed his capacity for wielding language;

33

but how can he call on a Muse who has been an exploded myth, an exorcised hobgoblin, for some two thousand years? Shall he invoke the shade of Solomon, who sang the praises of his love well enough? Alas, the higher critics of the Bible now assure us that Solomon probably never lived, and that if he did live he was a barbaric Syrian chief named Suleimo, and that in any case the Song of Songs is not by him at all, but is a clumsy Hebrew paraphrase of a certain well-known Greek love dialogue—so corrupted, it is true, as to be entirely unrecognizable—which only proves the backwardness of the Semitic adapters.

No, this is the twentieth century, and science alone can aid us; psychology, to be exact, which has developed the great principle of the association of ideas. This thesis states that if one thing is emphatically presented in juxtaposition with another thing, the animal and human minds (between which there is no distinction except unscientific prejudice) will inevitably come to connect the two. Shakespeare, for instance, in such lines as

"But soft! What light through yonder window breaks?
It is the East, and Juliet is the sun,"

was groping toward this principle which has been refined today into the subtle superposition of the picture of a partly clad girl's body on the billboard image of everything from motor cars to coffins. It is to psychology, therefore, and the association of ideas, that we turn to help us bring Laura Beaton before you.

Softly, softly, on viol, harpsichord, and flute, play the sweetest crystal melody that Mozart ever wrote. Blow, pink-and-white cherry blossoms, bravely blow in the sharp zephyrs of spring under a cool blue sky, and let little children laugh with silver glee, and let us hear their laughter faintly from afar. Open the fragrant chest of memory, and let us take out the most precious, muskiest remembrance, for now we are to recall the diamond moment of youth when we sat close to our secret beloved in the darkness, and heard the trivial song which had somehow come to imprison

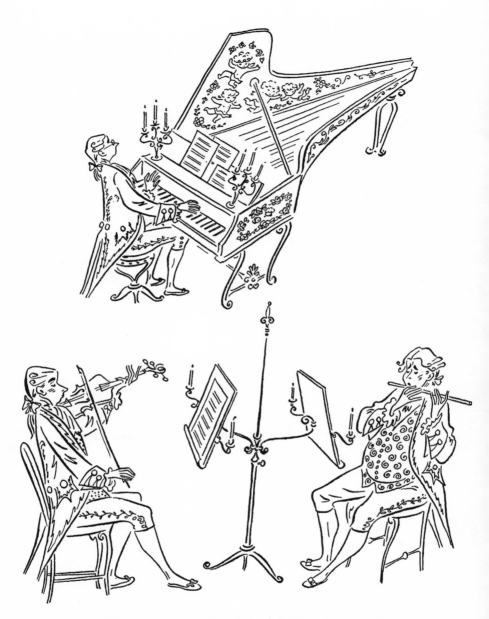

—The sweetest crystal melody that Mozart ever wrote—

the wild, piercing essence of first love . . . and our hands touched, and a delicious shiver shook us.

The curtain rises on Laura.

In a white silk slip she sat, brushing her glorious hair and talking calmly and cheerfully with her mother. Her hair was long and golden, and so heavy that she could not wash it without cloistering herself for a whole day. Her eyes, very large and gray-blue, and set wide apart under light, arched eyebrows and a square brow, had usually a frank and somewhat merry look; but sometimes, as now when her mother made a quaint and touching remark, they could all at once blink into a softness that might melt the heart of a corporation lawyer. She had a straight nose, and a jaw which might have had almost too firm a set, had not the sweet curves of flesh in her cheeks softened the line. Her inviting mouth, with its slightly protruding lower lip, was so lovely that cigarette advertisers paid remarkable sums to have their various brands photographed between or near those lips. (She always threw the cigarette away with a grimace when the pose was completed.)

But your eyes are straying to her other charms. Yes, that perfect bust which she confined habitually out of modesty and not to assist sculptural Nature, now stood out in clear beauty beneath the silk. Her body was straight, strong and tall as years of western outdoors and food could make it, and the sweet, exciting outward curve of her hips swept down into the finest, shapeliest, whitest legs and feet in the world. This rare being was encased in a smooth, healthy skin that looked as though it would be electric to the touch, and, as she was now wearing his engagement ring, it is not amiss to say that Andrew had once or twice found it so.

With infinite regret we must now go back twenty-five years. Briefly, you must know that she was the only daughter of a Congregationalist minister named Gideon James Beaton and his wife, Anna Wilson Beaton, whom he had found and married in Albuquerque, New Mexico, six months after he had arrived there in 1912 to preach the Word in that wide, sun-baked territory. Gideon Beaton had come from an eastern divinity school in answer to a letter from the shepherdless congregation to his dean. His first sermon, an abstruse dissertation on the Book of Jonah emphasizing the necessity of following the call to preach God's Word wherever it might be on pain of finding oneself in the dark hell of the fish's belly if one denied the call, was addressed to his inner self rather than to the congregation, to whom, indeed, it was not quite complimentary; but the flock, paying slack heed to the thread of his argument, was thoroughly won over by his deep, resonant voice, his pale yet manly good looks, and the intense sincerity of his words and gestures. No member of the laity was more impressed than Anna Wilson, gay and pretty daughter of a prosperous ranchman, who had reached the distressing age of twenty-five with her heart undented by the awkward assaults of the scions of local good families. Overnight her religious conscience awakened, and she realized with shame how she had neglected her duties to the church. She revived the languishing Junior Social Circle, volunteered to take the Sunday school children on summer picnics, contributed her sweet soprano voice to the choir, organized several suppers, and, in short, much to her astonishment, was proposed to by Reverend Beaton a half year to the day after he preached his first sermon. Her family consented with mixed feelings to this union with the cloth, and pretty Anna Wilson became the consort of a man of God.

In the years that followed, Anna's face gradually set in a permanent expression of puzzled and hurt surprise, so often were such feelings uppermost in her soul. Alas for the maidens who dash into wedlock expecting it to be an endless odorous lane of lilacs overhead and roses underfoot! The transition was very hard for Anna. Gideon Beaton was a religious man as well as a minister: gentle as a child in most matters, and adamantly willful as a child where principles of faith were concerned. It was his conviction that the Lord would provide, and he gave away all the money that came into his hands. Anna eventually learned to practice innocent deceptions and squirrel away occasional sums for the family's use, but to come to this from the insouciant, selfish spending in her parents' well-to-do home took years of bewilderment not seldom punctuated with tears. Deprived of most of the lighthearted self-indulgence of her girlhood, she developed a fantastic sweet tooth; her manner of nibbling at cakes, holding them to her mouth in two dainty hands, together with her practice of storing away money in hidden places, caused her husband to nickname her "Squirrel" in their private moments of endearment. These were many; indeed, they loved each other, and were innocent enough to be completely, unreflectively pleased with this love, not having any other experience with which to compare it and not being aware of the explicit standards set forth in modern treatises on the mechanics of connubial bliss, or the transcendent ecstasies hinted at in French novels. They grew old together in the unconscious contentment which the loose nomenclature of former days called happiness. Gideon passed away peacefully—after a heart illness of two days' duration—at the age of fifty.

Anna Beaton was left with their only child, Laura, then a ripening girl of eighteen. Her bachelor brother, Tom Wilson, who had inherited the ranch, urged her to come there to live, but Laura had other ideas. Already she knew that she was extraordinarily good-looking. Her mirror confirmed the testimony of the endless sighs and languishments of high-school and college swains. She knew, moreover, that she was lucky enough to have honorably vendible beauty; that is, she sensed that she was a born model, and was eager to go to New York to start earning a living. Her heart was completely her own. Had it been the fashion of the century, twenty boys in Albuquerque would have drowned themselves for her sake, but we live in trifling times, and they had all contented themselves with morose interludes lasting from a week to (in the case of the cadaverous, mustached high-school poet, Ed Hasley) four months, during which they had stupefied them-

39

selves with soft or hard drinks and violent jazz dancing, and had then all found other, more grateful loves. The fair Laura could therefore wish to leave Albuquerque without a qualm, since nothing ties down a young girl except family affection or romantic love. Not so her mother; she was as hard to uproot as the birch tree, which seems light and pliable, but has an iron grasp on its few feet of earth. In the clash of wills that resulted, Laura's character began to emerge from her aura of loveliness. When her mother saw her begin to carry out her threat to go to New York alone—Laura came into the house one afternoon followed by a truck driver carrying an enormous trunk—Mrs. Beaton burst into tears and yielded. Then the girl and the woman, who in that moment exchanged their life roles of protector and protected, fell into each other's arms and cried. And Laura, conscious of her new mastery, was sweetly penitent and insisted on staying; and her mother, who felt a strange mixture of vexation and warm, flooding relief at bending once again to a beloved will, was just as insistent on going. So the pathetic scene played itself out, and plans for departure were made and soon executed.

And thus, patient reader, we are back in the apartment of mother and daughter Beaton on Seventh Avenue in the upper Fifties in New York, pleasantly furnished with the aid of Laura's earnings and kept spotless by Mrs. Beaton's energetic, instinctive neatness; and Laura (now Honey) having completed her toilet, is putting on a simple black frock with a silver clasp at the throat, preparatory to going out to dinner.

"Well, Laura," says Mrs. Beaton, beaming at her child's beauty, which gladdened the trim, modernistic bedroom, "I always said you were going to marry a millionaire." (Indeed she *had* always said it; by actual count, perhaps five thousand times in the last ten years.) "It looks as though you're on your way to it, after all."

Laura turned deep, reproachful eyes at her. "Mother, how can you talk like that?"

"Stranger things happen here in New York," said the old lady with a very knowing look.

In an emphatic gesture, Laura presented her engagement ring within an inch of her mother's eyes.

"I haven't anything against Andrew; he's a lovely boy," said Mrs. Beaton in an injured tone, retreating and picking up a sugar wafer from a tray on the night table, "but there's many a slip—"

"Mother." A girl can put an exquisite edge on the homely word. "Stephen English is almost old enough to be my father. He only asked me to dinner because Mr. Marquis asked Sandra, and we were all sitting together. And if I so much as thought of him as a rival to Andy I wouldn't have said yes. I couldn't very well be rude to Mr. Marquis when we practically live off the account."

"What was Mr. English doing at the press party?" asked her mother.

"I don't know." As she talked, Honey put mysterious touches to her face, hair, and dress that seemed as necessary as colored spotlights on a rainbow. "This is the third time I've seen him. Every time Aurora Dawn starts a new program they throw one of these parties for about six awful looking radio critics and ten models and a few of the company bigwigs—and he's always there. Sandra says his bank owns Aurora Dawn, even though Mr. Marquis is president. Mr. English took Madge Anderson to dinner last time, and she told us he was perfectly lovely to her, and never so much as—you know, a thorough gentleman."

"I should expect so, with his background," said her mother. "And it's only natural for a man who's divorced to be lonely. They're really most susceptible then. I do hope you'll be nice to him. After all—"

"Of *course* I'll be nice to him," cried Laura impatiently. "Would I go to dinner with him if I expected to be unpleasant?"

"You know what I mean," said her mother. "You needn't act like an old married woman. I mean, you're still a young girl."

"Mother, if you're suggesting that I should flirt with Stephen English—"

"Laura, why do you always twist my meaning? If a wealthy and cultured gentleman is going to fall in love with you, you don't have to encourage him. Heavens, no man needs encouragement to do that. I don't blame Mr. English one bit for feeling as he does. But you should be kind to him."

"Mr. English is *not* in love with me," said Laura vehemently, "but you're beginning to make me think I'm being disloyal to Andy by going. Maybe I'll just telephone your precious millionaire and tell him I can't—"

"You'll do no such thing," her mother cried. "How can you dream of being so ill-mannered? Simply because I make a little joke about your marrying a millionaire—you know I've always said you would—you fly into the most dreadful temper! Really, Laura!"

The shrewd reader will guess from our heroine's irritability that her mother had prodded a tender spot. The fact is, Honey was aware of being a little more elated about this dinner engagement than she had a right to be, and, with feminine logic, she was angry at her mother for exhibiting precisely the same elation. Mr. English had not caused a ripple in her feelings she was sure—for they were a placid, bottomless pool of love for Andrew—but his reputation and wealth dazzled her, and his manner had been pleasant, even attractive, despite his graying hair and somewhat worn face. In the most unaccountable way she had found herself feeling sorry for him and desirous of pleasing him, so she had accepted his invitation to dinner with something like alacrity. This startled her as soon as she was aware of it, for it was the first time since Andrew had won her heart that she had felt anything but boredom in carrying out the social duties necessary to her bread-winning. She had known many moneyed men, if none quite so rich as English, so it was not merely the wealth that excited her, as it did her mother. But, whatever the cause, she knew she was a little disturbed, and was disturbed at the disturbance.

The ringing of the house telephone put an end to the silent soliloquy in which she had been acknowledging some justice in her mother's reproach. A hasty kiss on her parent's withered-apple cheek, and she snatched a sable-trimmed black cloth coat from a chair and went out—with the assurance that she would be home early—leaving her mother to answer the telephone and say that Miss Beaton was on her way down.

As she hung up the receiver and wandered into the kitchen to mix herself some chocolate milk, Mrs. Beaton reflected sadly that she would have liked to meet Mr. English. She knew that it was Laura's rule not to bring into her home gentlemen to whom it was expedient to be pleasant, and she took pride in the knowledge that Honey's closed apartment door was a jest among the other models; but she felt that the rule might have been waived in the case of the millionaire. (In the sense that he represented infinity in the scale of desirable sons-in-law, logicians would have verified Mrs. Beaton's instinctive belief that ordinary concepts could not be applied to him.) But how like her father Laura had been, thought the old lady, in her flare of temper at the idea of compromise with principle! The least suggestion of tampering with good faith, and the Beaton blood took to arms. . . .

Her reverie was interrupted by the sound of the front door opening, and Honey's voice calling gaily, "Mother, are you dressed? We have a visitor."

Mrs. Beaton's heart bounded. She glanced quickly at the reflection of herself in the glass of the cupboard, brushed a few cracker crumbs off the lace collar of her brown dress, straightened her skirt and trotted out of the kitchen, saying, "Laura, the house is in such a mess!"

"Don't fuss, Mother." Laura was playing with her gloves and smiling mischievously. "This is Mr. Stephen English."

English held out a lean brown hand, and firmly shook the timid little paw that Mrs. Beaton extended. "Don't blame your daughter, Mrs. Beaton," he said. "I asked if I might come up to meet you."

"Oh, I'm delighted, of course, Mr. English," said Mrs. Beaton. "If you'll make allowances, do come in and sit down for a moment."

Saying that he should like to very much, the visitor at once divested himself of a handsome tweed coat, which Laura hung with hers in the hall closet while her mother eyed English covertly. A very distinguished gentleman, she concluded immediately. How easy it was to tell breeding! His healthy, tanned face had something youthful about it, despite a heavy sprinkling of gray at the sides of his head and marked lines around the eyes and on his brow. His mouth was untightened as a boy's, and his eyes had an inquisitive, humorous look more suitable to a youngster of twenty-eight than to a man in his middle forties. His clothes, too, were youthful: smartly cut tweeds of a greenish brown mixture, with clipped tie and abbreviated collar of self-conscious elegance. He followed Laura into the apartment with an erect, supple gait. Not the least, not the *least*, bit too old for a girl of twenty-two. . . . Laura was old for her age, besides. (Thus Mrs. Beaton, to her inner self.)

"Will you have some sherry wine, Mr. English?" said Mrs. Beaton as they sat down in the living room. "I'm sorry we don't keep whisky. Mr. Beaton was the leading minister of Albuquerque when he was alive, and so we never—" As she paused, the guest said affably that sherry was his favorite before-dinner drink. He added, looking around at the neat room, "We really didn't walk in at such a bad time, did we?"

"Oh, that's Laura for you," said Mrs. Beaton. "She's such a wonderful housekeeper, I never lift a finger. Here she straightened the whole place before she left and I never even knew. Now don't you move, dear, I'll get the wine." With a radiant smile at her peerless daughter, she vanished into the kitchen.

"So your name is Laura," said English. "What an immense improvement over Honey! I'll never call you anything else."

"'Honey' was the Pandar Agency's invention, not mine," said Laura.

"A good one," said English. "When you're your own stock in trade, it's a good idea to have a brand name; but Laura . . . Laura—" As he repeated the syllables he smiled at her.

The smile tells all to the knowing eye. Palmistry is cant, handwriting analysis is fallible, and dreams give only a vague sort of information in Freud's fashionable revival of Joseph's art, but the smile is the key to character. Let a man but bare his teeth; he bares his soul. Much so-called feminine intuition is a direct, half-conscious estimate based on such subtle clues. English's smile left Laura in the dark. One corner of his mouth moved more than the other, so that while one side of his face was lit up with friendly amusement, the other side seemed to be waiting reservedly for the mirth to subside into care. His intentions for good or evil, which Laura had often surmised in men, without knowing just how, from a single expression around the mouth—these she could not read. A trace of wistfulness she thought she detected was so incongruous with all she knew of him that she was inclined to suspect his whole manner of being assumed, but she could not be sure. She found herself looking into his eyes and smiling back at him.

"I like your suit," she said.

"Thank you. I like your dress," answered English with a glance that backed up the remark with much sincerity.

Mrs. Beaton came brightly into the room, bearing a tray with a bottle of imported sherry, three tapering glasses and a tray of crackers. "Well, are you two growing impatient?" she said, setting the tray down on a low table in front of the sofa where Laura and her guest were lolling at ease. "Laura, you sit back, I'll pour." Laura had not moved, but Mrs. Beaton gave her a loving little push and proceeded to fill the glasses. "Heavens, if I left it to her

I'd never stir, Mr. English. I suppose it's the Wilson in her. I was that way with my mother. It never occurred to me to do anything but wait hand and foot on her, that is, until I married Reverend Beaton. Then he became the whole world, of course. Very old-fashioned, I suppose, but that's what we all are, just old-fashioned folks. Why, when President Wilson stopped at our ranch for three whole days—he did, you know, during his second campaign; father and he were first cousins—he was just the same. Plain? 'Fred,' he said to my father, 'if I find you putting yourself out I'll move into a hotel immediately. I want to eat when you eat, sleep when you sleep. I'm not the President here, I'm just one of the family.' That was a Wilson for you. I was just a youngster, but I remember it as though it were yesterday. You know, I've always thought Laura looked a little bit like Woodrow Wilson. Only around the eyes, of course. But that same keen, spiritual look—"

"Oh, Mother, really," cried Laura, gradually crimsoning through this discourse.

"Laura, you're so modest it's aggravating," declared her mother. "Honestly, now, Mr. English, for a girl who was voted the most beautiful in New York at the Photographers' Convention only last August, you'd think she was Plain Jane, and ready to die of shame. Of course it's becoming in a way, a Christian girl should always be humble in her heart, as her dear father used to say, but Laura carries it to such an extreme—"

"Well, I hardly blame her for disclaiming the resemblance to Woodrow Wilson," said English. "Still, I think I see what you mean about her eyes." Whereupon he availed himself of the opportunity to gaze so deeply into the fair Honey's orbs, that the girl felt no more blood could possibly crowd its way into her face.

"Of course, just look at them," said Mrs. Beaton (which suggestion was superfluous). "Reverend Beaton and I had decided before she was born to name her Woodrow; but wouldn't you know, she came along and fooled us," she added with an arch giggle.

"This conversation is embarrassing me very much," protested Laura truthfully, but not looking terribly displeased, as she sipped her wine.

"Well, you two young people had just better run along then," replied Mrs. Beaton with mock severity. "I'm sure Mr. English has other ideas than to sit around all night talking to an old lady. Although it was very thoughtful to pay me a visit," she said, glancing demurely at the guest.

"I am thoroughly enjoying myself," he returned, emptying his glass and settling back on the sofa. "Tell me more about Laura, Mrs. Beaton. Was she a pretty baby?"

"Well," began the mother, drawing a long breath, "you won't believe it, but for the first two months she was ugly as a monkey. Dear me, I'll never forget her Uncle Tom saying—" But here she was interrupted by Laura, who jumped to her feet, exclaiming, "We *had* better go. I am not going to agonize through the stories of my childhood."

English rose with her. "Some other time, I'd like to hear what Uncle Tom said," he smiled at Mrs. Beaton. "Thank you for the wine. I'm glad Laura brought me up for a moment."

"Do come again," said the mother, as English helped Laura with her coat and then donned his own. "You have no idea how seldom I have visitors. I don't know anybody in New York, and Laura almost never brings anyone here. Oh, a girl friend occasionally, but she's such a homebody she usually prefers just to set with her old mother; of course I like it that way myself. As for young men, she simply never lets them cross the threshold. I can't remember when I've seen one—well, I'm sorry you must go," she broke off, seeing Laura pull open the front door with noisy haste. "Good-by, Mr. English. Good-by, dear."

"Good-by, Mother," said Laura, with a wrathful overtone that escaped English but not her fond parent. English graciously repeated his thanks and Mrs. Beaton her invitation; and the door closed on the young people.

In silence they rode down the elevator, walked out into the street and stepped into a heavy Cadillac limousine. English gave the chauffeur the name of a little French restaurant built on the New Jersey palisades; the car nosed its way through the downtown traffic until it reached the Henry Hudson Parkway, then it moved smoothly along the black river strung with lights. Neither had spoken a word for perhaps ten minutes when Honey suddenly turned and looked at the reposeful English with determination. That gentleman was apparently deriving great pleasure from the spectacle of the George Washington Bridge, flung across the gorge of the Hudson like a great cobweb spangled with luminous dew.

"Mr. English." He turned eyes of genial inquiry upon her. "Why did you ask me to bring you up to meet my mother?"

English smiled at her, a pleasant smile conveying no information at all. "I don't know," he said. Then, as he saw her look vexed: "I liked her very much, and I like you. I'm delighted that we're having dinner together." And he looked at her in such an entirely friendly manner that Honey's mistrust subsided. She nestled back in the cushions and gave herself up to the beauty of the drive. The vision of Andy flashed upon her mind, but she was not tuned to a mood of self-reproach. She argued impatiently to herself that it was inconceivable for her to do anything untrue to Andy; and since she was doing this, it followed that there was nothing wrong with it. The vision of Andy did not look particularly satisfied with the line of reasoning, but nevertheless faded quickly.

Philosophers, ancient and modern, unite in disparagement of the character of woman. This has not materially lessened the popularity of the sex through the ages. Women, on the other hand, have had very little to say against philosophers—or for them, to be sure. In fact, except in rare instances beyond the aid of the

48

cosmetic art, women under forty generally pay no attention whatever to philosophers. This may shed some small light on the nature of philosophic opinion concerning them. Be that as it may, the author recounts with a heavy heart the spectacle of a girl like Laura, really a heroine of rare simplicity and virtue in a modern novel, beginning to behave in consonance with all the wry apothegms on womankind. Let us quickly return to our hero, and see if he is doing anything that may retrieve the situation.

CHAPTER 4

*Satisfying the reader's curiosity in some respects
but provoking it in others, and introducing
that remarkable character,
Father Calvin Stanfield, the Faithful Shepherd.*

*A*URORA DAWN!

The time has come, reader, for you to know the meaning of the title of this true and moral tale, and at the same time to learn the secret of Andrew Reale's mission to the Fold of the Faithful Shepherd. Learn, then, that "Aurora Dawn" was the name of a soap; a pink, pleasant-smelling article distributed throughout the land and modestly advertised as the "fastest-selling" soap in America. Whether this meant that sales were transacted more rapidly with Aurora Dawn soap than with any other, the customer snatching it out of the druggist's hand with impolite haste, flinging down a coin and dashing from the store, or whether the slogan was trying to say that its sales were increasing more quickly than the sales of any other cleansing bar; this is not known. Advertising has restored an Elizabethan elasticity to our drying English prose, often sacrificing explicitness for rich color.

Andrew's purpose was nothing less than to bring Father Stanfield and his Fold of the Faithful Shepherd on a nationwide radio program to make the fastest-selling soap in America sell even faster. Andrew was not employed by the soap company, but by the Republic Broadcasting Company, a vast free enterprise rivaled only by the United States Broadcasting System, another private property. These two huge corporations monopolized the radio facilities of the land in a state of healthy competition with each other, and drew their lifeblood from rich advertising fees which assured the public an uninterrupted flow of entertainment by the highest priced comedians, jazz singers, musicians, news analysts, and vaudeville novelties in the land—a gratifying contrast to the dreary round of classical music and educational programs which gave government-owned radio chains such a dowdy reputation in other countries. This is not to imply that the ingredient of culture was lacking in the American radio brew; for, in addition to exquisite opera and symphonic music broadcast on weekend afternoons—surveys having proved that more people listened at night, this time was naturally reserved for paying customers like coffee and toothpaste companies—there were numerous programs engendered and paid for by the radio companies themselves, called "sustainers," and having no other purpose than the uplifting of the nation's cultural tone. These bore such titles as "The American Forum," "You Can Love Music," "The Half Hour of Immortals," "Philosopher's Round Table," "God Behind the News," and so forth; occasionally, to everyone's surprise, one of these items gathered such a popular following that it attained commercial sponsorship, thus making culture useful as well as cultural.

Andrew was in the sales department of the Republic Broadcasting Company, and his job was to see that cordiality was maintained between the sponsors who paid such large sums for radio time, the network which gave them its gargantuan technical facilities in return, and the advertising agencies which acted as middlemen. He was assigned the supervision of several programs and kept a watchful eye on the hothouse blossom of personal relations in each of them, moistening and fertilizing as necessary. The requirements of his task were nine parts likableness to one part intelligence; if a young man began to exceed the proportion in favor of intelligence he was on his way to dismissal or an executive post, depending on how well his superiors enjoyed his company.

Andrew's affability and discretion, his expert golf game (which he had acquired, together with a high regard for the privileges of wealth, in years of caddying at the Colorado Springs course), his engaging smile, and a lucky capacity for swallowing large amounts of hard liquor without visible change in his manner, had endeared him to the powerful head of his department, the sales manager, Wilhelm Van Wirt. This chunkily built, hard-drinking gentleman, who spent his waking hours in alternation between gracious submission to the eccentricities of sponsors and heavy tyranny over his office force, suddenly conceived a deep, sentimental liking for Andy and took every means to be close with him. Starting with occasional lunches together, their intimacy broadened to include weekends at Van Wirt's home in Nutley, New Jersey, in company with his nervous, overdressed wife and a bulbously unattractive daughter of thirteen. Gradually dropping caution, the sales manager admitted Andy to the inner recesses of his life by making him a companion at the expensive and extremely private parties he occasionally arranged for the pleasure of certain clients who expected such hospitality as an informal rebate on large contracts.

The author, who is concealing nothing in this truthful narrative except the operation of his hero's stream of consciousness, is forced to admit that Andrew did not hold himself aloof from the questionable merriment, and indeed derived an extraordinary excitement and pleasure from this first encounter with the snaring luxuries of this world. I groan to tell you of the pretty but careless girls with whom he formed passing connections entirely unredeemed by spiritual values, and of the gallons of European wines and mellow whiskies which passed down his healthy throat

—An informal rebate on large contracts—

with ease. There must be among my readers well-reared young men in their early twenties who have not despised instruction, who have avoided these pitfalls, and who have the sense to be horrified at these revelations. Let them close the book at once and pick up something more advanced and profitable—Pascal's *Pensées*, or the poetry of Milton—they have no need of the simple moral which this story will teach.

Things were at this stage when Mr. Talmadge Marquis, president of the company which manufactured Aurora Dawn toilet products and easily the most peculiar curmudgeon of all Van Wirt's whimsical clients, conceived the brilliant notion of putting Father Calvin Stanfield on a commercial program. Stanfield was just then acquiring notoriety in professional radio circles by dint of having cut down the popularity of the colossal Ziff Soup Jamboree four and five-tenths percent in the West Virginia area. The Jamboree, including among its stars a movie hero, a stage heroine, a Metropolitan opera singer, and a burlesque comedian, as well as two miscellaneous guest stars each week, had so blanketed the hour from nine to ten on Saturday night for USBS, that the rival RBC had been unable to sell the time to any sponsor, and had given the hour back to its chain stations to fill in as best they could with cultural sustainers. Many of these local broadcasters, obliged to maintain a steady flow of intelligible sound during the hour at their own expense, had turned in their difficulty to religion, enhancing their credit in the community and padding the hour full of talk and music fairly cheaply—not very sparkling stuff, to be sure, but then they were reasonably certain that nobody was listening.

Father Stanfield had surprised everyone in the radio business. The managers of the RBC station in Wheeling knew little about him except that he was a lay preacher who ran a sort of community farm in the back hills of West Virginia and held revival meetings every Saturday night. After a brief survey of the field they offered him the time, and he accepted it willingly. They counted on an innocuous hour of revival singing and preaching, but they were unaware of the main feature of Father Stanfield's personal brand of religion, which was regular public confession by the sinners of the community. These were not necessarily members of the Fold: anybody who felt the need of cleansing his soul could come to Father Stanfield, tell his story, and request the privilege of standing up at his revival meeting to unburden his sins. A colorful ceremony attended the confession period which took up the last half hour of Stanfield's broadcast. On the left side of the raised platform of the Tabernacle sat the penitent sinners on low wooden stools, clad in gray sackcloth robes. One by one they came to the microphone and narrated their transgressions, and when they had concluded with the proper words of repentance Father Stanfield pronounced them pardoned and exchanged the sackcloth robes for snowy silken ones, whereupon they seated themselves on the right side of the stage on a gilt, plush-upholstered pew, while the congregation burst into a hymn of praise and joy.

The lively quality of these confessions, which laid once for all the sentimental notion that sin is confined to the great steaming cities, gained for Father Stanfield's hour, in two months, a popularity unequaled in the annals of religious broadcasting. The Father himself was no small asset to the program. After a twenty-minute opening of hymn singing and prayer he usually launched into a brief talk on some topic of the day in a style of rustic good humor and Godliness that occasionally took on a sharp edge of satire.

As Andrew trudged with his bag across the wide, dark, dewy lawn between the Tabernacle and the building known as the Old House, he was aware of a tingling across his shoulders and down his arms, signs of tension and excitement which his easy disposition showed rarely. The prospect of meeting the fabled Stanfield was partly the cause; much more than that, however, was the consciousness of what these next hours might mean for him. Van

56

Wirt was about to be promoted to a vice-presidency, and there were five assistant sales managers available for his place, among whom Andy was junior both in years and service. Van Wirt had deliberately given him this weighty mission with the intention of recommending him as his successor if he brought it off. There was more than the single program at stake. Talmadge Marquis had four of his six soap programs with the rival USBS, and only two relatively small daytime shows with RBC: "Meet Mother Murphy," wherein homespun Irish charm furthered the cause of Aurora Dawn Energized Soap Beads; and "Doctor Morris's Secret," a serial which had successfully advocated the virtue of Aurora Dawn Dubl-Bubl Shampoo for four years without bringing its listeners one jot closer to the nature of the kindly old horse doctor's secret. Now, Marquis had originally begun his radio advertising with RBC and had been won over to producing his major shows on the rival chain only by skulduggery, including relentless play on his weakness for tall, thin brunettes; there therefore lurked in the bosoms of Van Wirt and his superiors at RBC an unflagging desire to win him back, like the burning Irredentism of a Balkan state bereft of a border province.

Their great chance was at hand with the Father Stanfield incident. Marquis had originally ordered USBS to get the Faithful Shepherd for him, and that unhappy corporation had met with a flat refusal from the preacher to appear under commercial sponsorship. His reply to their clumsy representative—"The Saviour ain't for sale, Mister, not since Judas's little transaction, he ain't" —had circulated through radio circles with the speed of a sexy joke. Striking while the iron was hot, the executive director of RBC had ordered Van Wirt to devise a clever scheme which would bring the Fold of the Faithful Shepherd into the broader fold of Republic Broadcasting. (He had been vague on the details of the cleverness.) Van Wirt, equally vague, delegated the task to Andrew, giving him the alternative of a leap close to the top of RBC's executive hierarchy, in the thin, intoxicating ozone of twenty-five thousand a year, or possible ignominy and dismissal. Andrew had a plan, perfect as plans could be; its chances depended entirely on the correctness of his estimate of the character of Father Stanfield.

His heart quickening, Andrew mounted the steps of the broad farmhouse known as the Old House, and knocked loudly at the door. It was opened by a thin, meek-looking girl, innocent of the benefits of make-up and wearing a cheap gray cotton dress and a clean apron, who said, as Andrew stood blinking at the sudden rush of light, "You the young man from New York? Father expecting you," and motioned him to enter. She took the bag awkwardly from his hand, ignoring his murmured protest, while a hearty voice boomed from within: "That the young feller, Esther? Bring him in, bring him in!" Andrew barely caught a glimpse of an old-fashioned hallway with a full-length mirror near the door and faded green flowery paper on the walls, before he found himself in the dining room. Ablaze with the light from a glass chandelier suspended over a long, laden table, a-clatter with the noise of a dinner in full swing, the room seemed overflowing with food, people, and good humor. At the far end of the table sat a broad man with fair, straight hair and protruding ears, dressed in black, who stood up as Andy entered and strode to him, waving huge meaty hands in greeting. Andy was almost six feet tall, but Father Stanfield loomed over and around him; he was built on a massive scale and the mass was working weight, as Andrew knew the moment he shook hands.

"Saturday night's a good night to come to the Old House, son," cried the preacher, leading him by the hand to a vacant chair beside his own at the head of the table. "Esther, bring some hot soup. That food on trains don't do a man no good. We don't eat too bad here, son." With this he pushed Andrew into the chair and sat down in his own, picking up a fork and spearing a wide slab of fried steak from a metal platter as he did so. A plate of thick soup manifested itself under Andrew's nose, and its steam smote his nostrils like incense after the discouraging Pullman fish and the cold bus ride. Casting an appreciative eye around the board as he ate, he decided that in truth they "didn't eat too bad." There were plates heaped with corn, squashes, and baked potatoes; deep dishes filled with blocks of butter, halved lettuce heads, sliced tomatoes, peas, red beans, green beans, celery, applesauce, and stewed rhubarb; platters of steak, platters of pork chops, and platters of fried quarter chickens, all vanishing rapidly under the lunges of agile forks. Women rose from time to time with practiced dexterity to renew the supply and to refill the two tin pitchers of coffee that seemed never to stop in their rattling career around the table.

Stanfield glanced with approval at the speed with which Andy fell to. "Young man is all right," he commented, the comment somewhat muffled by steak. "Meet the folks, but don't reach to shake no hands." Starting at the head of the table, he introduced the men first, some as Elders, some simply by patronym, and, after he had made the round of male diners, he added, "The ladies alongside are the missus" which for some reason was greeted with a universal giggle. The men ranged in age from a white-haired farmer with seamed, blunt hands, seated at Stanfield's right, to a stout, pale-faced young man with heavy black hair at the foot of the table, who had been introduced as "Chico—he handles the machinery, and knows more about it than Hennery Ford." The men were all, it appeared, foremen or supervisors of various departments of the community farm, although the designation of Elder indicated that some were also religious functionaries in Stanfield's peculiar prelacy. Andrew was introduced as "The young feller from Radio City, New York, who's come down to see our meeting." The dinner passed in lively conversation, incomprehensible to Andy, aside from the jests of Elder Billingsley at the head of the table, who was the accepted wit of the synod. These invariably took the form of broad flirtatious remarks addressed at various wives, and everybody invariably roared except the twitted husband who invariably looked mildly surprised and foolish. There was a long discussion of a revised plumbing system in the New House (which, Andy gathered, was a kind of dormitory where the eighty families of the Fold lived) and a heated attack on the merits of a scientific cattle feed by Elder Comer, a very old man with a bald pate, and a back bent like a resilient bow. As soon as the dessert was cleared, Stanfield led a prolonged prayer of thanks, at the conclusion of which he rose, saying "Them folks a-waiting." Thereupon there was a great stir and bustle as every-one filed into the hall, donned hats and coats, and walked out across the dank lawn in the frosty March night to the Tabernacle.

The revival meeting was an unforgettable experience for Andy, tired and sleepy though he was. From his vantage point on the stage in the row of the Elders he watched with growing wonder the strange mixture of tent-show and religious service that was Stanfield's way of worship. As he listened to him deliver a sharp, rustically humorous diatribe against the growing tendency in the Fold to read popular magazines instead of the Bible—"Seems as how lately the Good Book is running a poor second to Red Book: I reckon the main trouble with the Gospel is, they ain't no part in it you can illustrate with a girl with her laigs up in the air"—Andrew felt an accession of confidence in his sincerity. This lessened considerably when, after the community singing and just before the confessions, Elder Pennington, a slight, gray man with a large fleshy nose and deep folds in the skin of his face, who had said nothing at all during dinner except "Pass the beans" or "More coffee," got up and made a desk-thumping appeal in a shrill, emotional voice for money to continue "the Fold's great work," and ordered baskets passed among the hundreds of tour-ists who crowded the Tabernacle to the last row of its narrow wooden-pillared balcony. The singing was real, and the confes-sions were real: the music was sung with uninhibited heartiness by the mountain folk of the Fold as well as by many of the visitors, the confessions came pouring straightforward from the people with directness of narrative, quaint turn of local speech, and touches of unexpected detail almost impossible to contrive. Father Stanfield absolved them, sometimes with gravity, sometimes with a rough jocular comment on their misdeeds, and evidently derived much pleasure from the showmanship of the ritual with the robes.

Reserving judgment, Andrew grew more and more positive that the man was accessible to the scheme he had in mind, and his prize of twenty-five thousand a year seemed drifting within his grasp. Momentarily his mind wandered from the strange pageant before him. He saw an apartment on Park Avenue in the Seventies, richly furnished, saw himself and Honey moving graciously among a gathering of radio and advertising executives, his guests; he smelled the hors d'oeuvres, he tasted the wine, his eye lingered on the clever matching of the dark maroon satin drapes with the Turkish carpet. He exchanged a casual word or two with a couple of his guests in a quiet corner of a room—just the word or two necessary to win a huge new account, doubling his income at a stroke and paying for the party ten times over. The apartment was cramping, after all. The house in Sands Point owned by Chester Bullock, of Bullock and Griffin, with the veranda facing sunsetwards over the blue Sound, was much more to his taste. Now he could afford to build one like it and start working toward his real aim, an advertising agency of his own. The first requisite, of course, was a home where he could do the large-scale entertaining which would open the golden gates. An aureate haze enveloped his thoughts. They lost coherence and became a series of broken images of luxury: a white motor yacht with a beautifully sheered bow, himself as skipper resplendent in a yachting uniform; Honey in mink, Honey and he in a box at the opera, bowing to the grand Davidoffs in the central box and being invited to join them for supper afterward; a two-month vacation at Colorado Springs, playing golf (he would always keep in shape, of course), being very gracious to his old friends and even to Curran, the flinty course manager who had gouged him so mercilessly in his caddie days; Honey the center of all eyes when they walked into the long, elegant dining room at night—except that Honey unaccountably was shorter and had black hair and thin, tense, active little hands like cats—but that was impossible—

He was roused from his dozing by a burst of music, the closing song of the repentance period, a lively air:

> *Their sins they were as scarlet,*
> *They are now as white as snow;*
> *Their sins they were as scarlet,*
> *They are now as white as snow—*
> *Their souls are back with Jesus*
> *And the devil hides below—*
> *For they're washed in the blood of the Lamb.*

The meeting broke up, following a benediction by Father Stanfield. With a rich noise of cheery converse the crowd went outside, where buses waited lined up to take them back to town. The people of the Fold melted into the gloom of the lawn. Conducted to a high, deep feather bed in a room in the Old House by Elder Pennington, Andy fell asleep almost immediately, to renew his visions of riches in the more brightly glowing hues of deep dreams.

Not being of the school of literature which deals analytically with the phantasms of slumber, this history makes no effort to follow our hero into the land of Nod, although doubtless the whole truth about him could thereby easily be laid bare under a skillful probe.

CHAPTER 5

In which the reader, by a magic older
and blander than that of the X-ray,
is permitted a glimpse into
the soul of Father Calvin Stanfield.

IT MAY BE, as Henry George said, that all religions (except yours and mine, friend) seem like the variously distorted apprehensions of a primary truth. Let us say here at once that the Faithful Shepherd's intimations of his Creator occasionally shaded into the grotesque; for such observations are not amiss in a history of plodding truth. Your novelist affects impartiality in order to lend verisimilitude to the phantoms of his brain, but a historian's allotted task is to blacken black, whiten white, force facts into his own view of them, and make enlightening comments along the way; for true life accurately retold would be a formless succession of accidents and follies, no more entertaining or improving than is your daily life, dear reader. So I say at the outset, Father Stanfield's cosmogony was bizarre; you may draw, from the events, your own conclusion as to whether this unfitted him for his post in the world.

The morning sun, which had officially risen seventeen minutes earlier according to local almanacs, now lifted itself radiantly over the eastern rim of the valley and slanted a white beam into the book-lined study of Father Calvin Stanfield, adding an appropriate luminosity to the picture of that divine on his knees on a large crimson cushion, deep in prayer. The sun did him the further grace of falling directly on the section of religious books opposite the window, throwing into clarity the titles of many substantial theological tomes, classical and current, and leaving in decent obscurity shelves of philosophical, biographical, epigrammatic, and fictional works that pertained wholly to the fleshly world. The taste thus shadowed seemed to range across wide areas of literature. The library had the jumbled appearance of one that is frequently and hastily referred to, and since the Father did not trouble to rearrange the books—and the faithful lamb who cleaned the room saw no incongruity—Spinoza rubbed bindings with Mark Twain, Jane Austen with La Rochefoucauld, James Joyce with Lord Chesterfield, Keats with Clarence Darrow, and so on, indefinitely. The last author's obsolescent books were very well thumbed; they furnished forth an army of familiar atheistical straw men for the Shepherd to strike down in his Sunday sermons.

In morning devotions the Father had a directness which might well be the envy of more polished clerics who sometimes struggle against a wicked intuition that they are mumbling into a void. He had not the slightest doubt but that he was in colloquy with his Maker, who, like himself, appreciated straight talk. It was his way to pray aloud and extemporaneously, alone or in the congregation.

"Lord, I'm doin' what I kin," he was saying, "but you know what I got to struggle aginst. You gi' me the call to preach, but you also gi' me a clownish soul, and I don't hardly know what's religion and what's my own doggone carryin' on half the time. All I know is, the Fold has prospered, and my people pray and read their Bible and live Godly lives with their families under these roofs you have blessed me to build; so no matter how unworthy a vessel I seem to be, you must know what you're doin'. Now this here young man from Radio City, New York, is a-comin' to tempt me with fine gold, yea, with much fine gold, to put our Saturday night revival meetin' on the radio. You know I kin use that money; we got seventy families on the waitin' list that we jest cain't take into the Fold 'cause they ain't no room. I could build a whole mess of nice little houses with that there radio money.

"But Lord, my soul is hungerin' fer the glitter and the glamour and the clamor of fame, and that's what I'm afraid of. Before honor must come humility, and where-at is my humility? I'm puffed up with pride and success, and if I take that money, I don' know but what I'm yieldin' to a temptation that's goin' to be the beginnin' of the downfall of the Fold. I rejected Temptation once, Lord, and here she is, a-walkin' back and forth in front o' me agin, Lord, in her black chiffon nightgown."

For a moment he bowed his head against his hands, which rested on the windowsill. Then he raised it again and spoke in a milder key.

"Lord, I ain't complainin'. If I didn' have no problems, it wouldn' be no glory to you if I triumphed. Only now and then I git cornered, and I got to holler to the Old Man for help. I jest don' know what to do. Nobody cain't tell me it's right fer to use the Gospel to sell things, but here I been a-prayin' fer money to enlarge the Fold, and here comes the old money, but with a long string attached where I cain't even see t'other end of it, and I don' know but what the devil's holdin' it.

"Well, lemme git off that fer a minute, I reckon I been layin' it on enough.

"Lord, I thank you fer the countless blessin's of my life. When I think of me, a-hangin' on to this spinnin' ball in black space, me smaller than a ant in yer eyes, the earth smaller than a ol' pebble, I wonder how I got the nerve to talk to you, and even more how it is you pay attention to me. *But I know you pay attention!*

When I laid in that mud-puddle in Belgium, Lord, with the shells a-screechin' ever' which way around me, and vowed if you got me out of that mess I would believe on you, you paid attention. A thousand fell on my left hand, and ten thousand on my right; unto me them shells did not approach. I knowed then that you had me marked out to do some work fer you on this li'l ol' round ball you got hung up in space fer man to act out his days on. I ben doin' my best, Lord, take it all around, except fer this clownish streak I got in me, which maybe I sometimes think you put there fer a purpose too, seein' as how I sure lay it over the regular preachers fer bringin' the folks in to meetin' and gittin' 'em worked up to the love of the Lord. Maybe to herd these mountain sheep you need a real crooked stick, Lord, which is me.

"You blessed me with everythin', Lord, except the greatest blessin' of all, a virtuous wife and children. I got no arrows to my quiver, and they ain't nobody risin' up in the gate to call me blessed. I ain't complainin'. I sinned with Gracie in London, I know I did. I dreamed of her last night agin, and she turned into thin air in my arms, same as always. Lord, I dunno if you ever stop to figger that I was unredeemed then and you cain't hardly hang me as high fer what I done then as what I might of done after. But thy will be done. Not as I will, but as thou wilt. Still, I ain't no Saint Paul, Lord. I ain't that pure in spirit, and I'm mighty lonely in the long nights, I don't mind tellin' you. Must I go on alone? Even Moses took a Cushite woman, and he was gittin' on to eighty-three when he done it. 'Course there it is. Him takin' her got the congregation all riled up and Miriam and Aaron murmured agin' him, and Miriam wound up with the leprosy and there was general hell to pay. Well, Lord, I reckon even if I did find Gracie after all these years and tried to bring a little English-talkin' Cockney gal in among these here folks it would bust up the meetin', is that the idea? I reckon you know best. I sure couldn't take no other woman, married as we are in yer eyes. I ain't no Mormon. Thy will be done, Lord.

"Thy will be done in everythin', Lord. On this here radio deal, how about tellin' me what to do? I don' want to take bad money, but I don't want to let it pass by if it's permitted me to take it. Will you guide me to the answer, Lord?"

Father Stanfield rose from his knees and walked to a little stand by his desk, on which there rested a large, worn Bible. It had been his practice for twenty years, in moments of extreme perplexity, to open the Good Book at random and put his finger blindly on a verse. If the verse thus isolated could possibly be construed as pertaining to the problem at hand he would abide by the answer with rigid resolve. The morning sun played on his hands as he placed them gently on the Bible, bent his head and said, "The Lord is nigh unto all that call upon him—unto all that call on him in truth." He opened the book near the middle, and his finger fell upon the forty-second verse of the second chapter of the book of Ezra:

The children of the porters: the children of Shallum, the children of Ater, the children of Talmon, the children of Akkub, the children of Hatita, the children of Shobai, in all an hundred thirty and nine.

Slowly and respectfully, the Faithful Shepherd closed the book, returned to his habitual place of devotion by the window, and knelt again. There was a faint smile on his face, good-natured and a little wry.

"All right, my Father," he said. "I gotta figger it out alone, is that it? I think the problem is too big fer me but *you* think it ain't, and so you tossin' her right back in my lap. Thy will be done. You know I'll do the best I kin. Inspire me to do the right thing fer the Fold, Lord. I ain't worth much, but the Fold is a fair work, a sweet home fer many folks who love God, and also much cattle."

His voice dropped lower, and he began to murmur rapid, indistinct prayers, evidently routine devotions.

Since we cannot hear him, and since you may suspect a touch

of extravagance in the picture of the Faithful Shepherd which we are drawing: a suspicion which, if unallayed, would cloud the veracity of our whole tale: we must fill in a detail or two of his background, at the risk of tedium. One of our beautiful young ladies reappears in the next chapter; you may skip directly to that if you believe unquestioningly all that has been said about the Father.

Calvin Stanfield was born and reared on the slopes of the valley, most of the arable land of which now belonged to the Fold of the Faithful Shepherd. His father was a farmer, remotely of English extraction like most of the valley people, who dug a small living out of an un-co-operative patch of soil, and sought no further satisfaction in the things of this world. The old Bible which we have watched the preacher use was his. As his farm was the only area of the earth that interested him, so the Good Book was the only acreage in the land of literature that seemed to him worth tilling. In his youth he had read two or three novels which had struck him as a lot of silly, protracted, and pointless lies; and he had returned with much satisfaction, and the resolve nevermore to stray, to the Book which could be depended on for truth, and which had such sound sense in it as, "Boast not thyself of tomorrow, for thou knowest not what a day may bring forth," and "The fool shall be bound with the cord of his own sins."

Calvin was his one child. The boy, hemmed in by his environment, inherited his father's two preoccupations: the farm and the Book. It was old Stanfield's habit to make Calvin read aloud five chapters of the Bible each night, and though the poor lad had treacherous going through the genealogies and the diatribes of the Prophets (for his father skipped nothing), he was well rewarded by the fragrant simplicity of the tales of the Patriarchs, by the gorgeous pageants of Joseph, Moses, and Joshua, and by the thrilling, bloody passages of arms in the books of the Kings. It happened that the boy had a sound, retentive mental apparatus, so that he grew to young manhood with a knowledge of Holy Writ

68

by chapter and verse which might have confounded divines in the cathedrals of remote cities.

At the age of eighteen came the revolt, that occasion in the life of each of us which seems an earthquake, and which is as commonplace as first love, and Calvin decided that his father was a fool, trapped in antique, useless habits of thinking.—How many of us marry our first love? How many of us retain the heady, delightful conviction that the old man was all wrong? How pleasant it would be, indeed, if each of us could strike across untrodden green meadows in the ancient journey! Good friends, who have broken your ankles and scratched your skins and fallen in holes in the green meadows before groping back to the old dirt path, was not that first leap over the stile, into the long grass, unutterably sweet?

Calvin found it so. The first World War took him off the farm and into the roaring excitement of a military camp near a city, and awe for the Good Book crumbled and vanished before the scathing profanity of the incredibly wise shoe salesmen and shipping clerks with whom he mingled. By the time he was transported to England, Calvin was an enthusiastic, even a crusading, heathen; but performance lagged behind conviction, as it usually does, and while in camp he actually did nothing worse than become very drunk two or three times.

Performance overtook conviction in London. The reader will forgive me if I omit the distressing particulars, but, as he may guess, there was a young lady named Grace. Suffice it to say that young Calvin Stanfield began to feel the unease of remorse at approximately the time that his life began to be endangered. It should not be a source of satisfaction to rational churchmen, as it seems to be, that men on battlefields return to their old beliefs: the cries of a scared child to its father have no logical or intellectual force: but anyway, Calvin Stanfield had a sudden great accession of faith while cowering in a shell hole during his first engagement. He quoted aloud psalms of David that were very much to the point, and he vowed that if he were delivered from this pit he would believe and do. He kept his word, and during the rest of that conflict which we once thought of as a Great War, he was known in his regiment as Holy Cal.

So much must be told in order that the reader may understand the motions of Father Calvin Stanfield. The rest would make an absorbing study for a few of my patient audience who are interested in folkways, comparative religion, and sociology. His return to his native valley, his growing reputation among the farm people for sanctity, his impulsive usurpation of the local pulpit and self-ordination when the starving minister abandoned the parish in the black time of the Depression, and the coagulation of a few acts of charity on his part into a self-sustaining rural communal settlement which rapidly expanded, all these things are not without color and excitement, but they took place entirely without the interposition of any pretty young ladies. It is plain and believable, I trust, that a man like Calvin Stanfield should become a lay preacher, and should take dispossessed rural families into his home to labor alike and share alike; and that such a group, fired by religious fervor and released from debt loads and competitive markets, should prosper and grow by degrees into a large, successful co-operative enterprise in agriculture. Such was the Faithful Shepherd, and such was his Fold. In the interest of brevity—for I am sure that some readers, accustomed to staccato loves, killings, hates, rapes, and reconciliations in the modern manner, consider me painfully periphrastic—I will omit recounting how the name "Faithful Shepherd" was acquired, since it would require my reproducing most of the text of Stanfield's first sermon, preached impromptu one gray Sunday morning when the flock arrived at the local church and found that the minister had quietly abandoned his post.

Father Stanfield has finished his prayers. Now he rises and goes down the wooden stairs of the Old House to the dining room, where he breakfasts with Aaron Pennington, the little large-nosed gray man who, you remember, thumped the rostrum so eloquently for contributions during the revival meeting. Esther, the plain girl whose face is as unmarked by bought color as her soul is by artifice, waits on them humbly and neatly. The two men speak in low tones of practical matters; the destinies of the Fold are determined at these breakfasts. So well do they understand each other that a reproduction of their conversation would reveal nothing. A few words of obscure reference, a grunt, a nod, comprise a discussion and a decision. Pennington is dry, dull, narrowly wise and devoted to the Fold and the Father. His tendency is to grasp and to build. Father Stanfield has gradually passed most of the administration of the Fold into his hands, but he retains a firm control over his manager, whose usefulness is limited by the fact that he has no intuition at all of the spirit of charity which animates the undertaking. This is not to say that Pennington's religion is anything but strict. In fact, were we to translate the cabalistic conversation between the men now, an exchange more animated and protracted than usual, we would learn that it consists of vehement objection by the manager to the presence of Andrew Reale in the Old House and to the implied consideration that the Father is giving to the prospect of going on the radio. It is a venture off the soil, into places of urban carnality, that offends Pennington's mode of thought. The Father is reassuring him that nothing will be done to hurt the Fold, but he will not promise to send Reale off without further discussion, and the breakfast ends in a silence that is not one of harmonious accord. Pennington moves dourly off to inspect the cattle.

Look well to your kine, Aaron Pennington, for I strongly fear that your master grows neglectful of his muttons. The smoothly-spoken young man from the city has descended to take breakfast and is talking to him now. The Faithful Shepherd is listening attentively and saying little, but every now and then he nods pleasantly. The young man grows warm and terribly earnest; his food is hardly touched; and now he has taken a paper out of his pocket and placed it in the Father's hands. The Father reads it with an expression of growing approval and pleasure. The young man falls silent. O, Pennington, Pennington, what is this? The stranger is taking a fountain pen from his pocket; the Father accepts it; he bends over the table; he puts his pen to the paper; he signs!

Does dry, gray Aaron pause in the midst of scolding a young farmhand for slovenly cleaning of his beasts, and does a chill of foreboding pass over his frosty spirit? Looking through the barn door, he sees the young man from the world of advertising, the red valley of Hinnom, walk out of the Old House with a cheer in his expression and a spring in his step that argue triumph. What has he said, what has he done, so completely to conquer the violent antipathy of the Shepherd to commercial radio?

At a bound, Andrew Reale has brought himself close to the riches that his soul desires. Father Stanfield has agreed to take the Fold of the Faithful Shepherd on the air—*under the sponsorship of Aurora Dawn soap.*

CHAPTER 6

*In which an important piece of the machinery
is set a-whirring.*

THE NEXT DAY Laura Beaton sat with two men at a table in the famous New York restaurant, "Le Boeuf Gras," on East Fifty-second Street, doing justice to a delectable luncheon and unconsciously spoiling the meals of a large number of people in her vicinity. She was painfully fair to look upon. She was a taunt to man, a reproach to woman. Faithful husbands felt a stir of mild grief as, against their will, they compared her to their spouses and knew that Fate had caged them forever in gray little traps. The flames of ardent lovers flickered and guttered as though the wind of truth had suddenly blown a gust into their overheated imaginations, and an odious little voice warned them that their rosy Celias were, after all, but so many muddy-complexioned, lumpy wives-to-be. Young bachelors fumed; old bachelors mourned. Not a woman within range but felt her presence as an indignity and took revenge in a patronizing analysis of her lure. Poor things, what did the details matter? They noted the cut of her dress, the style of her hair, the slant of her hat, the color of her nails; and each, even in the act of disparaging, resolved in her heart to correct one or more points of her person after the manner of Laura, as though these things counted a straw, and as though such trifles lent magic to the girl, instead of the other way around. Alas, when large and potent industries are built on that trivial illusion: the transfer of a young girl's charm to the articles hung on her body: how were these unhappy females to free themselves of it in the presence of Laura's murderous beauty?

Laura's escort was Stephen English; against the background of this expensive dining room his correct clothes, slightly worn handsomeness and general quality of good breeding rendered him as invisible as a chameleon. It is an indication of the quality of the third diner at the table that his identity was not entirely quenched by the girl's refulgence, and that the gaze drawn to her was eventually transferred, however briefly, to him. He was a pale, thin person in his early thirties, with a narrow face, black hair thinned at the forehead, and an arresting air of poverty mingled with arrogance. His clothes were shabby and unpressed, and a poorly-knotted, garish tie was twisted to one side of his soft shirt, of which the collar was open. His shoes were scuffed and his hair unruly; as he slouched in his chair with one hand hung over the back of it, exhibiting nails not innocent of dirt, his face shone with perspiration, and he waved the other hand about at a great rate, for he was talking, and had been talking almost uninterruptedly since the beginning of the meal. This picaro seemed no less in place in this retreat of moneyed people than the banker, English, but he dominated the scene instead of melting into it. The confidence in his eye and the ease in the attitude of his body belied his ill-kept garments—a second glance at which showed that they were of costly material—and his air of poverty was not unlike that of a monk from beneath whose coarse robe there might peep excellent and highly polished shoes. He was Mike Wilde, the celebrated painter.

"I will not paint this girl for you, English," he was saying, "until she promises to go back to Albuquerque on the day I finish, never to visit New York again until every hair on her head is gray.

I like this girl. I love her, without a shred of personal feeling. She is the central radiance. She breathes hills, and plains, and stars in a dying sunset, and everything that is clean and good a thousand miles from the city. The city, too, is beautiful, but it is a beauty to the taste of Baudelaire, a *fleur du mal*. This girl is a *fleur de la nature*. I love all beauty because I see with the eye of a saint, and there is no ugliness in the world, only beauty in varying patterns, harsh or gentle. I want her to go home because here she is incongruous, she is out of her pattern. When she takes on the patina of the city she will fade into something else and eventually glow with the beautiful phosphorescence of decay, which might be equally pleasing to my eye, but which will be hell for her. I speak now out of compassion, which is a high sentiment, and I tell her what my seeing eye sees. Beaton, will you go back to Albuquerque?"

"I will not," said Honey, industriously applying herself to a large steak. "Please pass the chili sauce."

"Why not?" inquired Wilde, belligerently.

"Because I'm making a lot of money," quoth Honey. "Stephen, the asparagus."

"A sensible reply," said English, handing her the dish with an approving grin.

"What the devil do you know about life, English?" growled Wilde. "You are insulated with so many layers of money that the electricity of existence has never shocked you into awareness. Wealth is a nonconductor of truth. It is the only condition of life more narrowing than poverty. You look at Beaton with the piggish eyes of desire, and you only see Beaton." ("Come, now, Mike," murmured English, but the protest was lost.) "I look at Beaton and I see every well-favored girl that has ever come to New York to make a lot of money as a model. I see them leaving the farms, streaming out of the hills, swarming from the small towns and funneling into the city's maw. I see the charm of young woman-hood being skimmed like sweet white cream from the nation and poured down the drain of commerce. It is a vast, terrifying picture. It is a subject for a symbolic panorama. I shall probably compose a double-spread cartoon in the manner of William Blake and sell it to *Harper's Bazaar.*—Beaton, go home, I beg of you!"

"May I have the celery?" said Laura to him politely. "Stephen, do you look at me with piggish eyes?"

"Not in the least, Laura," answered English. "Of course I think you're very beautiful—I'd be an ass if I didn't—and that makes your presence delightful. It's also the reason for this luncheon, despite the odd turn of the conversation. I think a painting of you in the character of Charity by Michael Wilde would be a perfect theme for the Community Chest drive. Knowing Mike as I do, I think we must give him his head for another fifteen minutes before he will come out with a rational answer."

"You talk of trifles while I am fighting for a girl's happiness," said Wilde, having paused just long enough to insert the greater part of a lamb chop in his mouth. "Beaton, listen to me, for I am a saint and can prophesy. I do not know to whom you are engaged, but the quality of your ring and the size of the stone tell me that he is some young man, simple in heart and not rich. If he is in New Mexico, go back to him. If he is here, marry him at once and drag him far from the city. You are in great danger. The virtue that breathes from you cannot last another year in this climate. You are selling your body in a way that the manners of the day pass as respectable—in photographs. You do not know it, but with each picture you are selling a little chunk of your soul. There is not the gulf that you imagine between hawking the shadow and vending the substance. The savages who refused to permit strangers to take pictures of them knew a deep truth that you poor, money-mad, fame-crazed models find out only too late. Go home, Beaton. Stop putting out your charms for hire to increase the sale of vanities. The money you are earning is the gold that drips from the hot walls of Hell. Go home!"

Laura put down her knife and fork, leaned back in her chair, and turned her renowned blue eyes on him in a long, serious look. "You play rough," she said.

Wilde reached into his pocket, drew out a bag of peanuts and offered them to her. "This is a better dessert than any you can order," he said. "English, I'll do her as Charity. It will be an abominable painting which will cause the whole town to praise me in the streets. Also, it will force me to postpone work on Talmadge Marquis's portrait, which will infuriate him. That is possibly the chief inducement. Peanuts, Beaton?" He rustled the paper sack.

"I don't want peanuts, thank you," said Honey, "and I'm not sure I want you to paint me. You're very strange."

"Her spirit is infected with urbanity already, English," said Wilde, proceeding to shell the nuts noisily. "In New Mexico she probably ate peanuts with simple gusto."

"Laura, you're making Mike very happy," said English. "Shocking people is his one delight, aside from hearing his own voice. He will pose as anything to achieve surprise—this Savonarola vein is a new thing which he seems to have cooked up just for you. Actually, he's a good fellow."

"I am not," said Wilde. "I am a still, small voice and a devouring fire, and my vision will one day be everyone's, but meanwhile I must suffer scorn like all true Evangelists. Next time we dine, young lady, I shall, for your especial benefit, devour a plate of locusts and wild honey. Perhaps then you will take me seriously."

Laura burst out laughing. English joined. Wilde's face remained impassive.

"Mike, you're splendid," said English. "For all your wind, you have just donated a gift worth many thousands of dollars to the Chest, not to mention the immense value it will have in the campaign, and all you're trying to do is cover up your generosity."

"All you're trying to do is seduce this poor girl," said Wilde. "I am pleased to observe enough force of character in her to resist you successfully."

"That charge, Mike, is plausible enough to be dignified with a denial. Laura, I assure you I have no such deplorable intention," said English, turning toward her.

"Matters stand much worse than I thought, then," said Wilde. "You are thinking of prisoning this child in the echoing golden dungeon of your wealth by marrying her. I am not at all sure she has the strength to resist that."

"Hello, Honey," said a new voice. The three diners glanced up. Andrew Reale was standing beside their table.

If the reader has been enduring Michael Wilde's nonsensical farragoes with half the impatience with which the author has been forced to set them down, he may wish to abandon the book now. I think it only fair to warn the audience that this harlequin is one of the key figures in the pantomime. It is regrettable, because he is capable of taking up an entire chapter with a speech (he does so, in fact, in Chapter 13); and were this anything but a true tale, I would surely remove him with surgical dispatch. As it happened, however, it was unquestionably Michael Wilde who started the great Aurora Dawn scand . . . but it is poor storytelling to anticipate.

Andrew, then, fresh from sleep in a luxurious Pullman compartment, glowing with the secret of his triumph at the Old House, had just arrived at Le Boeuf Gras to take a fortifying lunch before his appointed interview with Talmadge Marquis, a prospect at which men usually quaked. The fact that he was the bearer of good news reassured him only slightly, for it was known that the most pleasant conversation with Marquis could take a turn that would suddenly break a man's career and leave his children without bread. It was no great coincidence that brought Andy to the very eating place in which his sweetheart was dining with a millionaire and a well-known painter, for despite the number of restaurants in New York, there are only a half dozen at which a certain segment of the population will ever manifest itself, and, in the neighborhood of East Fifty-second Street, Le

Boeuf Gras is as much the place to go to as, say, Mahomet's tomb is in Mecca.

Honey introduced her fiancé to her companions, and he cheerfully accepted their prompt invitation that he join them at table. It was no new thing for him to find his sweetheart dining with strange and attractive gentlemen, for he was aware of the obligations of her profession. He trusted her utterly, with the careless confidence of a young man who has been permitted by a young lady to find out that she adores him. This reaction, predictable as the tendency of a man to stand with his back to a fire, is discerned by some young ladies early in life, and cynics say that occasionally they even use it to advantage, but this pen explores no such dark corners of experience.

It was not long before the conversation disclosed that both the painter and Andrew were to meet with Talmadge Marquis shortly after lunch—Wilde to observe his subject at work, and obtain what he called "the nasty dimension of truth" for his portrait; our hero, of course, to report on his foray to the valley of the Faithful Shepherd. They agreed to share a taxi to the Empire State Building, where, cutting a cross-section two stories thick across the upper part of the tower, the great enterprise of Aurora Dawn hummed.

While Andrew ate, the others were entertained by a harangue on the beauty of young love and the desirability of the immediate retirement of Honey and her betrothed from New York, of which Michael Wilde delivered himself without interruption, except as he paused to greet by name several wealthy, celebrated, or notorious people as they moved past his table. Since the reader is acquainted with his views on this subject, neither conscientiousness nor truth require the reproduction of his words, for which the laboring author is grateful.

The sermon was choked off by the arrival at the table of an anecdotal newspaper columnist, one Milton Jaeckel, who lived at the time by amassing and reprinting the witty remarks of well-known people. The value of a quotation being, for his purpose, always in direct proportion to the notoriety of the originator, it was often in inverse ratio to the content of wit, an excellent thing, since it saved the columnist's readers from puzzlement. This man of letters frequented the half-dozen dining places mentioned above, scurrying around the whole circle thrice during twenty-four hours: at dinner, after the theater, and in the early morning hours. He was rarely seen by day, but the feast of St. Patrick had altered his habits and activated him this noon. At night, the casual stroller along Broadway, taking pleasure in the agreeable contrast of the constellation of Orion and the electric cinema displays, would probably be startled and possibly knocked over by this pale, bird-visaged, stooping creature, scuttling through the gloom from one restaurant to another as though pursued by a fiend.

It was this same littérateur who, espying Michael Wilde, hurried to the table, drew up a chair, sat down without an invitation, and, pulling out a worn paper notebook, said, "Got something for me, Mike? Hello, Honey. Hello, Mr. English."—Nobody at the table seemed in the least surprised by this proceeding. Everything in the world is strange; singularity is only a matter of insufficient repetition.—Michael Wilde, hardly pausing for breath, switched from his exhortation of the lovers to a series of anecdotes about himself, one of which candor requires that we set down. A publisher, it appears, had asked the painter to write a history of American art. "You're too late," Wilde quoted himself as answering. "I have already sold the rights to my autobiography." The columnist's pencil swooped at this one; then he stood up, muttered an excuse, and vanished.

Luncheon over, the party rose from the table. Laura, with the utmost decorum, managed to find her way to Andrew's side and slip her fingers lightly through his, and out again. There were at least three men in the room who could have, and gladly would have, given a sum in excess of Andy's boldest aims for that touch and what it implied. Andrew was very pleased by it, to be sure, and whispered in return the one word, "Success!"—"Wonderful, come home to dinner," said Laura quietly. Andrew nodded. They walked out into the sunny canyon of windows and stone along which March was doggedly fighting its cold and windy way from the river. March came into Fifty-second Street like a lion at the bank of the Hudson, but, impeded by the buildings, usually was a very tired lamb at Fifth Avenue. This, however, was a vigorous March day, and there was a pleasant sting in the wind. Andrew Reale and the painter stepped into a taxicab while Laura took the arm of Stephen English and walked briskly by his side toward Radio City.

The reader may not approve of this pairing-off. I recount the events as they occurred.

CHAPTER 7

In which the reader has the privilege of meeting
Talmadge Marquis,
reigning satrap in the industrial realm of Soap,
and learns more of the truly fascinating history
of Aurora Dawn; but which he may skip if he
is only following the love story.

*T*HERE IS A school of philosophy which holds that there is no
such thing in the world as evil, and that what strikes the common
sense of mankind as evil is only "the absence of Being where
Being should be." The argument, simple and ingenious, runs so:
no being is perfect in this universe, except the Supreme Being;
all other beings are imperfect, and are constantly striving to become more perfect; but, in so far as they are imperfect they lack
true Being, and it is this imperfection which appears to us as Evil.
Adherents of this doctrine are quite obdurate. I once overheard a

—The absence of Being where Being should be—

two-hour argument in which one disputant was at last crowded to the wall with the instance of a drunken husband strangling his wife and two babies, and was asked whether he did not consider this an instance of evil? "No," he replied with great calm, "properly understood it is merely an absence of Being where Being should be . . ." and, in the shocked silence which ensued, he conceded, "a considerable absence."

Talmadge Marquis was known far and wide to suffer from a considerable absence of Being in this sense. To the unphilosophic view of people engaged in making soap and producing radio programs, he seemed (such was their lack of insight) to be an entirely evil bully, loud, capricious and mean, and as obstinately resistant to progress as a hundred square miles of mud. They saw this large man, with his large, red face, large, bellowing voice, and large indifference to reason and good manners as an epitome of badness, not having the scholastic training to recognize in him an imperfect Being struggling toward perfection. This grievous error was so widespread that he was hated by those he employed, feared by those he benefited, and despised by those who were beyond his power. The pity was that, for all his upward striving, he seemed to acquire no Being whatever, because in the twenty years since he had inherited the Marquis company at the death of his father he had only become more perverse and noisy in the opinion of all who knew him, whereas he had started with no small endowment of these qualities.

It is important to emphasize that although Marquis was a soap manufacturer according to his income tax return and his own innermost belief, he knew less about the article than a first-year student of organic chemistry, and could no more have manufactured a piece of passable soap, given the necessary materials and apparatus, than he could have written a sonnet cycle on the subject. Aurora Dawn, the soap and the industrial plant alike, had been created by his father. A man of power, Talmadge Marquis, Senior, would, in other centuries, have organized a crusade, or rifled the Indies, or won a throne, or founded a religious order, or led a revolution; having erupted out of the well of eternity into nineteenth-century America, he made and sold soap. He understood better than the chemical engineers in his employ what the essential problem was. They saw it as a matter of producing a saleable cleansing substance. He saw it as a matter of creating a new popular habit. He smashed at the populace with all manner of powerful sermonizing in journals and on billboards, playing on strings of fear, love, and hope in their souls, until he had a good number of them broken like children to an obedient trotting to drug stores at regular intervals for the purchase of his little pink bars. He won a domain for himself out of the national economy in this democratic way; and in his old age, shrewdly estimating his son as a man of very mediocre parts, he buttressed his conquest with talented managers and careful lawyers, and died in the comforting faith that the principality would endure, despite the new prince.

Talmadge Marquis, who had smarted for years under his father's low opinion of him, took up the scepter with a flourish. He had been in power for less than a year when, by fiat, against the advice of all his father's counselors, he changed the color of the soap to white and ordered the spending of two million dollars to popularize the slogan, "Snow White, Snow Pure." This caused the resignation of the general manager of production, a genius of chemical engineering named Abraham Serf, who had adored "Old T.M.," and who had quietly effected the smooth running of the plant and the excellence of the product for several decades. The sales of Aurora Dawn soap dropped forty percent in a single year, and the value of the Marquis Company stock sagged. On the verge of a breakup, Marquis was rescued by a banker, none other than our acquaintance Stephen English, who purchased a controlling interest in the corporation, rehired Serf and politely ordered Marquis never again to overrule the general manager in matters of technical policy. The presidency of the company and the entire outward picture of control were left as before with Marquis at the head. The original roseate hue of the product was restored, and two million dollars were allotted to popularize the slogan, "There Is Nothing Purer Than the Dawn—and the Dawn Is PINK."

Thus balked in his first effort to assert his rule, Marquis became so irascible that within six months he lost his wife and half of his office staff. He made up the defection of his spouse with a procession of young women strikingly similar in dimensions, coloring, and morality, changes occurring, as a rule, when intimacy with Marquis strained the large tolerance of these companionable damsels. In time an office force evolved around him made up of people with a limitless capacity for bearing contumely so long as they were well paid. The arrival of Marquis in his office was the occasion of a series of white-toothed smiles as he passed along the desks, implying as much friendliness as the snarls of cougars. He was aware of this, and usually found a curious pleasure in moving through the atmosphere of impotent hate.

Two years after the snow-white-snow-pure episode, an event in the life of Talmadge Marquis restored his credit in the industry, changed his way of work and, in no small measure, wrought a revolution in national habits of living: he discovered the radio.

Far from being the roaring colossus it is now, broadcasting was an industry on a small scale when Marquis decided to try vending his soap by means of wireless entertainment. Although he was later hailed as the "pioneer" of radio merchandising, when he took the first step he was as innocent of its implication as he was of the workings of God's laws that made possible electric pulsing of sound through silent space. An imaginative radio entrepreneur persuaded him to attend an audition of entertainers, and Marquis was so enchanted with the homage paid him by these people, well known to him through his devoted attendance at musical comedies, that he could not resist acquiescing to this dubious experiment in popularizing Aurora Dawn.

No American except a congenitally deaf one needs to be reminded of what followed. Sales of the soap increased so sharply upon this first venture that Marquis realized he had stumbled into El Dorado. During the next five years, while conservative manufacturers were debating the propriety of invading private homes with spoken pleas for their products, Marquis started program upon program, and harnessed the full strength of this vast new selling machine to drive Aurora Dawn soap up to a fantastic level of popularity. His mathematical charts of sales became Andes, Himalayas of new peaks, while his competitors fumbled in the foothills of journalistic and billboard selling. In time they all imitated him, but in the interim Aurora Dawn had soared into the advertisers' Ninth Heaven of "household words," beyond compare; and the pink bar became almost as usual a phenomenon in American homes as running water.

It is safe to say that during all this Marquis had not a glimmer of what was happening, namely, that a very old institution, the medicine show, was being revived in a mechanized form. The basic motion: attracting the attention of idle people with amusement, and then diverting that attention to a commodity: was old in Oriental bazaars when Abraham went forth from Ur of the Chaldees; the slight innovation of radio lay in its use of the mystery of electromagnetism to make its way into the hitherto sacred privacy of family circles, there to perform its tricks and cry its wares. Talmadge Marquis, however, knew only that he had been wafted to a Prophet's Paradise of groveling attendance, infinite puissance, and unending indulgence of appetite. Fawned on, flirted with, bowed to, he lost whatever sense of proportion he had and became as whimsical as Nero. Riding this mighty new selling engine, it was impossible for him to make a mistake. His decisions, which diverted golden streams of dollars one way or another and therefore called forth the most desperate efforts to please and placate him, were choices between Aphrodite and Helen, for he was first in the field and had the entire range of

American amusement at his command. He could afford to offend skillful artists until they threw his rich contracts into his face, for there were always others to grasp for his money; he could indulge with safety the urge to meddle, which had proved so disastrous when he applied it to an obdurate substance like soap, for the quicksilver spirits of comedy and music slipped through his fingers, and, while satisfying himself that his ideas were improving his programs, he actually did them only slight harm. The whole development was as lucky a turn for Aurora Dawn as Old T.M. might have prayed for on his deathbed. Marquis abandoned all but the faintest pretense of being concerned with the making and distribution of soap, leaving those matters in the hands of his father's brilliant oligarchy of managers, much to the increase of their happiness and efficiency. He spent his days as the arbiter of merit and taste in all the entertainment for which he was paying and soon acquired among the gossipy folk of the amusement world a legendary fearsomeness combining features of the reputations of the Marquis de Sade and the Erl King.

In all this I am, of course, striving only to reproduce the impression which Talmadge Marquis made on unphilosophical minds unable to perceive that, in truth, he was suffering from an absence of Being where Being should be.

This chapter is an example of how the teller of a true story is hampered. Absolutely nothing has happened. Laura Beaton and Stephen English are still walking up East Fifty-second Street, leaning forward into the March wind; Andrew and the painter are still in their taxicab. Unless I make the excuse that the taxi has been held up by a traffic jam in front of Saint Patrick's Cathedral during all this time, I must plead guilty to the sin of having permitted the story to come to a standstill. Yet, friend, had you been ushered without this dull explanation into the presence of Marquis, you would eventually have hurled the book across the room, revolted by its implausibility. No writer of fiction could be forgiven for carving such an odd puppet, but the Creator's extravagances we accept *de facto*. The praying mantis exists; so does the bat, so does the cuttlefish, so does the duck-billed platypus; and so did Talmadge Marquis, of whose history your author is but the wide-eyed and humble recorder.

CHAPTER 8

In which, to make up for our previous discursiveness, there is nothing but pure plot.

*T*HE ATMOSPHERE was oppressive with Power.

In Talmadge Marquis's inner office on the seventy-eighth floor of the Empire State Building were gathered four masters of men: Marquis himself, Wilhelm Van Wirt (whom the attentive reader will remember as Andrew's mentor, the sales manager of the Republic Broadcasting Company), and two gentlemen named Walter B. Grovill and Thomas Leach, whose joined patronyms formed the name of an advertising firm known wherever anybody ate the bread of broadcasting. As to these two new figures on our stage, we are determined to leave description and proceed with our tale. You must be content, then, to know that Grovill was large, fat, and pale, and ended most of his utterances with a conciliatory giggle, while Leach was small, bitter-visaged, and pale, and incessantly twisted a college ring around his third finger by flicking it with his thumb. Some day, if spared, we may tell the story of these two although it will not be so wholesome and improving a tale as this one, containing, as it must, considerably more human error and fewer interludes of innocent romance.

The daunting array of four great men sat on one side of Marquis's wide leather-topped desk, rather in the aspect of a general court-martial; and facing them on the other side sat the fearless Andrew Reale. (Stretched on a large blue sofa at the other side of the room, gazing out of the wide windows at the noble panorama of the city of stone and rivers, reclined the disheveled Michael Wilde, whose presence had been explained by Marquis and quickly forgotten by everyone.)

"Andy, you'd better redeem me," Van Wirt was saying with worried joviality. "I presumed on Mr. Marquis's time to arrange this meeting simply on the basis of your telegram saying you'd signed Stanfield."

"I have signed him," said Andrew. He took from his breast pocket the paper to which Stanfield had put his signature the previous morning and unfolding it carefully, he extended it to Marquis. The soap maker scanned the document. As his eye fell on the Faithful Shepherd's signature a grin of triumph broadened his mouth, but as his eyes traveled through the typewritten paragraphs his expression changed, and his physiognomy began to approximate the appearance of cirrus clouds, shifting winds, a falling barometer and other signs of an approaching storm.

"I'll be G——d," he exclaimed. "Van Wirt, do you know what's in this G——d agreement?"

"Why, no," said the unfortunate sales manager, with the look of a man in a frail craft running before the gale, "I entrusted the entire arrangement to Reale. Of course he's a little young, and he may have slipped up on a detail or two, but nothing that can't be—"

"A detail or two?" roared Marquis. "Why, G——n it, how about reading what your company is trying to get me into before sending out your G——n wet errand boys on a man's business?" He threw the paper to Van Wirt.

(It should be said here that Marquis's conversation, regarded solely as a numerical achievement in violations of the Third Commandment, was remarkable; and, as sophisticated readers would be fatigued and innocent ones baffled by repeated dashes, and as we do not intend to offend by printing his oaths, we will simply ask the audience to assume the single blasphemy, "Goddamn," inserted in his every third phrase during moments of anger, fear, excitement, surprise, or pleasure.)

Van Wirt pounced on the paper and his head moved from side to side in short jerks, so eagerly did he examine it. Dismay dawned on his face. The ring on Leach's finger increased its speed of rotation, and Grovill's smile solidified.

"Andy!" said Van Wirt in a tremulous voice, "no commercials? What does this mean? You exceeded your authority—"

"I know I did, Mr. Van Wirt," said our hero, with oleaginous deference. "Please hear me out, gentlemen—and first, notice that that paper does not in the least bind us, except as to the manner of presentation of a *proposed* program. It only binds Stanfield."

Marquis took the document out of Van Wirt's hands with a glare at him, and ran his finger along several lines; then he passed it to Grovill and bent a glance on Andrew Reale in which the barometer was still falling rapidly.

"Gentlemen," said Andrew, "when you want to induce a religious fanatic to come on the radio to sell soap, after he has already declared publicly that the Saviour isn't for sale, you are facing a rather unusual problem in personal relations. I was given *carte blanche* on this problem and told that my career in my company would advance or end according to the way I solved it. I accepted the challenge, and devised a presentation which, I thought, would cause Father Stanfield to agree to come on the air under commercial sponsorship. As you see, it worked. The remaining question is, will this manner of presentation still sell soap? I think it will sell vast quantities of it.

"That paper binds us to limit our commercial identification to a single sentence at the beginning and at the end of Stanfield's half hour of broadcasting, to this effect:

"The Marquis Company, makers of Aurora Dawn Soap and Aurora Dawn Soap Products, have turned over the next half hour

93

of radio time to Father Stanfield's Fold of the Faithful Shepherd, as an Aurora Dawn contribution to the religious life of America.

"There is to be no further reference to the product."

As he said this, Andrew Reale rose to his feet and, pressing his fists on Marquis's desk, proceeded with great earnestness. He had the attention of everyone in the room, not excepting Michael Wilde, who sat up on the sofa and leaned forward.

"Now, it is my belief that such a gesture will create an amount of good will for the product that could not be approximated by sledge-hammer sales talks. America is a religious country, despite the atmosphere around radio studios. Every pastor and every churchgoer in the land will speak with favor of this uniquely unselfish act on the part of a soap company. The word-of-mouth advertising will be colossal, and it will be solid selling of Aurora Dawn, gentlemen, because, if you will notice, in that brief announcement Father Stanfield has accepted six mentions of the name: three at the beginning of the program, and three more at the end. Six times your product is identified, Mr. Marquis, tied to the selling power of God himself. I don't think that's a disservice to Aurora Dawn."

Mr. Marquis's face began to undergo curious and indecipherable alterations of expression.

"I realize, however," went on our hero, with vigorous assurance, "that this is a radical selling approach, based on an opinion of mine. I don't propose, gentlemen, to induce you to accept the idea on such a flimsy basis. Despite the paper which Mr. Leach is holding—" as this was said, Leach dropped the paper to the desk as though it had suddenly developed a voltage—"we will tie an old-fashioned, double-barreled, two-and-a-half-minute straight commercial into Father Stanfield's broadcast; and he will never object to it, and probably never even know it!"

Van Wirt ran his tongue around his lips and said, "Now wait, Andy, you're talking about the impossible—"

"Hear me out, Mr. Van Wirt," said Andy. "Mr. Marquis, you

94

have, in the Bob Steele comedy show on USBS, one of the most popular half hours on the air. The time in which we of RBC propose to place Father Stanfield is 8:30 to 9:00 Sunday evening—the best spot of the week. We know as well as you the prestige value of this religious marvel, and we intend to enhance our network's standing with it.

"Now, here's the crux of the matter. It happens that in the 8 to 8:30 Sunday evening spot on our network, Durfee's Yeast Cake Jamboree *does not intend to renew*. That hour will be free on April the first. My idea is this, Mr. Marquis: shift the Bob Steele show to our network in the 8 to 8:30 spot. At the *end* of that program—at the time when every follower of Father Stanfield will be tuning to our station—put in the longest, strongest commercial that the brilliant staff of Grovill and Leach can produce. You will then have a solid Aurora Dawn hour in the best spot of the week—the second half will be a terrific good-will stroke that will take America by storm—and, for insurance, you will cash in on the entire religious audience, by slipping in your straight commercial *at the end of the preceding show*.

"If that is not the only way to handle Father Stanfield—and if it is not an effective sales idea—then I'll willingly give up my position with you, Mr. Van Wirt, because my judgment in these matters is meaningless."

Andy sank into his chair and sat poised, his eyes on Marquis. Grovill, Leach, and Van Wirt seemed hypnotized. Not a sound, not a flicker or a gesture indicating approval or disapproval escaped any of them. Even Leach's ring ceased its rotation, lest it seem in some obscure way to suggest an opinion. Marquis leaned back in his chair and gazed intently for perhaps a full minute at the end of his cigar. Then he looked around at the waiting faces and said, in deliberate tones: "Gentlemen, that is the greatest idea for radio promotion that I have ever heard."

This statement acted upon Van Wirt, Grovill, and Leach like a starting gun. They jumped up, dashed at Andy with shouts of joy and praise, shook his hand, pounded his back, shook each other by the hand, pounded each other on the back, laughed, cried, capered, and generally conducted themselves as though a war had just ended. Marquis observed this demonstration with a calm smile, while Mike Wilde's eyes widened like a child's at a zoo when he comes upon a dancing bear. Van Wirt twined his arm affectionately around Reale's waist and refused to remove it. "He's my boy, my boy," he kept repeating. Grovill observed with many happy giggles that he would steal this young genius from RBC; Van Wirt defied him to try it. Leach's ring spun furiously, and Leach himself made several centrifugal tours of the room in the manner of a dervish, thus releasing the energy which the others expended in laughter, a form of activity of which he had apparently lost the muscular pattern.

When the jubilation had abated, Marquis said to Leach, "Tom, will we be able to shift the Steele show? USBS can plaster us with lawsuits. The contract gives us another year on that half hour."

Leach's face tightened into its accustomed lines. "I don't think they'll struggle too hard," he said through his teeth. "Not with four daytime and one other evening show still on their nets. I'll talk to Wolver. It'll be all right." His manner of saying this left no doubt that it would be, and indicated that his "talking" to the unlucky Wolver would be in the tradition of persuasion followed by antique monarchs with the aid of quaint machines.

"Even so," mused Marquis, "it's obviously vital that no word of this deal get out until it's all arranged. I hope, Reale, that you warned Father Stanfield to be discreet."

Andy said the Faithful Shepherd had himself observed that he desired secrecy to be maintained, if possible, until all was ready for him to go on the air.

"And I presume," went on Marquis, "that you have discussed the matter with no one?"

Van Wirt, his arm still around the small waist of his protégé, broke in with: "Why, he never even told me about it! Andy's the deepest boy in our organization. He's a Sphinx, a silent tomb!" He gave the silent tomb a heavy paternal squeeze.

A small box on Marquis's desk came to life with a woman's voice and said, "Mr. Marquis, Carol is here." Marquis touched a button on the box and said, "Tell her to come in." "Yes, sir," said the box. This bit of Oriental fantasy went totally unregarded. Electricity is ending all mystery. How can we impress children any longer with Aladdin's djinn? He was simply televised, and worked by remote control.

The door opened and a young lady entered. Andrew's heart bounded and his head swam so that he all but collapsed in his chair; he stared at the girl with dropping jaw as Marquis said, "This is my daughter, Carol, gentlemen."

It was impossible to mistake the sweater, the hair, the face, the paint, the hands. Carol Marquis was no other person than the Beautiful Brahmin of the train; the inquisitive stranger to whom Andrew Reale had disclosed, with many disparaging comments on the peculiarities of Talmadge Marquis, his entire scheme for the capture of the Faithful Shepherd!

CHAPTER 9

Containing the story of Bezalel,
with some of Stephen English's ideas about life
and people—and a little more plot.

At this exact moment in time—no, that is not correct, for late research indicates that there is no such thing as an exact moment in time; but it is very hard for the clay feet of history to keep up with the winged sandals of science—at this inexact moment, then, Laura Beaton and Stephen English were standing in a gallery of the Museum of New Art on Fifty-third Street, gazing at a painting by Michael Wilde. It was a beautifully executed horror of arms, legs, breasts, and faces disposed in a circular pattern. The color was subtle and rich, and the design, could it have been voided of its charnel-house content, would have been entirely pleasing. The title of the painting was: "He Looked Again, And Saw It Was A Letter From His Wife."

"I hope," said Laura, laughing, "that he isn't going to make me appear like that."

"Have no fear," said the millionaire. "Mike is guilty of many apish tricks like this one, but he knows exactly what he's doing all the time, and, as you must see just from his work on these walls, he's a good painter."

"He Looked Again, And Saw It Was A Letter From His Wife"

Said Laura, with puzzlement putting a charming furrow between her brows, "But why does he take so many silly or nasty themes? And why the elongated titles?"

"I can explain all that, but it would require a little time," said English, taking her arm and starting to walk down the gallery, "and you must have work to do this afternoon."

"All I have to do is check in at Pandar Agency, and I can attend to that by telephone. Do tell me about him."

"There is nothing I would enjoy more," said English, with just the ghost of a smile. "Come."

With this he turned abruptly to the right, and Laura found herself stepping into a small automatic elevator. The banker pressed a button marked "Roof," whereupon the doors closed, the little elevator sighed its way up three stories, and the doors opened again on cold air and blazing white sunshine. English led Laura through a garden crowded with curious statues, some all curves, some all angles, some all planes, none particularly resembling any sublunary object. At the other end of the garden was a penthouse, the door of which, as they approached it, was opened by a smiling little gray-haired lady in a very starched, very green apron.

"Good afternoon, Mr. English; good afternoon, Miss," she said, as though she had been expecting them for half an hour. "There's a nice fire, Mr. English. Will you be having some tea?"

"Later, thank you, Mrs. Brennan," said English, as he and Laura stepped inside. They were in a small vestibule, with doors opening to the right and left. The beaming Mrs. Brennan went to the right, and following her with her eye, the girl caught a glimpse of a committee room decorated in the modern style and furnished with a long table and many chairs, and beyond it a swinging door leading to a kitchen, into which the old lady vanished. English led Laura to the left, and together they walked into a sunlit, old-fashioned library which might have been transported detail by detail from a cinema setting for a story of rich Tories in the American Revolution. It was, in fact, a replica of one of the replicas in the Williamsburg restoration of colonial homes; the wraith of a wraith, its quality of other-worldliness heightened by its forlorn setting atop a building full of fearfully New things. A real fire burned in a real stone chimney, and a wisp of real smoke even brought a sting to the eyes, due to a really faulty draft.

English and the girl seated themselves on the deep-cushioned sofa that faced the fire. Neither spoke. English contemplated the dancing flames, pale in the sunlight, and Laura contemplated the millionaire, waiting for him to begin his explanation of the work of Michael Wilde, and wondering not a little at his curious manner with her, particularly his custom of long, placid silences. Perhaps for five minutes they sat so, then English looked up at her, and smiled the baffling smile that made her feel an absurd, pitying kindness toward him.

"Take your hat off, Laura," he said.

After a moment's hesitation, Laura in a quick movement unpinned the nonsensical little bonnet from her yellow hair and laid it on the arm of the sofa, saying, "Well, but what does my hat have to do with Michael Wilde's painting?"

"Nothing at all," said Stephen English, leaning back comfortably in the sofa. "It's surely no secret to you that I enjoy looking at you. The hat is becoming, but I find the unadorned hair more so. Now, about Mike. You have seen him referred to as Bezalel, haven't you?"

"Yes, many times," said Laura. "The columnists are very fond of the name. I've seen his illustrated Bible, and I know the reason for that."

"That incident," said the millionaire, "is Wilde's career in miniature. But be sure that you are quite comfortable, because, like Scheherazade, I intend to spin out my tale, to postpone the cutting off, not of my head but of this agreeable scene into which I tricked you and which I should like to last as long as possible. This then, is

THE STORY OF BEZALEL.

It has always entertained me (said Stephen English) to listen to a furious discussion among aesthetes, with one side maintaining that Michael Wilde is a poser and a charlatan, against an equally heated assertion that he's a brilliant artist. The reason for such disputes, of course, lies in the assumption that the two descriptions are contradictory. In Mike's case it's obvious that they're both true.

Mike was born in the Irish slums that used to exist around Ninety-sixth Street and Columbus Avenue in New York. He has, therefore, the poignant love of money that's reserved only for people who've known poverty. Rich people respect money because it's their safety, but to poor people money is freedom. Never forget that when you analyze the behavior of someone who used to be poor; there's a friskiness about such persons which is only the lightness of limb that comes from taking off chains. Mike's antics, of course, have further, more self-conscious motives.

Really, Mike carries on the way he does because it helps to sell his paintings. It's true, of course, that he's enormously conceited and that he has a natural taste for being the life of the party, but such characteristics are commonplace. In most careers they must be severely repressed, because the aim of a man is to give an impression of reliability, steadiness, and a sense of propriety. Artists—in all the arts—are exempt. Successful artists today must be crowd pleasers, and its the opinion of the crowd that artists are a little crazy, so a man of talent who plays up to that opinion will unquestionably make more money than one who doesn't. He'll be talked about and he'll gain stature. Mike stumbled on this open secret in Paris when he was nineteen. Have you ever seen the ballet he designed, "Chanson de Moi-Même"?

(Laura said that she had not; and, shifting a little in her corner of the sofa, she tucked her famous legs under her skirt, folded her hands in her lap, and regarded English with the clear, serious eyes of a listening child.)

Well, at the time, he was in the thick of the impecunious artistic set that you used to find sitting around in front of the Dôme in the evenings, drinking *fines* and arguing about everything. He fell into the hands of a celebrated première danseuse, who was well on the nostalgic side of thirty, and he became a pet of the ballet people. The choreographer of the company was inspired to do a ballet based on Walt Whitman's "Song of Myself"; and, thanks to the intervention of the danseuse, Mike was commissioned to try his hand at the *décor*.

He was an entirely irresponsible kid then, spoiled both by his talents and his attractiveness. He had come to Paris after working in an advertising agency for a year, just long enough to accumulate the money to travel, and in that year, by the way, he acquired his single vicious prejudice: get him started on the subject of advertising, sometime, if you want a jeremiad. Anyway, in Paris he habitually followed only impulse in whatever he did. In designing the ballet he was seized with the whim of taking the title literally, and he proceeded with some pains to sketch out a weird, extravagant set consisting of nothing but reproductions of himself. The center piece was a colossal bust of Mike Wilde with the lower part formalized into a Greek temple; the trees were graceful, gnarled versions of himself; even the rocks were worked into profiles of him; and the dancers all wore masks in his likeness. Well, Freud was a fad then, ten years ago, so the choreographer was rapturous, and worked out a dance on the theme of Narcissus which really wasn't bad. The ballet was a sensation in France and in America. It's odd that you never saw it.

("I was twelve years old ten years ago," said Laura demurely, "and the ballet didn't stop in Albuquerque.")

At any rate Mike found himself and his work suddenly in demand. He had the pleasure of selling to dealers who had snubbed him, the very pieces they had dismissed. The newspapers also came after him, and Mike, realizing that they were looking for bizarre behavior and ideas, just gave rein to himself and furnished them with all the copy they could use.

You've seen his Bible. He did most of it before the ballet, as an exercise in dramatic sketching and coloring, and I've always thought the pictures ordinary; they bear many traces of his advertising drudgery, in fact. When he came to America with the ballet, he was approached by one of those enterprising publishers who make a business of exploiting a new genius or a new word game each year. He promptly hauled out his portfolio of Bible pictures, to the ecstasy of the publisher. Mike won't admit it, but I'm sure he put in the controversial pieces that brought all the bishops and ministers down on him—Ruth at Boaz' feet, Judah and Tamar, that scandalous Magdalene, and so forth—*after* he'd sold the portfolio to the publisher. He did once tell me that he inserted the portrait of himself in Old Testament dress as Bezalel, the divine artist of the Tabernacle, because he thought "the excitement would make the book go better." Of course, you know what happened. It sold more than half a million copies, and it still goes into a new edition each year—all at eight dollars a copy.

("My father preached a sermon in favor of the Wilde Bible and we had a copy at home," said Laura. "Mother came after it with the scissors to cut out Judah and Tamar and some of the others, but Dad fought her off. They compromised by locking it up until I was seventeen.")

The very worst time to let you look at it, but you seem to have survived the exposure.—Well, there you have Mike Wilde, Laura. He does have a bent for perverse flamboyance, but instead of checking it, he exploits it. He takes horrid themes because they cause talk; he uses long, pointless titles for the same reason. He blathers about goodness and beauty and his own genius for the same reason. To bring the thing off as well as Mike has done requires address, I grant you, and a gift for mountebanking; but it must be great fun, once he overcomes the loss of face involved in making an ass of himself in public. Nobody can commit the impropriety of public self-praise without losing personal dignity and integrity, but, in the field of the arts, it's a common sacrifice. You see the pattern repeat itself two or three times in each generation. A man of moderate talent proclaims, "I am a genius," and backs his assertion with colorful social and artistic eccentricities. These have nothing to do with genius, but the crowd thinks they do, and so his claim is improved. Shakespeare, Bach, and Blake didn't find it necessary to use the technique. Mike's an excellent painter, and his work will last his time and keep him well-to-do, but his mouth long ago outsped his brush. I've said these things to him, so I'm not violating our friendship in telling you the truth about him. It's nothing you wouldn't have seen for yourself, anyway, in a year or two.

* * *

The fire was dying. Stephen English rose, poked it up, threw two small logs on it, and, as the flames snarled gratefully around the dry wood, he sat again near the girl and gazed at the brightening blaze in silence. The sunlight now slanted above the fireplace, and for the first time Laura noticed the painting hung there. It was a portrait of her companion. Beneath it was a medallion reading: "Stephen Allworth English, President of the New Art Foundation—Portrait by Michael Wilde." The likeness was vital, and, as Laura looked at the face, she felt again an unaccountable, sympathetic condescension toward the subject. She glanced at him, sitting beside her, absorbed in the pleasant spell of the flames.

"Stephen," she said. He turned his head toward her, a slight lift in the eyebrows that were faintly tinged with gray. Laura hesitated for a moment, conscious of a great impulse to say something kind. "I think you're very decent and wise."

Stephen English laughed aloud, and Laura realized that she had not heard him do so until now. It was the kind of short, reluctant mirth with which someone joins in a joke at his own expense. He took her hand; Laura did not protest, nor did she wrest her hand away from him. They sat thus in a new unspeaking intimacy looking at the fire, and thus they were still fifteen minutes later when Mrs. Brennan rustled starchily into the room, decorated with the broadest of all possible smiles and bearing an exquisite service of tea.

It will be very hard, surely, to justify to the gentle reader what must seem a looseness in our heroine's behavior. Remember, then, that even Noah, the only man deemed worthy of being saved from a world's destruction, was described as being merely "righteous in his generation." The manners of the time and place in which Laura lived took an exceedingly frivolous view of the importance of holding hands, and indeed of other, somewhat more searching liberties. Morality is eternal, but its modes fluctuate. A Japanese, they say, thinks nothing of bathing naked in the same tub with a stranger of the opposite sex, but a clasp of hands between the two would be a turning point. We ourselves observe with great calm our young ladies walking on beaches with all but a half-dozen crucial square inches of their skins exposed; an hour later, we are shocked to see one of them come in to dinner wearing a skirt which ends an inch above the knee. Laura was, beyond doubt, righteous in her generation; yet, betrothed though she was, she permitted Stephen English to hold her hand. That this was an inadvisable kindness will perhaps be seen in the sequel.

When Laura returned to her apartment at sundown, she observed with surprise that her mother was setting the dinner table for two. "I telephoned you that Andy was coming," she protested.

"Andy telephoned at three o'clock and said he was sorry, but he suddenly found that he had to take someone to dinner for business reasons," said Mrs. Beaton, smoothing the tablecloth daintily. "How was lunch with Mr. English and that famous artist? My, you're moving in high company nowadays. You'd have been right at home with your uncle Woodrow in the White House."

"Lunch was very pleasant," said Laura, with a sinking at her heart which she could have in no way explained. "Did Andy say he would be here later in the evening?"

"No, he said he was afraid he was going to have to make a night of it. Strange that a millionaire finds time for you and a young fellow like Andy is so occupied," said the mother, and was about to continue when she observed a dangerous gleam in her daughter's eye, whereupon she prudently disappeared into the kitchen.

The telephone rang. Laura leaped at it; the radiance on her face as she put the device to her ear was the expression the old masters were always struggling for when they painted angels. The disappointment that quickly succeeded it was like the dropping of a curtain. "Hello, Stephen," she said. "You're much too kind to me. Thank you, but I'm having dinner at home." A silence followed during which she was clearly being subjected to persuasion. "Stephen, I don't like to be serious over the telephone, but don't you think that it's not proper for me to see you so often?" Another silence. Laura's expression changed to one of resignation. "Yes, of course I'd enjoy that," she said at last. "Do come up for a while after dinner. You can't stay long because I have to work early in the morning. Good-by."

As she put down the instrument her mother came out of the kitchen, carrying plates of bread and butter. "Who was that?" she inquired with the elaborate innocence of the eavesdropper. Laura told her wearily that Stephen English had asked permission to pay a call after dinner, and that she had been unable to think quickly of a gracious way to refuse him. Mrs. Beaton observed with gravity that she was sure it was perfectly proper, otherwise a fine gentleman like Mr. English would not suggest it, and furthermore, she was confident it would be a short, pleasant and *very* harmless little visit, and much nicer than sitting alone, wondering what Andy was doing. She returned to the kitchen as she said this, and no sooner had she passed out of her daughter's sight than she executed a caper that was slightly at variance with her remarks and quite singular in a lady of advancing years.

No heroine, surely, should consider entertaining in her home a man other than the one to whom she is betrothed, but there's such a majesty doth hedge a millionaire that one must deal lightly with a maiden whose sense of propriety falters before him. Yet I fear that this apology may be misplaced, and that all too many of my readers, even as Mrs. Beaton, only feel that Laura is at long last beginning to use her head.

CHAPTER 10

*In which Andrew Reale improves an acquaintance,
and eats one Magic Dinner more than is supposed
to be healthy for a young man.*

𝕋HE SNOW IS FALLING in a whirling veil in Central Park tonight. It has been falling steadily and heavily since sunset, and
the trees are laden with a decorative burden, while the lawns
and asphalt roads are blanketed in silent whiteness. The lamps
are haloes around which dance innumerable snowflakes, fluttering
ever down and down like dying little white moths. So thick is
the snowstorm that beyond the lamps nothing can be seen of the
artificial cliffs which march grimly to the four brinks of the park
and halt there, baffled by the charm of Municipal Ownership; and
tonight the park might be a thousand square miles of whiteness
instead of a few besieged acres. Snow . . . snow . . . snow. The

automobile traffic is all diverted to the straight avenues flanking the outside of the park, where monstrous machines thrust the snow aside as fast as it settles to the wet stone. The winding roads inside the park are deserted, and, as they gather the whiteness undisturbed, they are gradually merging into the lawns out of which they were first gashed. It is with difficulty that the ancient driver atop the ancient hansom cab—which intensifies the solitude by being the sole moving thing in it—can see his way through the sooty night and the milky storm, but the sense of the horse is better than the cabman's eye, and he plods surely along straightaways and around curves that are stamped into his muscles. The noise of his hoofs is muffled to a padding such as might be made by a giant cat. The cabman utters no sound and thinks no thought. Inside the cab, the young couple are as completely alone as they might be at either Pole. This is well, since they are locked in most affectionate embrace.

It is with regret that I must identify the couple as Andrew Reale and Carol Marquis.

They remain thus, mouth to mouth, clinging to each other as the cab rocks them gently, for a length of time that is better imagined than specified. At last Carol takes her burning mouth from his, and, leaning back in his arms, whispers, "I know all about you. You're engaged to Honey Beaton. Why are you doing this to me?" Andrew's eyes are looking into hers. "I don't know why I'm doing it. Shall I stop?" he says. A little white hand steals into the plentiful fair hair on the back of his head, and his mouth is softly pulled down on hers once more. The cabman blows snowflakes out of his gray mustache and notices mournfully, through a rift in the storm, the straight line of lights on One Hundred Tenth Street, which tells him he is only half way around the park; and his slow mind, oscillating for a moment between wonder at the foolishness of his fares, and gratitude for the twenty-dollar bill with which he was bribed to accommodate their eccentric impulse, settles into a numbness matching that of his fingers and toes. Snowflakes drift inside the cab through a small opening of one window and settle unheeded on the girl's fur coat. And it is cold inside the little wooden box, but there is no numbness in here, no numbness at all.

Sweet friend, may Heaven preserve you from error and keep you safe in the good paths of life; but if you are fated to stray, in order to learn the bitter lessons of straying, may one of your sins be a hansom cab ride through Central Park in a snowstorm, wrapped in the arms of a young creature who is not yours.

The chain of circumstances that had brought Andrew Reale into such peccant activity was curious, in that each link but the very last could be regarded as innocent—and probably was, to his best discernment. Confronted with the apparition of the girl in Talmadge Marquis's office at a moment when a word from her could have engulfed all his hopes, he had seen no other course but to say to her, in a swift aside during introductions, "Mum's the word, and I'll take you to dinner at the Ferrara." The girl had given him a single mischievous glance and muttered, "Done!" and thereafter had feigned indifference to him, and had made no mention of their encounter on the train. It developed that she had come to her father's office to meet Michael Wilde and obtain an interview with him for her college newspaper, and shortly after her arrival she left with the talkative painter to visit his studio. The business meeting continued with a discussion of plans for the Stanfield program, and ended in an atmosphere of hearty good feeling as rare in Marquis's office as conversations in ancient Hebrew—a complete triumph for Andy. In the spangled firmament of advertising, a new star was unmistakably beginning to glimmer.

The Club Ferrara, like the setting of the "Decameron," was a pleasant retreat where aristocrats gathered to escape a spreading epidemic—in the older instance, bubonic plague, in the present one, equality. The proprietor was a chevalier dauntless in the tottering cause of privilege, and his prices formed a steep wall which only the stoutest purses could scale. Outside, the throng sweated and pressed, and one or two of the hairy mob might even fight their way each evening inside the walls, but always they were confronted in the outer hall by this Aramis, skilled in parrying the bludgeon of raw gold with the pliant steel of insolence. It followed, naturally, that the Club Ferrara was considered the most desirable place in New York at which to dine. The interior of the club was decorated with murals depicting the life of Lucrezia Borgia, but the research and toil of the artist went for naught, since at the club the animal act of feeding was veiled in a fashionable gloom which obscured his work and also, mercifully, the coloring of many of the patrons.

Andy's offer to take the Marquis girl to the Ferrara had been an inspiration, for it was the very shrine of the Beautiful Brahmins. A devotée who came here twice in one week acquired thereby an increase of caste and was distantly envied by her sisters who could contrive to immerse themselves in this Ganges only once, limited as they were to collegian escorts of good family whose weekly allowances were consumed like stubble by an evening at the Ferrara. Andrew was a familiar figure at the club, for in the entertainment of clients his purse was the exchequer of the Republic Broadcasting Company itself. The proprietor bowed and spoke pleasant words of greeting to the couple, and conducted them to a table directly beneath a panel depicting Lucrezia and Pietro Bembo in a guilty kiss.

No reader under thirty-five will fail to agree that a thousand dinners at restaurants may go by, undistinguished one from another, and then, suddenly, one will come that is fatefully perfect. The wine invigorates like Ponce de Leon's fountain, the roast chicken is a miracle of brown excellence, the asparagus is green as emeralds, the rolls are warm snowballs in a crust of gold, and there never was such a swooning sweetness of ice cream; and all this, by the luckiest of coincidences, happens on the very evening when one first dines with a young person who is destined to become of Great Importance. Andrew Reale had eaten such a magic dinner once before, six months earlier, when he had taken the pretty Dixie Cigarette Model-of-the-Month, Honey Beaton, to dinner. It did not occur to him at all now—for he was, truthfully, in an unreflective stage—that there was anything more than delight in the fact that tonight he was eating another one.

The note struck in the relationship between a young man and a young lady in the first hour of their acquaintance often persists unchanged until stilled by separation or death. This dinner was the breakfast on the train all over again for Andrew and Carol, with the added warmth of renewal, and a merriment engendered by their conspiracy to hide his folly from her father. The girl archly threatened to expose him whenever, as she pretended, an item of the dinner displeased her, as, "This rice is cold. I'm going to tell my father everything," whereupon Andrew never failed to produce extravagant and ridiculous pleas for mercy. This inexhaustible joke kept them gay, and Andy, feeling again the buoyancy that the girl inspired in him, proceeded to talk about himself with abandon, and found the subject fruitful, with the youngster's attentive dark eyes fixed on him. Again there were the short, pertinent questions dropped into his pauses for breath, urging him on to further self-revelation; again there was intense laughing appreciation of every point and sympathetic admiration of each opinion or plan. Once or twice, with a vague sense of the lack of balance of the dialogue, he tried to shift the focus to her, but the girl impatiently dismissed herself as "just a school kid," and brought the conversation back to the topic on which he was never unable to resume his eloquence.

The dinner vanished, together with two quarts of champagne. Carol's laughter at Andy's wit grew louder and more prolonged, her threats to inform on him more frequent, his miming of a suppliant more absurd. Between bursts of mirth she told him that she had decided to fix his fate by the quality of his rhumba dancing: if he proved the best with whom she had ever danced,

—Murals depicting the life of Lucrezia Borgia—

her lips were sealed, otherwise he must face Talmadge Marquis's fury. Andy took up the challenge. He was accustomed to the assurances of young ladies that he was, as they invariably put it, "a divine dancer." Which member of the Trinity he was supposed to resemble in this attribute had never been specified, to the knowledge of the recorder.

They proceeded, accordingly, to the Krypton Room on the roof of the skyscraping Hotel Saint James, where brown South Americans played the music of their continent, to which, at that time, citizens of the land of the free took pleasure in agitating their bodies. Andrew and Carol were soon weaving happily under the strange whitish light of the fluorescent tubes filled with krypton gas, which gave the room its name. (The title was first selected by the hotel manager under the impression that Krypton was a metal with which the walls could be decorated: the mistake was discovered only subsequent to an extensive publicizing effort, and the krypton-light tubes were ordered at great expense, as the name was considered most smart and modern. The lights had the effect of making anyone who stood directly under them look extraordinarily ill, and feminine habitués like Carol exhibited much ingenuity in maneuvering outside their scope.)

Since the dance called the rhumba resembled nothing so much as a stylized fertility rite, and since the music to which it was danced was in a congruent mode, our hero soon found himself regarding his partner with sentiments that did him little credit. If the large quantities of wine which he shared with her were intended to quench these feelings, they were unsuccessful. Carol Marquis did not become giddy, but her eyes took on sparkle, her cheeks reddened and she danced in a manner that might have won applause from the Indians among whom the inflammatory rhythms were born. Andrew was swept up in the flood of her energy. Higher and higher rose their spirits. During a break in the music they walked into the foyer to enjoy the view of New York for which the Krypton Room was known, and, as they gazed out on the splendid panorama of the towers of light, a snow cloud rolled in from the sea, and all vanished except an electric glow, rose-within-white. Clouds of such appearance must float around the near approaches of Heaven. Huge flakes began to hurl themselves against the window and cling there. "Oh, Lord, look at the snow now!" cried Carol, and grasped Andrew's hand impulsively with warm, tense little white fingers that scratched a bit, so long and sharp were the nails. "Let's go out and roll in it!"

To fetch their coats, to drop seven hundred feet, to rush out into the storm and feel the tiny stabs of snowflakes on their faces, was the work of a minute. Holding hands, laughing, shouting, and singing, they ran the two blocks that separated them from the lawns of the park, where snowdrifts were already beginning to pile. The many people walking along the cold street with their faces buried miserably to the eyes, people unwarmed by wine and the rhumba, wondered who these noisy fools might be, and passed on. No sooner had Andrew and Carol gone by the stone wall that divided the snarl of city traffic from the dark stillness of the park, than the girl, true to her word, threw herself on the ground and rolled around in the snow like an animal. Andrew regarded this spectacle with astonishment for a moment, then flung aside his hat and imitated her, finding the crunch of the snow under his chest and shoulders a very exhilarating sensation. A few moments of this, and the girl jumped up, shaking the snow from her hair and her furs. "This is wonderful. I want to ride in a hansom cab. Come on, there's a dozen at the plaza." She gave a sharp little tug at his hand to help him up, and they ran along the path to the plaza through the thickening storm.

Most of the cabmen had abandoned their posts in the face of the snowfall and had sheltered their ageing steeds in the warmth of stables; but a few necessitous or inert drivers still sat on their high seats, huddled in blankets to the armpits, wrapped in shawls the rest of the way, shrinking from the snow under their ancient top hats, and exhibiting out of all this protection a minimum of red nose, as a sort of shingle to indicate that, weather or no, they were open for business. Dashing up to the reddest of these, Carol shouted, "How much to ride around the park?" A pair of eyes only slightly less red than the nose appeared dimly from under the brim of the top hat, and gazed at the girl with filmy wonder. "What, in this storm?" spoke a voice, its indignant overtones somewhat lost in traversing two layers of thick wool. "Yes, in this storm. How much?" said the girl impatiently. The eyes vanished for a moment while the driver looked into his soul, then reappeared: "It's cruelty to the poor horse. I was just fixing to take her to the stable. I couldn't do it for less than twenty dollars." Carol whirled on Andrew. "You've got twenty dollars, haven't you?" she said, but the green bill was already whipping in the cold wind on its brief journey from Andrew's wallet to the cabman's pocket. The girl leaped into the rickety vehicle, her escort followed, and the equipage moved off into the white curtain that was masking the world. Scarcely had the carriage passed from the cloudy brilliance of the street lamps into the gloom of the park, when Carol and Andrew moved into each other's arms without a word. Mouth found mouth; and thus they remained, with few perceptible changes, until the moment that opens this chapter, when the unhappy author was forced to intrude upon this desperate scene, in order to move his story along.

These events will inevitably recall to many readers, I am certain, Immanuel Kant's important distinction between *arbitrium sensitivum* and *arbitrium brutum* in his inquiry into the possibility of free will and moral responsibility. This philosopher's belief that the human will, while influenced by sensuous circumstance, is not coerced by it, places the blame for what is happening squarely on our hero. Determinists, however, would hold that Andrew Reale was but a helpless tennis ball, batted out of moral bounds by the racket of Causality. The essence of Determinism in the field of morality is contained in the phrase, "I'm only human, after all." Readers who have availed themselves of the maxim will be pleased to know that, like the Bourgeois Gentleman, they have been speaking philosophy all their lives without knowing it. But neither Determinists nor Kantians, surely, can be quite comfortable about leaving Andrew forever in Carol Marquis's arms. Back to our tale.

The hansom cab and the old horse were now making no sound at all, so thick was the snow on the road, and the strange carriage glided slowly like a black ghost through the white night. At last, the diffused radiance of Columbus Circle could be dimly seen through the cloud of snowflakes, heralding the end of the circuit, and the driver rapped twice, discreetly, on the roof of the cab. Carol opened her eyes and looked over Andrew's shoulder out of the window; then she loosened her arms, leaned back, and regarded him quizzically.

"This has been very crazy," she said softly.

"It has," agreed Andrew.

"But fun," said the girl, with a small laugh.

"Yes," said our hero.

"I won't tell Honey Beaton on you," Carol promised, and, disengaging herself, she produced a cosmetic kit and proceeded to restore the ravaged paint on her face with remarkable speed and deftness, while Andrew removed remnants of her earlier effort from his ears, nose, cheeks, mouth, collar, and shoulders as best he could.

Thus it was that, a half hour later, they presented a reasonable similitude of casual innocence when they spun through the revolving door of the Café Armand, near the park, in search of drinks to warm them, and ran head-on into Laura Beaton and Stephen English, just gathering their coats to leave. Really, Andy's demeanor was especially decorous, and should have deceived any eyes, even those of a fiancée.

Readers must now contemplate a picture that will strain credulity, particularly if the readers are modern young ladies. It is Laura, our heroine, having just said good-by to Stephen English in the hallway of her apartment house, riding up in the elevator with a fixed expression, and, as soon as she steps inside her door, bursting into violent sobs and flinging herself on the living-room couch face downward, in an attitude of entire misery. I say that the celebrated Honey Beaton, the transcendentally gorgeous model, is crying bitterly and muffling her cries in a cushion to avoid waking her mother, for all the world like any plain, fat girl who grieves her unlucky fate; as though she had never come to New York, as though she did not make two hundred dollars a week, as though her face and form did not bloom on paper from one end of the land to the other like a pretty, rampant weed, and, most improbable of all, as though she had not just returned from a date with a handsome millionaire who was in love with her. Where is happiness, where is fulfillment if not with Honey Beaton? What mean these tears?

The house telephone rings. Startled, for it is one o'clock in the morning, Laura goes to the instrument and speaks into it a hollow, mournful "Hello?" Then her expression changes wildly. "Andy! But it's so terribly late!" Pleading sounds from the diaphragm. "I'm not sure there's any point to explanations—and anyway, can't they wait until tomorrow?" Tones of emphatic protest vibrate the receiver. "Yes, I suppose so. Come on up." She puts away the telephone and glances at the mirror. One hand darts professionally to her hair and another to her eyes; but, in a moment's pause, she evidently decides that tear-stained disorder is not inappropriate to the occasion, for she refrains from changing it. As a matter of fact—such is the grace of these blessed damsels—it *is* rather becoming than otherwise.

Must we record exactly what Andrew says to her in this interview? Is it not enough to observe that, approximately fifteen minutes after his arrival, she places herself in his arms and permits him to console her with kisses? Andrew finds her kiss inexpressibly gratifying, as always, but there is tonight a taste he has never known in it before. It is the faintest touch of salt.

Let young men who envy our hero his culling of the sweetness of two such mouths in one evening observe the sequel with attention.

CHAPTER 11

*In which a great deal of history is compressed
into a very little ink, and the author indulges
in a short digression into a theory of literature
—fair warning to impatient readers.*

EACH OF US, manifesting himself as an entity on the earth, is
given a corporeal frame which can be expected to be serviceable
while the terrestrial globe makes twenty thousand turns on its
axis. It is rather unfortunate that some three thousand spins are
reeled off before we know this, and perhaps ten or fifteen thousand more before we believe it. It is even more unlucky, and very
odd, that the last five thousand spins are whirled away at what
seems to be a highly accelerating speed. Formerly this was considered an illusion, but the march of science is treading under
even that small comfort, since it now appears that there is no
absolute standard for measuring time, that all quantities are relative to the observer's "system," and that, consequently, when a

spurned young lover thinks the days crawl, while an ageing author finishing his masterpiece imagines that the very same days are whizzing, both may be perfectly correct. One person, whose identity is perhaps obvious, is the only figure in this tale who actually counted spins as they were expended. The rest went about their concerns as though the world were a flat, immovable platform lighted, with pleasing alternation, dimly and brightly, and as though their bodies were as permanent as a true philosophical idea.

Our story has all taken place, thus far, in the space of three spins; truly, no more, good friend—Saturday, Sunday, and Monday. Permit the author to make amends now for his leaden pace, by whirling his spherical stage through sixty complete revolutions in a single paragraph. Whrrrrrrr. The snow melts. The wind dies. Days lengthen. The air warms. Grass comes. Trees sprout. Flowers open. Insects wake. Food grows. Animals leap. Young ladies become demure. Young men become urgent. Every breathing human being has paid sixty spins out of his allotment and has bought with this odd coinage the privilege of being alive in the green, pleasant month of May.

The appearance of Father Stanfield and his Fold of the Faithful Shepherd on a broadcast under the sponsorship of a soap company was the wonder of the radio business, but his success was a marvel that exhausted the adjectives of even this fecund environment. There existed an enterprise, the Hooley Institute of Public Sentiment, devoted to compiling information on the popularity of programs and stating the results as numbers; an idea calculated to appeal to business people who were bewildered by the intangible standards of entertainment, but who worked under the rule of numbers, struggled for numbers, schemed and lied for numbers, were rewarded with numbers, judged each other by the size of their numbers, and left to their children when they died, as the fruit of their lives, numbers. This Hooley Institute, four weeks after the start of the Stanfield program, announced to the gasping industry that the Faithful Shepherd's "Hooley" was fifty-one. An idea of the astronomical size of this figure will be suggested by the fact that the President's annual message to Congress usually achieved a Hooley of thirty-nine. All established principles were confuted. Successful advertising executives, who held as an article of faith that the radio world rested on the four pillars of laughter, light music, notoriety, and sex, were staggered to observe that religion was more popular than any of them. Many argued that it was a sign of unhealthy times. Others were aghast at the sacrilege of demeaning Holy Writ to sell soap, and none exhibited this commendable taste more than executives who were producing programs for other soap companies.

The first two broadcasts were made directly from the Tabernacle in the remote West Virginia valley, but when an electrical storm caused a local power failure, blotting out most of the third, it was decided to avoid such risks in the future by bringing the Father and his followers to a large studio in Radio City each weekend. The expense was ponderable, but the program remained much the cheapest evening show on the air, and even if it had not, no expense would have been considered excessive for the maintenance of the majestic, the incomparable Hooley of fifty-one.

It soon appeared that Father Stanfield, like the machine gun or any other remarkable new thing which at first promises to upset all tradition in this old world, had his drawbacks. He was impervious to direction or management, and, although he acquiesced readily to the shift to New York, he was as much his own master among the great towers as he had been among his native gentle hills. In one of his first New York broadcasts he launched an extemporaneous attack on the city styles of feminine clothing, which he found too provocative. "Don't see how I kin go on bringin' the Fold up here," he said, "less'n I put blinders on the married men and check reins on the single ones. Dunno what they got theayters fer. Seems a feller'd pay to get out of the theayter and look at what's goin' on in the streets. First night I come up here I thought some big hotel was on fire and a lot of ladies got turned out of bed in a hurry—but no, seems they was wearin' evenin' gowns. I ain't no authority on the subject, but seems like the only difference between evenin' gowns and nightgowns in New York is, you don't have to marry the ladies to see 'em in evenin' gowns. When I say *in* 'em, I mean *out* of 'em. The Good Book don't say how much of her bodily temple a woman can reveal and still be decent, but I say, the less room she leaves fer doubt that she's a female, the more room she creates fer doubt that she's a lady." There was much more in this vein, culminating in an admonition to the women of the Fold to remember that "Babylon was much bigger than Jerusalem, but the Almighty allus has had sorta small-town ideas."

Of course, this sally called forth violent objections from the New York press and pulpit, varying from indignant defense of the decorum and virtue of metropolitan females to excoriation of Stanfield as a fraud. On the other hand, press and pulpit outside the great city chorused hallelujahs and amens to the rebuke. It was astonishing to observe that ministers of identical denomination in New York and New Jersey, united in creed and divided only by the Hudson, could hold absolutely opposed views on the topic—a reassuring evidence of lack of regimented narrowness in the church. On the whole, since there are more people outside New York than there are in it (I refer skeptical Manhattanites to a late World Almanac), the episode was supposed ultimately to have been a good thing for the sales of Aurora Dawn soap, at least so it was decided at a conference of his executives hurriedly assembled by Marquis. At the same time, uneasiness was expressed by Grovill and Leach lest Stanfield's next bull-like charge carry him into a more dangerous china-shop of popular opinion. Accordingly, they determined to ask the Faithful Shepherd to write out his sermons in advance of the program and forward them to the agency. Andrew Reale, who was assigned the ungrateful task of bringing this about, approached the Father with some misgivings, but found him tractable. "Dunno but what I might git some good suggestions that way," said the Shepherd, and cheerfully agreed to comply. The incident closed to the satisfaction of everybody (except a few million New York women) when the Institute of Public Sentiment disclosed, a week later, that Father Stanfield's volcanic Hooley had erupted to a new high mark of fifty-seven.

Of all the myriad events that occurred during the sixty days which we recently compressed into a paragraph, only one other will interest the reader. Before setting it down, I must admit in passing that this old-fashioned tale is violating the accepted literary rule of the day, Realism. To show life "as it really is" is considered the only significant task an author can perform. It seems curious that life "as it really is," according to modern inspiration, contains a surprising amount of fornication, violence, vulgarity, unpleasant individuals, blasphemy, hatred, and ladies' underclothes. A perverse observer might say that these things had become conventions almost as strict as the shepherds, shepherdesses, flutes, fruits, and flowers of early French poetry, but this would be carping; one must grant the sincerity of the authors and concede that their lives undoubtedly are composed in large measure of these very ingredients. But that is not necessarily life "as it really is," except for them. I hold that only one author has ever succeeded in recreating life as it really is: the Author of all things: and that he recreates life exactly as it is each day, to the wonderment of a few poets and philosophers, but without greatly impressing ordinary folks, and that all other authors, both great and insignificant, merely select from His work a few fragments that have impinged forcibly on their sensibilities. The true history of Andrew Reale underscores a very old moral truth that has impressed me, and so, to the exclusion of his life "as it really was" during those sixty days, this chapter focuses only on an event or two that bear along the line.

One more digression, the last for many pages, I promise. It will be noticed that I spoke of being struck by a moral, not a historical truth. You may scent quibbling, but upon my word, in this distinction I see the reason for my work and the justification for the breed of scribblers. For example: "The wicked are punished, and the good rewarded," is a great moral truth, but, you will all agree, a most indifferent historical one. In this life, the gap between moral and historic truth is only to be bridged by faith, wine, or art. We who write books toil on everlastingly at this task, side by side with the vintners and the priests. So much for theory. I might better have placed this effusion in a preface, but I wanted somebody to read it.

During the months of April and May, there germinated and blossomed in the mind of our forceful hero, Andrew Reale, the notion that he might marry Carol Marquis, and thus realize all his dreams, except one, at a stroke. To be sure, this one exception was the vision of holding the unadorned charms of Laura Beaton in a conjugal embrace, and the prospect of sacrificing such bliss gave him great pause. Nevertheless, the young heiress, if less dazzling than the famous Honey, was a sweet, exciting damsel, and much more attractive to Andy than he had supposed any other member of the sex could be, after the star-gemmed night on the rocky promontory under the George Washington Bridge when he had given Laura his engagement ring and had receiv in return, for the first time, the full surrender of her kiss. The interval between this excellent moment in his life and the initial still, small whisper, "Maybe I could marry the Marquis girl," was exactly four months and twenty days.

The thought crossed his mind under circumstances which made it exceptionally scoundrelly, for he was sitting by the side of Laura at the time, and her pretty white forearm was, in fact, resting ever so lightly against his. The occasion was the first performance in Radio City of Father Stanfield and his Fold. Watching this important event from a soundproof room through a glass wall

—Life "as it really is," according to modern inspiration—

facing the studio stage, was a select company that included Talmadge Marquis, Carol, Andrew, Laura, Grovill, Leach, Van Wirt—also about a dozen other people of the radio and advertising crafts who perpetually danced in Marquis's wake like scraps of paper behind a thundering subway train.

Fifteen hundred people filling the wide, bleak studio barked with laughter all at once. A sinner in sackcloth, a little, thin, weary-looking farmer, admitted he had given another man's spouse a hug and squeeze in the vestry of the Tabernacle the previous Sunday. Upon being asked who his partner in guilt was, he indicated a burly housewife on a penitential stool nearby, whereupon Father Stanfield asked whether he was confessing to coveting his neighbor's wife or laboring on the Sabbath. As Carol Marquis leaned back her head and laughed, throwing her hair in a black shower on the gold stuff of her gown, her eyes chanced to look full into Andrew's, and in that exchange of glances, for reasons of the human spirit which could not be fathomed by ten empiric psychologists running a hundred rats through a thousand mazes for ten thousand days, Andrew felt that this girl was his for the taking. Since the famous night of the snowstorm he had seen her only once, on a Friday evening when she had suddenly telephoned and spoken thus: "Hello, Teeth, I'm in from school and I want to rhumba tonight. Take me to the Krypton Room or I'll tell everything." But the tête-à-tête had proved decorous in the extreme, and he had returned the willful maiden to her doorstep without so much as brushing her lips with his. All the more curious, then, was the unmistakable content of this historic glance. The girl's dark brown eyes had laughed into his; then become fixed; then flickered for the merest instant to Laura; then looked profoundly into his eyes again, for perhaps five full seconds; and then, with a laugh and a toss of her head, she was regarding the stage once more. Our hero, stirred to his toes, gazed thoughtfully at her small white ear, and the artful tumble of thick hair pulled back to expose it, and from some gloomy crypt of his soul he heard a slow, clever voice say, "Maybe I could marry the Marquis girl"; at which precise moment the exquisite hand of Laura softly closed over his with quiet affection.

There is little that could be called heroic about our hero at this point, but worse is coming, and that without delay. In descending to the next level of infamy, let us follow the example of an illustrious predecessor, and begin a new Canto.

CHAPTER 12

*The Dinner Party: I—Containing a skein
of many colors.*

*N*ATURAL PHILOSOPHY has reached a stage of progress at which
it can predict with confidence that the mixing of certain sub-
stances will produce a material capable of detonating, to the
detriment of the persistence of life and property within a known
radius. Unfortunately, that branch of philosophy dealing with
human reactions, known in our time as psychology, has arrived
at no such level of certainty, human spirits proving, for some
reason, less amenable to systematizing than gases or metals. That
this is only a temporary setback, and that eventually science will
be able to predict the behavior of a middle-aged Caucasian as accurately as it can that of hydrogen, no one doubts, but in the meantime the margin of uncertainty makes many undertakings risky,
and not the least dangerous of these is the composition of a dinner

party. Talmadge Marquis, no close reasoner on human relationships in any case, can therefore not be blamed for inadvertently compounding a brew of souls which went off with an explosion that shattered several lives and brought his own pleasure dome down on his head in a tinkling heap.

Andrew Reale and Honey Beaton, in evening dress, stood at the threshold of the Marquis home on East Seventieth Street in New York, on a warm and humid evening in early July. The old three-story house had been designed by a naïve architect of the last decade of the nineteenth century to whom walls were not walls unless they were soundproof, ceilings not ceilings unless twice a man's height intervened between them and the floor, and fireplaces not fireplaces unless they were places for fires; while his taste in exterior decorations ran to such things as ornate ironwork and white stone lions. As Andrew rang the doorbell his fiancée glanced at the evidences of old fashion with surprise, for our hero had been praising the splendors of the Marquis establishment for a month. Andrew saw her expression and said quickly, "Pay no attention to the outside. It's all been done over inside, and—" the opening of the front door interrupted his sentence and rendered further description unnecessary, for, as Laura stepped past the butler through the doorway, the wonder itself lay before her.

The brass horse in the hallway caught and held her eye immediately. He was not a horse as the lions were lions, ploddingly taken from life. Oh no! He stood on a severe table before a huge round bronze-tinted mirror imbedded in the dark blue wall, and he was a horse streamlined, unhorsified, geometrized until nothing equine of him remained but the toss of his head with which he looked back at his body, contemplating that arrangement of cones and cylinders with vacant dismay. Andrew took Laura's arm and led her to the living room, where Marquis stepped out of the group of chatting and drinking guests to welcome them.

Laura's eyes, as she entered the room, were treated to the sight

—*The brass horse in the hallway*—

of a riotous marriage of mathematical forms and pastel tints, a nuptial delirium of Euclid and Iris. The low tables were planes tangent to and resting on metal circles; the carpet was a vast gray square, innocent of designs; the chairs were upholstered green parabolas; the huge sofa was a hollowed tan parallelepiped; the drape masking the far end of the room was a single yellow oblong; the very flower vases and ash trays were coppery polygonal prisms; and all was lighted from concealed sources with a diffused radiance that cast nothing so irregular and uncalculated on the scene as a shadow. While Laura scanned these objects of her beloved's admiration, the soul of the display came tripping up to greet them in the form of the fair Carol, climactically fashionable in a gray silk gown topped with a wine-red-lined cowl which she wore demurely over her jetty hair. She greeted Laura familiarly, for she had become friendly with her at Michael Wilde's studio, where her presence as a worshipful art student had been tolerated by the painter while he was depicting Laura as "Charity." Indeed, Wilde had at first taken some pleasure in reviling the youngster for being a parasite and in exhorting her to become a nun, but upon seeing that everything he said was received with groveling and meaningless admiration he left off the uncontested argument in disgust and had permitted the young ladies to chatter. Thus it was that these positive and negative poles in Reale's career had become "Carol" and "Honey" to each other. The greeting of Laura by the young hostess was a long, effusive business, while the welcome to Andrew was a brief "Hello there" and a briefer squeeze of the hand, which was all very proper.

Gathered around the honored guest of the evening in the center of the room, a knot of brilliantly bedight ladies and elegant gentlemen were all talking at once, and like a cornered bear among dogs, Father Stanfield loomed great among them, his shoulders as high as most of their heads—for you must know, reader, that this feast of Belshazzar was in celebration of the renewal of the contract between Aurora Dawn and the Faithful Shepherd, after twelve weeks of unique success, with a Hooley which still floated lonely as a cloud in the cerulean reaches of the high fifties, while the comedians and jazz singers whom he had overtopped bobbed impotently around thirty-five, like balloons which have reached a height where the thinness of the air nullifies the buoyancy of their gas. When Laura and Andy arrived, the Shepherd was undergoing a bantering attack for his views on ladies' clothing and was defending himself with a high good humor which had already sent one blushing matron to the privacy of a bedroom to revise the steepness of her décolletage. The other guests, drinks in hand, pressed around him to argue and to laugh.

Now dinner was announced, and the banqueters, their souls wafted on the pleasant fumes of the red, brown, green, blue, yellow, purple, or orange versions of alcohol they had consumed, marched hilariously to the dining room, which might have shocked them, had they been in a less hedonic state, with the suddenness of its change in style from the living room; for it was "done" with painful authenticity in the English manner of a hundred and fifty years ago, as though the decorator had indulged a taste for allegory to testify that, however modern *living* might become, *dining* remained an old-style affair. Each guest was graciously pointed to a place by young Miss Marquis, and the dinner began.

It will be well to trace how the characters were disposed in this fatal symposium. At the head of the table sat Mr. Marquis, of course, and facing him at the other end was his winsome daughter, the cowl now thrown back from her raven coiffure. On Marquis's right hand bulked Father Stanfield. On his left was a lady known to all present as Mrs. Towne: a tall, slender brunette of perhaps twenty-eight summers, who had little to say but said that little good-naturedly, and who had not been seen to arrive at the party, having been in the living room, very much at home, when the first guests came. Beside her sat Stephen English, and next to him, the fair Laura. Walter Grovill, the fat advertising man, giggled at Laura's left side. In an effort to overcome his self-conscious stiffness at being in his master's home he had rapidly swallowed four drinks, and his geniality-mechanism, broken loose from its moorings, was carrying him away helplessly. Next to him was Mrs. Leach, wife of his small, bitter partner, who seemed to have shrunk in the course of years from a normal stature to that of her spouse, acquiring all the discontented wrinkles of his face in so contracting. Since scarcely a day went by wherein this good wife did not calculate how much richer she would be, and how much more elaborate a household she could afford, if the advertising firm were Thomas Leach, Incorporated, instead of Grovill and Leach; and since she had already decided this evening that she could easily have a living room like Marquis's were it not for the sums that went for Grovill's salary and dividends; and since she hated Grovill with a separate, entirely altruistic hatred because of his recent marriage, for reasons which will be clear when the focus shifts to Mrs. Grovill; her juxtaposition to her husband's friend depressed her far beyond the poor power of alcohol to add or detract, and rendered her fully qualified for the ancient office of the Death's head at the feast.

Between Mrs. Leach and Carol sat Michael Wilde, facing, as he protestingly pointed out, his own handiwork, the portrait of Marquis which hung on the wall opposite: "I'm perfectly familiar with the piece," he said, "and placing me here is depriving someone else of the pleasure and profit of contemplating it": but the wily Carol who directed the seating would have him no place but at her right hand. On her left sat Mr. Van Wirt, most unhappily sandwiched between Carol and the strange Mrs. Grovill. The latter, a very tall, strikingly handsome red-haired young lady about twenty-five years of age, was an old friend of Laura's, and had been known in her days of work for the Pandar Model Agency as Flame Anders. Walter Grovill had wooed this auburn beauty doggedly for two years, and had been startled one day by a sudden and utter capitulation. Edith Grovill—for "Flame" had been quenched at the altar—worked as a model no more, dropped her former friends, acquired a rich wardrobe, and spent most of her time in shopping, or in lying around Grovill's apartment in undress, reading novels. She also gained a singular reserve, and could go for days without speaking, except when addressed. At this dinner party she had not as yet voiced a syllable, having answered all greetings and gallantries with a mechanical but dazzling smile that was as acceptable as the best repartee of the newest wit in town. The astute reader will perceive with no further instruction why this creature was hated by the wife of her husband's partner, and why Grovill, like a moon, received some of the reflected green rays of this hatred. But, we were sympathizing with Van Wirt. The efficient administrator was in a difficult case, since neither short arrogance nor scrambling humility, his two natural bearings, quite served with these two females, nor was his wide experience with demireps of much avail. Carol, in her determined prodding of Wilde to elicit remarks she might quote, ignored Van Wirt as though his chair had been vacant, while Mrs. Grovill paid no more heed to his hard-wrought pleasantries than if she had been deaf. To be simultaneously snubbed on the left hand and on the right by two beautiful young ladies is possibly the least congenial experience a man in his late forties can be made to undergo; and therefore, at least to the outward observer of the group at dinner, Van Wirt, of all present, was most to be pitied.

On the left side of the red-headed Sphinx sat Andrew Reale, and beside him, due to the numerical unbalance of males and females, was placed Mr. Leach. The sad downward lines of Leach's face were softened by the alchemist warmly at work in his veins, and he occasionally interjected a remark in the main conversation which indicated that it was no mean mother-wit that he had dammed and channelized into the uses of advertising. The ring on his finger rotated in a steady, mellow motion. As to Mrs. Van Wirt, Carol had shown her shrewdness in seating her on

Leach's left hand, next to Father Stanfield; for that lady was bulging, brightly-clad, middle-aged, and of an inoffensive church-going suburbanity—of all the females of the party, much the safest for insulating the unpredictable preacher—a layer of lead to screen the X-ray of his feared humor.

This, then, was the array of the dinner.

What a tangled knot of interest and passion was here, in this gathering, this blithe rectangle of fourteen polite people! Supposing that human relationships, instead of being impalpable tensions of spirit, had suddenly materialized at this table in the form of colored silken threads, a color for each feeling—red for desire, blue for greed, yellow for fear, green for hate, black for envy, brown for disgust, orange for pride, purple for deceit, and, of course, white for love—would they not have had a most gorgeous and not-to-be-unraveled skein among them? Reader, if such a materialization were a risk that all such gatherings faced, with how many of our friends would you and I sit down to dinner? Has a soul walked the ground since time began, all of whose threads, going and coming, would be white?

The fowl had been served: roast duck à l'orange, hugely successful, and quickly reduced to many little heaps of bones. Talmadge Marquis rose, glass in hand. "Ladies and gentlemen," said he, "I'm a man of few words." He proceeded to prove this assertion in a tribute, lasting seventeen minutes, to "that great religious leader, Father Stanfield," to "that great financier and patron of the arts, Steve—you don't mind my calling you Steve in front of friends—English," to "that great artist and painter, once you get to know him, Mike Wilde," and to "this great staff of advertising people who have put across this great show"; his words were few, a vocabulary of possibly two hundred, or one hundred ninety-six if "an-honor-and-a-privilege" were regarded as one (as Mr. Marquis clearly regarded it); so few, that he contrived to fill out seventeen minutes only by the most ingenious permutations and combinations of them.

At last he sat down amid approving murmurs. Now Michael Wilde, at the other end of the table, cleared his throat, and, rubbing his fingers around the brim of a wine glass, began—

But what comes now is crucial. Let us draw the fresh breath of a new chapter.

CHAPTER 13

The Dinner Party: II—Containing Michael Wilde's
famous "Oration Against Advertising."

W E EXIST IN A curiously touchy age. No work of fiction dares
to peep out on the stage of literature today without first timidly
poking forth from the side of the proscenium a placard proclaiming that the story to follow is a lie from one end to the other, and
that no person in it actually lived or lives. Now I freely affirm
that this history is truth, every word of it, and that every character
in it is a breathing human being whom I have seen and talked to,
and whom I have named by name. Let any impostor who has the
conceit to imagine that one of my people is a parody of himself,
beware; I shall bring him to justice for defaming my work by
implying that any part of this serious narrative belongs in the
frivolous racks of fiction.

MICHAEL WILDE'S ORATION AGAINST ADVERTISING

(Running his fingers absently around the brim of a wine glass,
Michael Wilde began thus:)

Marquis, while you were talking I looked around this table and saw that with the exception of the ladies, a banker and two men of God—Stanfield and myself—everyone here wins subsistence through the activity called advertising. Now, I realize that you invited me in the absence, enforced by your sedentary ways, of stuffed tiger heads or other trophies on your walls, a live artist being the equivalent of a dead beast as a social ornament. I will not question your motive because it has given me a chance to do a beautiful and good thing. I should like to entreat all these gentlemen to redeem the strange, bittersweet miracle of their lives, while there is yet time, by giving up the advertising business at once.

Has it ever occurred to any of you gentlemen to examine the peculiar fact that you find bread in your mouths daily? How does this happen? Who is it that you have persuaded to feed you? The obvious answer is that you buy your food, but this just states the question in another, less clear way, because money is nothing but an exchange token. Drop the confusing element of money from the whole process, and the question I've posed must confront you bleakly. What is it that you do, that entitles you to eat?

A shoemaker gives shoes for his bread. Well. A singer sings for her supper. Well. A capitalist leads a large enterprise. Well. A pilot flies, a coal-miner digs, a sailor moves things, a minister preaches, an author tells stories, a laundryman washes, an auto worker makes cars, a painter makes pictures, a street car conductor moves people, a stenographer writes down words, a lumberjack saws, and a tailor sews. The people with the victuals appreciate these services and cheerfully feed the performers. But what does an advertising man do?

He induces human beings to want things they don't want.

Now, I will be deeply obliged if you will tell me by what links of logic anybody can be convinced that your activity—the creation of want where want does not exist—is a useful one, and should be rewarded with food. Doesn't it seem, rather, the worst sort of mischief, deserving to be starved into extinction?

None of you, however, is anything but well fed; yet I am sure that until this moment it has never occurred to you on what a dubious basis your feeding is accomplished. I shall tell you exactly how you eat. You induce people to use more things than they naturally desire—the more useless and undesirable the article, the greater the advertising effort needed to dispose of it—and in all the profit from that unnatural purchasing, you share. You are fed by the makers of undesired things, who exchange these things for food by means of your arts, and give you your share of the haul.

Lest you think I oversimplify, I give you an obvious illustration. People naturally crave meat, so the advertising of meat is on a negligible scale. However, nobody is born craving tobacco, and even its slaves instinctively loathe it. So the advertising of tobacco is the largest item of expense in its distribution. You must wage continual war against the natural cleanliness of human beings, or the use of nicotine would almost stop. It follows, of course, that advertising men thrive most richly in the service of utterly useless commodities like tobacco or under-arm pastes, or in a field where there is a hopeless plethora of goods, such as soap or whisky.

But the great evil of advertising is not that it is unproductive and wasteful; were it so, it would be no worse than idleness. No. Advertising blasts everything that is good and beautiful in this land with a horrid spreading mildew. It has tarnished Creation. What is sweet to any of you in this world? Love? Nature? Art? Language? Youth? Behold them all, yoked by advertising in the harness of commerce!

Aurora Dawn! Has any of you enough of an ear for English to realize what a crime against the language is in that very name? Aurora *is* the dawn! The redundancy should assail your ears like the shriek of a bad hinge. But you are so numbed by habit that it conveys no offense. So it is with all your barbarities. Shakespeare used the rhyming of "double" and "bubble" to create two immortal lines in Macbeth. You use it to help sell your Dubl-Bubl Shampoo, and you have no slightest sense of doing anything wrong. Should someone tell you that language is the Promethean fire that lifts man above the animals, and that you are smothering the flame in mud, you would stare. You are staring. Let me tell you without images, then, that you are cheapening speech until it is ceasing to be an honest method of exchange, and that the people, not knowing that the English in a radio commercial is meant to be a lie, and the English in the President's speech which follows, a truth, will in the end fall into a paralyzing skepticism in which all utterance will be disbelieved.

God made a great green wonderland when he spread out the span of the United States. Where is the square mile inhabited by men wherein advertising has not drowned out the land's meek hymn with the blare of billboards? By what right do you turn Nature into a painted hag crying "Come buy"?

A few heavenly talents brighten the world in each generation. Artistic inspiration is entrusted to weak human beings who can be tempted with gold. Has advertising scrupled to buy up the holiest of these gifts and set them to work, peddling?

And the traffic in lovely youth! By the Lord, gentlemen, I would close every advertising agency in the country tomorrow, if only to head off the droves of silly girls, sufficiently cursed with beauty, who troop into the cities each month, most of them to be stained and scarred, a few to find ashy success in the hardening life of a model! When will a strong voice call a halt to this dismal pilgrimage, this Children's Crusade to the Unholy Land? When will someone denounce the snaring allurements of the picture magazines? When will someone tell these babies that for each girl who grins on a magazine cover a hundred weep in back rooms, and that even the grin is a bought and forced thing that fades with the flash of the photographer's bulb, leaving a face grim with scheming or heartbreak?

(At this moment the former Flame Anders had the ill luck to

146

upset a glass of wine in a purple waste on the white cloth. The painter continued on, unheeding; it is questionable whether he would have heeded the simultaneous sudden deaths of the entire party.)

To what end is all this lying, vandalism, and misuse? You are trying to Sell; never mind what, never mind how, never mind to whom—just Sell, Sell, Sell! Small wonder that in good old American slang "sell" means "fraud"! Come now! Do you hesitate to promise requited love to miserable girls, triumph to failures, virility to weaklings, even prowess to little children, for the price of a mouth wash or a breakfast food? Does it ever occur to you to be ashamed to live by preying on the myriad little tragedies of unfulfillment which make your methods pay so well?

Why are we all here tonight, if not to celebrate the ultimate outrage of advertising: the people's yearning toward God harnessed to make them yearn toward a toilet article? You, Reale, have been rendered so insensitive by your education and environment—for I think you are not truly bad—that you are proud of the device with which you made this improper thing possible, instead of burning with shame at it. What if Father Stanfield in his innocence is satisfied that he is doing no merchandising for you? You know better, for you yourself arranged to place another Aurora Dawn program ahead of the Fold hour, and that scheme was in your mind when you signed the Father to appear on a program nominally without sales lectures. It was not well done. It was crafty. You spoke with a divided tongue to a simple man, and won him to your uses. It will profit you nothing at the last, because wickedness is empty.

I trust that I am offending everybody very deeply. An artist has the privileges of the court fool, you know. I paint masterpieces because I see with a seeing eye, an eye that familiarity never glazes. Advertising strikes me as it would a man from Mars, and as it undoubtedly appears to the angels: an occupation the aim of which is subtle prevarication for gain, and the effect of which is the blighting of everything fair and pleasant in our time with the garish fungus of greed.

If I have made all of you, or just one of you, repent of this career and determine to seek decent work, I will not have breathed in vain today.

* * *

Coming to this good-natured conclusion, Michael Wilde gravely poured himself a glass of wine, and proceeded with composure to cool his throat. The company sat in stupid silence. Van Wirt's jaw, which had dropped open in the first minutes of the painter's rodomontade, still hung so loosely that it seemed a little push would set it swinging gently up and down. Marquis had gradually turned a vivid scarlet, such as is produced by the boiling of shellfish. Stephen English and Andrew Reale were impassive, but Father Stanfield scowled and worked his laced fingers violently against each other. The powerful partnership of Grovill and Leach was singularly affected. Grovill, whose eyes had met his wife's at the instant of her spilling of the wine, had sunk in his chair, looking old and ill; while Leach's face was lit with a peculiar inner glare, and his ring rotated rapidly in a reverse direction for the first time in years.

The hush that followed the harangue had lasted for an eternity audibly recorded by the house clock as some forty seconds in length, when Stephen English turned to the painter and said, in a matter-of-fact, friendly tone, "Mike, it's a pity that talk doesn't register on canvas. If piffle were painting, you'd be Michelangelo."

This frail jest broke the tension like a lightning spark. A deluge of laughter followed. Marquis howled and whooped, Grovill reached across the astonished Laura's lap to pump the banker's hand, the ladies added loud silver tones to the merriment, and Wilde himself reluctantly chuckled. The dinner was over. With one accord the guests rose, laughing and talking excitedly, and moved back into the living room.

Father Stanfield was the last to leave the table. He rose slowly, and walked out slowly. Of all the guests, he alone had displayed no symptom of mirth amid the general laughter that had cleared the air.

CHAPTER 14

*The Dinner Party: III—Containing a variety of
opinions on an important subject.*

Y̲OU CAN DEPEND ON IT, anyone who says, "I have no opinion
on the matter," is dissimulating, because every man forms an
opinion on everything that comes within his ken. Some enterprising thinker, in quest of a succinct description of Man, more
exact than the traditional plucked-chicken picture of a "featherless
biped," laid down that "Man is an animal capable of forming
opinions." In the interest of precision he might better have said
that Man is an animal incapable of *not* forming opinions. Your
human being is the phrase "Now, *I* think," surrounded with arms,
legs and obduracy. The guests at the Marquis dinner party, all
common clay webbed into human shapes, were no exceptions to
this rule, and each one had something to say about Michael
Wilde's Oration Against Advertising.

Honey Beaton and Stephen English were sitting on the tan
parallelepiped in the living room, sipping cherry brandy. Andrew
had disappeared during the exodus from the dining room, and
English had quietly appeared at the girl's elbow and assumed the
burden of her company. "I never know whether Wilde's serious
or not," said the entrancing Honey. "It seemed to me he was getting pleasure out of being spectacularly rude."

"That was part of it," said the banker, "but Mike was also airing a venomous prejudice, which stems from the year in which he slaved under some stupid bully for twenty-five dollars a week. What he said was true enough about certain unsavory details of the business, but he missed the real point. Advertising exists because it creates demand, and demand is the solar energy of the American system. He also missed the obvious fact that our people like advertisements. They like to look at pretty girls' pictures, they like to be promised the moon in a bottle of mouth wash, and they enjoy the pleading for patronage implicit in all advertising copy. However, I thought Mike was in excellent form, and I confess I was ungraciously amused at the modulations of Tal Marquis's complexion."

Mr. and Mrs. Van Wirt, Mr. and Mrs. Grovill, Mrs. Towne and Talmadge Marquis were taking their liqueurs in a semicircle before the fireplace, where a fire smouldered halfheartedly in the steamheated air looking as though it felt sufficiently silly being lit and could never be persuaded to blaze under such ridiculous conditions.

"It was just a lot of radical communism," said Grovill. "These artists are all radical communists. Mind you, Mr. Marquis, I think Wilde is a genius—that painting of you in the dining room is a real masterpiece, and plenty lifelike, too—but that's just it. All these geniuses have crackpot ideas because they're not down to earth. I know some advertising fellows who are every bit as brilliant as Michael Wilde, and honest men, too, and I sure wish one of them had been here to talk up to him."

Said Mrs. Van Wirt, "Van, I just sat there and kept praying you wouldn't explode. Thank Heaven you behaved yourself. You know," she confided to everybody, "Van is a holy terror with all these radicals and communists. I wish I'd brought a clipping of the speech he made at the Nutley Municipal Outing on the Fourth. It was just fireworks! Really, Van, I don't know how you held yourself in." The good lady rested her large hand in a gesture of relief on the orange silk of her bodice.

The holy terror cleared his throat and explained that he supposed any man who was a guest of Mr. Marquis had a right to his own opinion, however strange it might be, and that he always had as little as possible to do with artists, singers, and such people, and didn't take any of them seriously.

Mr. Marquis said that his good friend Steve English had warned him long ago about Wilde's funny ideas, and that if the man who ran the English Trust, Incorporated, made a friend of a radical there couldn't be anything very dangerous about him, and anyway, he believed Wilde's bark was worse than his bite, because he never saw him any place but at the best restaurants and clubs with the best people, who all accepted him.

"Dear," said Mrs. Towne, putting her hand affectionately on Marquis's, "why don't you tell them about Aurora Dawn? You know, how the name started, the way you were telling me the other night. I think it answers that painter perfectly."

"Oh, well, there you are; just goes to show how a fellow can shoot off his face without knowing what it's all about," said Marquis. "We of the Marquis Company are perfectly well aware that Aurora means 'dawn' and that the name is repetitious. What Mike Wilde doesn't know is that the name of the soap was just plain 'Aurora' at first, when Dad started to make it, but he was afraid too many hicks didn't know what it meant or even how to pronounce it, so he decided to take no chances. The original trademark on the package had 'Aurora' in a gold arch over a rising sun, and Dad just put the word 'Dawn' in big black letters in parentheses under 'Aurora.' Well, wouldn't you know, every dumb housewife who bought it began asking for Aurora Dawn soap. This went on for ten years, and then they held a board of directors' meeting and decided to cut out the parentheses and use the double name. It was my idea, by the way, to have the girl put into the trademark. I got it in college when I read about the dawn being a Greek goddess. Everyone knows that those goddesses ran around naked, so it was a perfect opportunity for some glamour, but classical, you know, not offensive. Dad was conservative, but I talked him into it. I've heard it said that we have the most tasteful yet eye-catching trademark in America."

"It is pretty," said Mrs. Van Wirt.

"And I'll bet the girl who posed for it did all right," said Grovill in an aggrieved tone. "What has that fellow got against models? Edith here was a fairly well-known model in her day, and she's none the worse for it."

"Not judging by her looks," said Marquis gallantly, and was rewarded with a glowing smile, which encouraged him to proceed. "What did you think of Wilde's little speech, Mrs. Grovill?"

Said the former Flame Anders pleasantly—and it was the only time she spoke during the evening—"I have no opinion on the matter." With this, her smile died away as gently as a winter sunset.

To the left of the blue foyer where the bronze horse contemplated his geometrical rear with distaste, there was a miniature wood-paneled barroom decorated with old-fashioned sporting prints, drinking slogans, and tolerably ribald designs, wherein Michael Wilde and Father Stanfield had established themselves with a bottle of brandy and a large glass bowl of salted peanuts between them.

"Shepherd, I like you," said Wilde, burying his hand to the wrist in peanuts and withdrawing a fistful. "You are a clown and a fraud, but you lie in Abraham's bosom all the year, despite yourself. I envy you your relationship with the Almighty, which is what redeems your nonsense and even gives it the white effulgence of sanctity. I suppose in a land where radio comedians are the ultimate custodians of utterance, God, too, must speak through an instrument of brass. Perhaps we're close to the Last Judgment, Shepherd, for in you the scripture is fulfilled, 'The Lord ascendeth in the noise of a cornet.'"

The massive cleric refilled Wilde's glass from the half-empty bottle of brandy.

"Son, you gi' me plenty to think about tonight," he said. "I reckon I kin tell when a feller is really mean and when he's jest actin' up outta pure love of fun or springtime, and yer rough talk don't bother me none. You was worryin' them folks fer the hell of it, but you was worryin' them with the truth, which is the best worrier they is. I want you to know, son, that afore I signed that there contract I prayed fer a solid quarter hour to the Lord to open my eyes, if I was a-reachin' fer devil's money. Every one of these here soap dollars is goin' into new buildings fer the Fold. Gain is trash to me, but I am ambitious fer the growin' of the Fold. Maybe my ambition carried me away."

The painter drank off his glass. "Look, Shepherd," he said, "your hands are clean. It's old Dubl-Bubl and his auxiliaries who must burn for buying and selling the Word. Whatever you're doing on the air is good. Your merry-andrew preaching gets to thousands of deafened ears and reawakens them to the sound of the still, small voice. You're a cheap and tawdry horn, Heaven knows, but Gabriel is blowing you."

"I got one thing to thank you fer, son," said Stanfield, leaning his chin on a heavy hand and gazing far off, his lips compressed. "Until tonight I had nothin' to say in next week's broadcast fer a sermon. Now I dunno—"

Mr. and Mrs. Thomas Leach were holding a colloquy in a guest room upstairs while Mrs. Leach renewed the perishable charms of her complexion.

"Hell of a lot in what he said, even if he is a crazy painter," said Tom Leach, his face dark, his ring still rotating in reverse in eccentric jerks. "I hate advertising. I've always hated it. Sometimes when I come to the office and see Grovill's pig face I get so sick of myself I want to die. I'd be happier if I went back to Detroit and got myself a thirty-dollar-a-week job as a reporter."

"It's Grovill who poisons the business for you," said his spouse, carefully painting a crimson mouth on the pale ribbons of her lips and addressing Leach's image in the dressing-table mirror. "How can you enjoy your life while you're carrying a dead elephant on your shoulders? You do all the work for both of you, and split the reward. He should be your office boy, not your partner."

"Walter took me into his office in the first place," muttered Leach unhappily.

"Are you going to pay for that with your life? He took you in because he saw that you were a gold mine, and he's been working you ever since. You'll never get any pleasure or peace in life until you push him out. But when you do, and when you're Thomas Leach, Incorporated, with the biggest name and the handsomest home of anyone in the business—a house as good as this show-place of Marquis's, or better—*then* you'll like advertising, Tom, you'll like it fine!"

There was in the rear of the Marquis domicile a thing as strange in that area of Manhattan as a camel or an igloo would have been; namely, a garden. An unlikely series of real estate transactions had reared two huge apartment buildings on either side of the little plot, and these grim sentinels had preserved the breathing earth from obliteration between them by rendering construction in that narrow space forever unprofitable. The sun shone into the garden for only a little longer each day than it might have illuminated the bottom of a well in those latitudes, but all the prisoned creativeness of earth, held down in every direction by asphalt and brick, seemed to burst jubilantly up through this tiny oblong open to the sky, for the garden, with no very expert tending, flourished luxuriantly. It was full of rose bushes, a memento of the sentimental taste of the divorced mother of Carol, and during the summer months it was altogether the most exotic, the most entirely Keatsian bower of sweet scents and amorous leafage that ever a taxicab roared by in a cloud of fumes. Urchins with destructive hearts and itching fingers came and went with the years, eyeing the fragile, blooming wonderland impotently through knotholes in an exceedingly stout and high fence and venting their bafflement by chalking improper adjurations as tall as themselves on its sturdy boards.

Curious readers can verify in the Nautical Almanac that on the night in question—July 9, 1937—the moon was three days away from fullness, and at an extreme northerly declination. At about ten-thirty that evening, therefore, the satellite was almost directly over the Marquis rose garden, pouring a flood of rare silver radiance down the bleak shaft between the apartment buildings. Project yourself in imagination into the heart of this leafy, moonlit, odorous retreat, this perfumed fragment of Eden hidden at the very core of the stony desert of Babel; and then, succumbing as you must to the spell of the blossoms and the compassionate lunar radiance, forgive what you see.

Our hero (for he remains such, despite his grievous errors) sat on a marble bench beside Carol Marquis, breathing the rose-scented air, gazing at the girl's palely luminous charms, and expressing his opinion on advertising. The newest-burst rosebud on the topmost spray in the garden was not more sweet and chaste than the maiden as she sat with her little hands folded neatly in her lap, listening attentively to his discourse. Fixed on him was the largest pair of brown eyes ever misappropriated from the species Deer and bestowed on a human being. Andrew Reale was speaking quickly and nervously. He had been disturbed by the painter's talk somewhat as a pious novice, raised from birth in a convent, might be by her first encounter with a sneering atheist; a bottomless black hole had suddenly opened before him in what had always seemed the solid ground of Reality, and he had felt himself tottering on its rim. What would happen to the world, he had wondered uneasily at table, if anybody but painters held such ideas? The burden of his rapid lecture to the girl was that advertising was just his way of getting to the top, and that it was no better or worse than any other way, so far as he could see. If he could get ahead faster in advertising because he had the knack of pleasing people and making ideas convincing, what was wrong in that? As long as there was business there would be advertising, and he was going to be the leading executive in the game (the moonlight glinted in his eyes as he said this) before he was thirty-five years old. As for the painter's philosophy, maybe it was too deep for him, but it sounded like a lot of showy speech with no substance; and furthermore, as far as that went, there was nobody in America more successful in advertising his own self than Michael Wilde.

Andrew stopped talking. A warm, languid breeze fought its way past innumerable buildings into the garden, and stirred the roses so that they shed their sweetness tremulously upon the air. The moon was moving all too quickly from one side of the canyon overhead to the other; already one wall was black while the other gleamed with moonshine. A slant ray slipped through the tangle of a trellised bush and haloed the dark head of the girl. Turning her eyes away from his face, she looked modestly at her hands and said in a small, distant voice, "Teeth, old boy, shall I tell you what *I* think?"

"Please do," said Andrew.

"I think," said the young lady, with dainty deliberateness, "that he was talking at you all the time."

Startled, Andrew said, "I felt that, too. But what on earth was his purpose?"

"I think," went on Carol, her eyes still downcast, her face shadowed by her hair, which fell forward as she slightly bent her head, "that all he was doing was making fun of you for my benefit . . . because Mike Wilde likes me . . . and . . ." her voice was little more than a whisper ". . . because he thinks I like you."

A perfume came to Andrew's nostrils, clear and poignant through the scent of the roses, like the trill of a piano over violins. And this odor reminded him of a train speeding south at four o'clock in the morning, and a white small hand in black hair; it reminded him of fur and warm breath and twining arms in a silent universe of falling snow, and the muffled sound of a horse's hoofs on thick snow— He caught Carol's hands. "What a baby you are!" he said with difficulty. "Mike Wilde is just about twice your age."

"A girl can have an opinion," came faintly from the hidden face.

Andrew put his hand under her chin, and turned her head so that she was looking into his eyes once more.

"Do you like me, Carol?" he said.

The eighteen-year-old miss held her breath for an instant, and then spoke very softly. "Teeth," quoth she, "I think Honey Beaton looks very beautiful this evening. What do you think?"

The answer of our hero was to gather Carol Marquis in his arms, a deed eased by the fact that she merged into his bosom the moment he touched her. There followed a kiss: for details of the duration, intensity, and nature of which the reader is referred to his or her single sharpest and most heartrending memory of the April years.

"Carol, dearest," said Andrew Reale, as his mouth parted from hers, "I want to marry you."

The girl's eyes opened to an unnatural wideness, then her lids drooped until they were nearly closed, and she smiled a slow smile in which the future advertising king could see her small, regular teeth. "Andy, darling," she murmured happily, "you don't really want that," and forestalled immediate remonstrance with the effective seal of her mouth on his.

As we pass into the late years we incline to remember the kisses of youth as blinding blazes of feeling wherein all movement of mind was blotted out, and "the lips sucked forth the soul." My young readers will back me up, however, in an assertion that this is far from true, and that, on the other hand, a kissing man is not unlike a drowning man in this respect, if no other: in that an indescribably clear and rapid succession of images and ideas may flash through his consciousness in the few moments that the honied pressure of a maiden's mouth is wafting him to Paradise. (I speak of the man only, having stated earlier in this consistent work that I make no pretense of describing the activities of young ladies' minds.) Andrew Reale was in precisely such a case. As Carol lipped him and clung to him, the warmth of her thin arms coming through the cloth of his dinner jacket, he found himself reviewing his situation swiftly in all its aspects, for all the world as though he were about to make a daring bid at contract bridge. Foremost in his thoughts was the looming loss of Laura Beaton; insistent, too, was the echo of Michael Wilde's invectives against advertising and the odd sickness of heart he had felt to hear them; with almost a physician's detachment he savored the lips of Carol Marquis and realized that irrevocably he preferred those of his first love; and meanwhile the clever voice that had suggested the alliance with the Marquis girl months ago whispered to him that he had won, won, *won,* and that with a little firmness of nerve in this hour, a little resolve to remain unswayed by sentiment, he was a millionaire. A clever hand that went with the voice flashed a colorful image on the screen of his mind: Laura, happily married to Stephen English, attired and jeweled as she could never be with him. She would fare better, severed from his fortunes, he silently averred. He would supplant Grovill and Leach, he promised himself, in a set of offices he would open in one of the high towers of Radio City—"Andrew Reale, Advertising"—ARA, flashing on and off in a smart blue neon monogram—ARA, ARA . . .

Carol Marquis stirred in his arms and rested her cheek against his.

"Teeth," she murmured, "what about Honey?"

"She's the sweetest girl I'll ever know," said Andrew, adding hastily, "except one. She'll be happier with someone who deserves her more. When will you marry me, Carol?"

The moon had vanished behind the westernmost of the two apartment-cliffs, and the garden had only the faint illumination of starlight and diffused moonshine. Andrew could not see the girl's face as she leaned back on the bench, took his hand in hers, and spoke. "I'm so young! I've never thought of getting married. I like you, Teeth, you're sweet and darling and good and I don't know, maybe I love you, but all this is roses and moonlight, it isn't real. You'll take Honey Beaton home tonight and laugh at me in the morning."

"I will never see Honey Beaton after tonight," said Andy, and his heart pounded so that he could hardly breathe as the words passed his lips. "Whatever happens, I owe her that much decency." He put his hand to his face in a quite classic gesture of shame. "I must say I feel swinish about that part of it."

Swiftly, Carol Marquis had her arms around him again, pressing him affectionately. "Andy, don't say any more about it. I think I do love you. If you still feel tomorrow morning the way you do now with the smell of roses all around us in the darkness, come and have breakfast with me. If you don't come I'll understand and eventually I'll forget you. I'm just a kid, luckily for me. . . . I'm going inside," she broke off in a different tone. "Don't forget —lipstick." She ran her fingers in a light caress over his mouth, and disappeared into the blackness.

These, then, were the various opinions passed on the important oration of Michael Wilde against advertising, the sole purpose of this chapter being to illustrate the proposition in its first sentence, that there are as many opinions as there are people in every event. Did we linger a disproportionately long time in the rose garden lighted by the lamp of Cynthia? Good friend, was it not a pleasant place—perhaps even a little nostalgically familiar to you?

CHAPTER 15

The Dinner Party: IV—The aftermath,
in which three books are closed.

*T*HE DITHYRAMBS OF all the imitators of Walt Whitman notwithstanding, there is something unheroic about our times. Samson went down in the temple of Dagon; Hector was destroyed before the walls of windy Troy; Hamlet died in the presence of the Danish royal court; and must our hero fall in no statelier setting than the back seat of a yellow taxicab? Well, this is a true story, and the author will not stray one hair from the facts on the plea of poet's license. Let not the most trivial detail of this terrible event go unrecorded, but let us not attempt to rhapsodize over dreariness, but simply say: it was in Yellow Cab 774, license 606-683-41 New York 1937, driver Morton J. Kupelsky of 1422 Brenner Avenue, Queens, that Andrew Reale was predestined on the day of his birth to inform his one true love, Laura Beaton, that they must forever part. (That this predestination in no wise altered his free will, *ergo* his culpability in the matter, is a scholastic commonplace that we have touched on before but that cannot too frequently be emphasized.)

The dreadful thing, which the girl had anticipated no more than a collision of the earth with a comet, and which her faithless lover had been half-consciously planning for weeks, had just happened. The taxicab was speeding through the deserted Sixty-sixth Street underpass from the east to the west side of the park. Honey Beaton cringed in a corner of the back seat as though she had been struck, her face tear-stained and bowed, her left hand tightly gripping a metal bracket, her whole body shrinking against the side of the car as though she feared nothing so much as that Andrew Reale might touch her. Indeed, this gallant had endeavored to quiet her grief with a caress, only to be repulsed with a vehemence that startled his very soul. Now he sat in confusion, gazing at the appalling havoc he had wrought. There was little in the girl's appearance to recommend her to the buyers of beauty now, as she wailed, clutched her tumbled yellow hair, gnashed her teeth and contorted her face in the fury of a death-wounded heart. In vain did Andrew attempt to interject words of comfort or apology; she seized on every phrase as it came from his mouth, twisted it into a bitter denunciation and made it an occasion for a fresh paroxysm of misery. The taxi swung around corners, stopped like a trained metal beast at the flash of red lights, and moved again with a grinding whine of old gears as the lights snapped to green. The broad back, round head, and wide ears of the driver might have been made of the dead substance of the automobile, for all the acknowledgement he made of the horrid scene behind him, and for all the attention that the agonized lovers paid him.

The girl's passion, after raging for twenty minutes in mounting crescendos, began to spend itself; her sobs subsided, her wild and incoherent utterances ceased and she fell to quiet weeping, her face averted from Andrew. He, still stunned by the force and surprise of her outburst, dared not speak. The sight of the balanced, placid Laura as a maddened female had been a disturbing one, and (as he thought), he felt immense tenderness, sympathy, and regret for her, but he had no doubt of the wisdom of his course, and no intention of being diverted from it by the overpraised power of a woman's tears. Not only had Honey Beaton's luster been dimmed by her lapse into hysterics, but he even felt a strange, obscure glow of satisfaction, of which the storm he had raised in this desirable breast was somehow the cause. When the taxicab drew up before the girl's apartment building and she automatically moved to get out, Andrew suddenly felt that he did not want the exchange to end. He had to persuade Honey that he had done well, for her as well as for himself, and sensed a confidence in the reasonings that quickly gathered to the portals of his tongue. Gently he detained her in her seat, and began to talk. Drying her eyes, Laura listened with wan attentiveness in an otherwise immobile face.

The meter clicked on and the driver sat with the patience of an old priest, his eyes looking straight ahead at the dark, lonely avenue splashed here and there with the electric sign of a tavern or delicatessen, as the ambitious young man poured forth his apology. After all the declarations, proposals, jiltings, seductions, ruptures, reconciliations, and dénouements which the driver had heard in the rude confessional of the front seat, screened by the perfect anonymity of the back of his head, he was as wearily wise as Ecclesiastes, and he scarcely had an ironic sigh left for the pattern of words which Andrew Reale was earnestly improvising under the impression that it was the first time in history that a decamping lover had ever been so considerate and lucid.

For the rest of Andrew's life, the smell of a taxicab, mingled of the odors of gasoline and leather, would unfailingly bring before his mind's eye this scene: the broad avenue, quiet in the night, with its far-stretching row of alternately red and green lights; the silent girl, her face marked by grief; the clicking of the meter, the persistent sound of his own voice, the shaken feeling within himself of rounding a tight corner in life, and—this to his dying hour—Laura's figure under the green silk of her evening dress which was draped unheeded about her tired body, a sword-sharp loveliness entirely his own but two hours ago, already beyond reach and receding like a sun-shower rainbow with his every word.

He spoke of the necessity of thinking of the future and of being practical. He exposed the illusion of there being but one man for each woman and vice versa in this crowded world. He pointed out how accidental their meeting had been, and how short and trivial the eight months they had known each other must eventually appear in the perspective of a lifetime. He assured her that they would have a laugh together over this absurdly tense scene some day in the near future. He did not fail with great tact to bring in the name of Stephen English, and to acknowledge humbly that that patrician was much more worthy of her charms and could give her more happiness than himself, a poor, struggling advertising man, and noting by a brief change in Honey's expression that this point went home, he dwelt on it with considerable "selling power." He concluded with a tribute, not far from poetry, to the beauty of the interlude they had shared and an assurance that it was graven on his heart forever. As he spoke, he had the relief of seeing the taut lines of grief completely fade from Laura's face; and when he finished, she was looking at him intently with very bright eyes. He leaned back on the arm rest, conscious of a difficult task ably done, and waited for her words without fear.

"Andy," said Honey, after a pause in which she ascertained beyond a doubt that his peroration was done, "do you love Carol Marquis?"

(For he had not said so. In the sad moment of disclosure he had told her only that he was going to marry the Marquis girl.)

To this question our hero, peculiarly enough, found nothing to say immediately.

. . . Come, Andy, speak up! To think on your feet, to answer on the spur of the moment—the ready reply, the quick and pleasant phrase—it's the heart of the game, man, and you're going to the top of the game! Speak, Andy, and meet the challenge of this sentimental question. You've parried thousands of harder thrusts before! What, not a word? Do you open your mouth and stupidly close it again without a sound? Do you stare helplessly at Laura as though she had knocked out your breath, and—oh, no, man—do your eyes drop before hers? You can't lose countenance, man, or you lose the sale!

Andy, Andy, look up and say something quickly! Tell her that love is just a word, that you can't make lifelong decisions out of blind passion, that all women are alike in the dark, that there are things more important than love, that love dies but money remains, that you can't live on love, that any two young people can come to love each other in time, or that sensible marriage will always outlast a love marriage. Or tell her that you love Carol Marquis! What is love? Who cares what love is, or whether it is anything? Honey is prettier than Carol, but Carol is richer than Honey. The older Honey gets the less pretty she will become. The older Carol gets the more rich she will become. Put it logically, Andy, and how can any reasonable person fail to see it, particularly with your selling power behind it?

But man, whatever you're going to say, say it quickly. That's the game, you know, and you're the most promising young man in the game. *Talk!* . . .

Andrew's eyes were still on his hands and his silence was still unbroken when he heard Laura say, in tones of a timbre unlike any he had ever heard issuing from her throat—as though she were addressing an unattractive strange man—"I think that what you're doing is contemptible." He heard a metallic click, and when he looked up the door was open and she was stepping out into the street.

This chapter and this first volume do not end, as they might, with the picture of our hero, free at last of the burden of commitment to a moneyless girl, gazing, presumably with relief, at the high corner of the building where Laura's apartment is, his eyes fixed on the yellow square of light in her remembered bedroom, glowing against the dusky violet dawn of the New York sky. Nor does it end with the snapping out of that bright square, leaving him looking at the gray face of a cliff full of sleeping people for a moment, and then turning and walking slowly up the brightening avenue, as the pallid street lamps go out unnoticed in the morning light.

No. Our end comes the next evening when Laura Beaton stands with Stephen English on the green terrace of his majestic apartment overlooking the East River, and when, with the most curiously positive sensation that her body is somebody else's, she feels it quietly embraced, and feels the strange lips of the banker on a pair of strange lips which are, to outward appearances, her own. It is at this pleasant moment that the first book closes—in her life, in our hero's life, and in this true and moral tale.

PART 2

The Hog in the House

CHAPTER 16

Consisting of a digression about Heroes,
which the reader may find helpful, but which he
need not peruse if Andrew Reale seems to him
a thoroughly agreeable and lovable person.

OOD FRIEND, having come thus far in the amazing true history of Aurora Dawn, you may find yourself disturbed by the author's application of the term "hero" to young Andrew Reale, who seems nothing but a cunning simpleton; one of a swarm that can be found in the administrative and executive offices of the land in all fields of work, narrowly shrewd in self-seeking, blind to God and goodness. How can such poor English usage be explained? Setting aside the tempting answer, always available as a last recourse, that the author is an ignoramus, please examine the suggestion that you have a mock-heroic chronicle here, a literary form in which the hero may be a madman, a thief, a scoundrel, a scamp, a coxcomb, a busybody, in fact anything but a hero in the received sense of the word.

The mock hero is interesting for his deficiencies, as the true hero for his virtues. Don Quixote turned sane, Gil Blas turned honest, Pickwick turned sociologist by imprisonment, are dull as spinach. Should Andrew Reale ever see his errors for what they are (whether he will or not is still the author's business, if you please) the story would at once be over. Meantime he has a redeeming quality, which should enable you to read on with forgiveness, and which distinguishes him from the parcel of cads and Doll Tearsheets who hold the center of the stage in current romance: he knows not what he does, and is acting vigorously but innocently according to the values which he has breathed in with the atmosphere of his times.

This aside to the reader would have been unnecessary, by the way, had this work made use of "the stream of consciousness." An inspection of the acts of modern heroes to whom this avenue of expression is available shows that, while they may and generally do commit all the grosser sins in the arsenal of wickedness, such as infidelity, stealing, blasphemy, disrespect to parents, violation of the Sabbath, envy, false witness, killing and the like, the events are so obscured by the heroes' protracted maundering to themselves, usually rendered by the artistic machinery of broken phrases, bad grammar and no punctuation, that the reader comes to sympathize with the rascals, or at least to overlook their garish misdeeds. Poor Andy, however, is never permitted to drivel in this way; his faults are set forth in straightforward storytelling, and by his acts you must judge him. Remember this, and when the tale is told, think back and decide whether he really deserves less sympathy than the pack of adulterers, adulteresses, and arrant law-breakers of every description who swish and swash and talk to themselves in the popular reading of the day, and pass for heroes and heroines.

As a matter of fact, the story may be said to have a true hero, as well as a mock one, but the discerning reader has observed this point, long ago.

And now, enough of this talk about the contents of the puppet box. Probably you care not a fig for all the analysis of art in the world, so long as the play amuses you. Therein you are quite right. Music! Lights! The glorious epic of "The Hog in the House" already seethes behind the curtain.

CHAPTER 17

*In which nuptials are rushed by one couple
and deferred by another, and Carol Marquis
takes a lesson from the queen of Persia.*

Rᴇᴀᴅᴇʀs ᴡɪʟʟ ɴᴏᴛ have forgotten the literary figure who
scurried briefly across our stage early in this history: Milton
Jaeckel, the anecdotal columnist. On the Wednesday morning following the events just related, the daily column of this respected
craftsman opened with the following paragraph:

*"Honey Beaton, noted glamorous model, will wed Stephen
English, noted millionaire and philanthropist, some time this
week. This news will surprise many people, including young
radio executive Andrew Reale, but it won't surprise any of my
followers who read my columns of March 28 and May 19. Coming events cast their shadows before—in Jaeckel's Jotings."*

For historians who may find access to newspaper files of the
period difficult, here are pertinent extracts, first, from the column
of March 28: *"Seen at Boeuf Gras—Stephen English, Honey
Beaton, Andy Reale, and Mike Wilde, chumming together"*; second, from the creation of May 19: *"Seen at the Community Chest
Ball—Stephen English and Honey Beaton."* Since Mr. Jaeckel
listed almost a hundred such pairings in the course of a week's
journalism, he could with all justice claim to have predicted nearly
every conspicuous marriage in New York. In fact, he did make

such a claim, and, as nobody came forth to dispute it, the distinction was his by default.

In this instance, his forecast was as accurate as a modern astronomer's promise of an eclipse. Behold, reader, Laura Beaton, dazzling as the sun in a white bridal gown, standing in the center of her living room while her mother and two seamstresses fuss uselessly around the garment, which drapes her young form with Grecian perfection; dazzling as the sun, but languid, as though sensing the approach of the dark disk of matrimony, soon to roll between her and the world. Inexorably as a cold satellite, the event moves nearer and nearer to Now. What straining philosopher ever got as good an intuition of the onward flow of time as does a hesitant bride while her sands of maidenhood run swiftly out?

The day is named, Friday. The elaborate clockwork has come to life, dancing the gay jig that ensues in our community upon the utterance of the magic word "Wedding." The printing press sighs and groans in stamping out the announcement as though it were a disapproving cousin; the disapproving cousins spread the news as though they were printing presses; the dressmakers descend, hard of eye and quick of tongue, to sell the virgin more dresses than she has ever owned, in honor of the occasion of her casting the charms of dress aside; the pastrycook, proportioning the number of layers in the cake to the number of digits in the bridegroom's fortune, is at work on a terraced pyramid bearing an unfortunate resemblance to Purgatory; the musicians are hired, the caterer instructed, the wine ordered, the flowers assembled, the ring selected, the minister informed, the guests bidden; Stephen English has an efficient secretary, and were it possible formally to remind angels to be present it would certainly be done. Nothing else essential to holy union has been left out.

Deferring to his bride's wish, the banker has projected a quiet wedding: the ceremony in a small church, and a handful of friends at his home afterward; but the handful has yeasted already, mainly under the warmth of Mrs. Beaton's enthusiasm, to more than a hundred people. The state of mind of Mrs. Beaton, with the prospect before her of the marriage of her daughter to a New York millionaire, is not within reach of ordinary comparisons. Mothers with marriageable daughters will understand her feelings, and all other readers are referred to the writings of Plotinus or any other classic author who is reputed to have caught in words the nature of the Mystic Vision. Observe Mrs. Beaton —a plain little, round little woman in a shapeless rusty dress—as she critically fingers the folds of her daughter's bodice, and learn how a humble surface may hide a privileged being; for here is a soul contemplating and soon to experience vicarious union with the One—followed, in this instance, by at least six ciphers.

The doorbell rings. The happy mother trots to the door and opens it, and recoils with a little shriek of dismay. Breathlessly choking "Excuse me," she snatches a long blue velvet evening cloak from the hall closet, runs into the living room and throws it around her daughter as though the girl were naked. Then she calls out, "You can come in now, Mr. English." For it is the bridegroom himself, and were he to see the wedding gown before the ceremony, calamity would surely ensue. Mrs. Beaton is shielding her daughter from this, as from all the profound mistakes one can make upon entering the married state.

Here comes the bridegroom, then, handsome and correct as before, but with a new air of stunned delight about him, as though he had just inherited a million dollars—or rather, as almost anybody else might look who had just inherited a million dollars. The wonder and pleasure, the pride and hope with which he looks at Laura are nearly boyish, and combine so oddly with his reserved deportment that a less busy hostess than Mrs. Beaton might wonder how a man who has so much can want anything so deeply. But she is occupied in a flurried explanation of her gesture with the blue cloak, while English wordlessly walks up to Laura, takes her hands in his and compliments her. The maiden's demeanor lacks nothing in the way of modesty, propriety, and shyness; in fact, her behavior toward her future husband is remarkably like what it was before their engagement, except that she has lost the trick of smiling frankly at him—a logical change prior to the serious step of marriage.

The mother dismisses the seamstresses and, while Laura changes her dress, reviews the details of the wedding with her son-in-law, in the conviction that she is attending to the affair as a bride's mother must, with the convenient help, as it happens, of English's domestic staff. When Laura reappears, the loving couple proceed to an earnest discussion of honeymoon projects, the mother busying herself to serve tea. The visit passes in a bright description by the millionaire of the pleasure places of the globe —for he proposes nothing less than a trip around the world to ensure the happiness of his bride—to all of which Laura gives her respectful approval. The world has been toured in talk from Antibes to Zanzibar, English has just risen to leave, and Laura is accompanying him to the door, when the telephone jangles a summons.—It would certainly be breaking literary ground here to insert a sublime apostrophe to the telephone; modernists would scoff at the manner, and classicists at the matter; but I put it to my readers to grant, in the teeth of pedants of all stripes, that the ringing of the telephone has filled human hearts with more intense emotions in our time than any of the accepted objects of rhapsody, such as windswept hills, the ocean, flowers, music, kisses, and such stuff. Nevertheless, to avoid controversy the tribute shall die in the inkwell.—For no clear reason, I say, the sound of that telephone set up a tumult in the breasts of the three people who heard it. English looked sharply at Laura; Laura stopped moving and stood like a statue. Mrs. Beaton, nearest the instrument, picked it up, listened briefly, glanced at the other two, and then, saying "I'm sorry, but you have the wrong number," hung up. There was the slightest silence, broken by English, as he courteously bade them farewell, kissed Laura, and left.

The girl walked back into the apartment and said, with no

perceptible shade of feeling, "That was Andy, wasn't it, Mother?" Mother and daughter being females, there were certain matters in which deception was impractical. "Yes, it was," said Mrs. Beaton. "I'm sorry, but it seemed the best thing. Did I do wrong, dear?"

Our heroine moved to the window and looked down at the street. Twelve stories below her she saw English's limousine, parked on the very spot where the Yellow Cab 774 had stood, somewhat more than a hundred hours ago.

"You were quite right," she said, in a voice a little fainter than usual. "Thank you, Mother." She kept her face turned to the street for some time, but it was not to hide the bright tears starting out of her eyes and rolling down her cheeks, for she was not aware of them.

In this rude way did Andrew Reale discover that his relationship with the Beaton household had changed. Having jilted the daughter, he might have anticipated a cooling of sentiment toward him in that quarter; but, such is the lag between action and understanding in a rising young man, he was surprised not to encounter the same generous forgiveness and forgetfulness which he had wanted to express to Honey concerning her forthcoming marriage. He hung up the telephone slowly, baffled in his desire to do a kind deed; and, as he returned to the table at which Carol—

But in order to bring the reader up to the moment in our hero's own marital fortunes, we must briefly retrace our steps.

The decisive breakfast with Carol on Sunday morning, following the unfortunate but necessary occurrence in the yellow taxicab Saturday night, proved to be less than decisive, after all. Andrew arrived at the Marquis home at what he hoped was a logical breakfast hour—eleven o'clock—groomed to the tips of his ears, excellently dressed in a soft blue English cashmere suit which had cost him two hundred and twenty dollars, with a snowy white shirt and a happy choice of maroon knitted tie, truly the complete wooing male, his plumage as attractive as the taste of the time permitted. The world looked clean and golden and the air smelled sweet as he marched to the Marquis threshold, and his pulses quickened painfully as the door opened and he stepped in past the butler and the geometrical horse to claim his bride. Almost instantly, however, his pulses slowed, for it was obvious that the supreme moment would have to be delayed. He could hear from the living room the voices of Carol, Talmadge Marquis, and Michael Wilde.

Scampering out to meet him came the soap heiress, her hair carelessly pinned back, her eyes shining, her face aglow, looking oddly wholesome in a smeared white painter's smock. "Hello, Teeth, you darling," she whispered, kissing him and pressing his hand for a moment against her soft side, "I talked Mike Wilde into staying overnight to look at my paintings this morning. He's ripping them apart. What fun! Come on." She tugged him into the living room, saying, "Look, here's Andy Reale. Go on, Mike. What's the matter with that red one?"

The artist sat in a deep chair, holding at arm's length a painting about two feet square representing, all in tints and shades of red, a rolled up piece of carpet, a chair, a box of strawberries, and a shawl. Around on the floor, or leaning against Wilde's chair or propped up on other pieces of furniture, were more specimens of Carol's inspiration: oils, water colors, pastels, and pencil sketches, crudely mounted and very much the worse for careless handling. Wilde was regarding the red picture with a pained expression, while Talmadge Marquis watched his face like a hound striving to fathom human speech.

"Young Marquis," said the painter, not looking at Carol or Andrew, "there is no use in my spending any more time on this stuff. I would say you have not an atom of talent, except that the atom is no longer believed the smallest particle in the universe, and 'not an electron of talent' sounds forced. Your draughtsmanship is inferior to that of an advertising comic strip, and your sense of color, which you think is your main point, is banal, so that your effects are either oversweet or disgusting. Asking me to criticize these things is like asking Einstein to correct high-school algebra papers. Give me coffee and I shall go home."

"You don't think I should encourage her in her art courses, Mr. Wilde?" said Marquis.

"Don't be an ass, Marquis," said the painter. "Keep her at it until the day she marries. The Victorians, at whom we sneer, knew the value of wrapping a girl in the cotton wadding of aesthetic studies. It's the only way to keep fresh the sparkle of her ignorance, virginity's chief charm. A girls' school today sullies and dulls young females to a middle-aged familiarity with sex machinery and domestic management before they have been authentically kissed. Let her paint or act or sing or write until she charms and weds a young man as rich and untalented as herself. Only, in all charity, never expose her products again to a man of taste. They are puppy yappings."

Our hero, glancing around at the paintings, opened his mouth and spake on behalf of his loved one thus: "Well, I don't know much about art, but—" whereupon Wilde interrupted him with, "It would be cruel of anyone to suggest that you do, Reale, and to ask you for an opinion on the subject. Join us in coffee."

The breakfast which followed, served on the terrace of the rose garden, bore small resemblance to the lovers' tryst that Andrew had planned, consisting as it did of a disquisition by the painter on the theme that flowers were higher in the evolutionary scale than man, a stand which he maintained with such arguments as, "We give flowers to each other as tributes, whereas, if it were possible, it would be ludicrous and offensive in a rose to present another rose with a nosegay of human beings." Talmadge Marquis, stuffing himself with pancakes and sausages, hardly listened; Andrew sulked; Carol drank in his words with wide-eyed attention. Time for young Reale seemed shackled. He thought it took three hours before the painter left and Marquis withdrew with a brief grunt, whereas the unreliable sun had changed its position by twelve degrees, exactly as though only fifty minutes had passed.

—The value of wrapping a girl in the cotton wadding—

Privacy brought no relief to his bursting bosom. The black-haired maiden chattered on about painting as though the great Bezalel were still present or, rather, she seemed to be venting all the conversation which had been dammed up by his loquacity. Andrew, with a heart strained by suspense, was forced to listen to an hour of enlightenment about "plastic form" and "color orchestration" and "space values" as much to his purpose as extracts from the Babylonian Talmud; and what was worse, the girl handed all her works to him one by one, compelling feeble, increasingly morose compliments from him.

It is hard to say that Carol Marquis habitually followed patterns of action found in the Bible, or that she had conned the Book of Esther before this breakfast. Certain it is, though, that in this case she adopted the Persian queen's scheme for stretching male curiosity to the breaking point, by inviting a questing gentleman to one meal only to invite him to another. When Andrew finally, desperately, brushed two small oil paintings out of her hands with the surly exclamation, "Now look, Carol," she laid her hand on his mouth and said, "Not a word about anything big. I have to drive out to our country place with Dad now. I'll be back in town Tuesday. Meet me here at ten o'clock. We'll ride horseback in the park and have lunch at the Tavern-on-the-Green, and then I'll say what you want me to say—I think." Her arms went around him; her lips were on his, off them, and vanishing into the house with the rest of her before the ambitious lover could gather his wits to pursue the tender topic. Evidently he was in a new, heady intimacy with her: she permitted him to find his own way to the door.

It was to a table at the Tavern-on-the-Green, therefore, to which Andrew Reale was returning to join Carol, three days later, following the unsuccessful telephone call to Honey which was described above, and which came about thus: The heiress, all during the horseback ride around the reservoir, had maintained an irrelevant vein of chatter until Andrew felt on the verge of a violent act; and as they sat down to lunch on the outdoor terrace, he had clenched both fists on the sides of the table, leaned forward with sparks in his eye and taken a deep breath to deliver an ultimatum when the girl suddenly produced a folded newspaper sheet from her wide purse and thrust it at him saying, "Haven't you seen this yet?" It was a piece of the morning paper, with "Jaeckel's Jottings" heavily outlined in Carol's lip rouge. Staggered when he read it—for he had been too distraught to glance at the day's news—Andrew brought out a broken sentence about his pleasure at the development and his desire to congratulate his former fiancée, and marched off to be rebuffed at the telephone.

Older readers know the natural tempo of misfortune: long peace, followed by a brisk series of increasingly heavy blows. When Andrew returned to the table the head waiter was there with a note. It was a telephoned summons from Van Wirt to abandon lunch and come to the office of Talmadge Marquis at once, a desperate crisis having arisen concerning the Father Stanfield program. Silently cursing his error in having told his secretary where he would be for lunch, Andrew bade adieu to the object of his desires, who accepted the note as very sufficient excuse for his departure, and said sympathetically, "Watch out for Dad. When he's bad he's ghastly."

With the burning question of his life still unanswered, with no food in his stomach, with a sick fear in his breast of the legendary terror of a Marquis rage, Andrew Reale rushed to his apartment, changed his clothes and set his course into the teeth of the gathering storm.

CHAPTER 18

In which the Marquis office undergoes
a Christopher Situation,
and Andrew Reale flies forth to save the day.

*T*ALMADGE MARQUIS WAS BELLOWING, and the buildings of New York skipped like rams. He roared; the foundations of the city were moved. At least, such was the impression of the people who gained their livelihood by a capacity for staying in proximity to Mr. Marquis throughout his tantrums. Given the choice, they would probably have endured a bad earthquake rather than one of his frenzies. Indeed, an office wit had performed an immortal prank (a few months before the nervous breakdown which ended his business life) by telephoning Fordham University after Mr. Marquis's paroxysm brought on by a poor comedy program, and inquiring whether any disturbance had registered on the seismograph.

From his inner office the muffled shouts and imprecations of Mr. Marquis could be heard this afternoon. Pending the arrival of Messrs. Grovill and Leach, who had been hurriedly sent for, the soap manufacturer was releasing his high energy on the nearest handy human being, a girl secretary who had brought him a letter with a typing error in it. Meantime a hissing whisper went through the whole Aurora Dawn floor of the Empire State Building—"Christopher Situation!"

The employees of Talmadge Marquis, like any other group isolated from the rest of mankind by a peculiar destiny, had evolved a folklore, which taught that in their master's rages, known as "situations," there were three ascending orders of magnitude: Albert, Boris, and Christopher. The reader will notice that the initials of these three names are the first three letters of the alphabet. The nomenclature of the situations was essentially a warning code, containing a wealth of information that could be passed in one word, and so indissolubly united were Mr. Marquis's unphilosophical employees in hatred of their master, that none had ever been recreant enough to betray the secret. Many a time had one subordinate, leaving the Presence, said to another in low tones as he entered, "Albert" or "Boris," thus giving at least a slight chance of preparation for the onslaught that was almost certain to follow. Superstitions had arisen; it was commonly said that nobody could confront the soap man during a Christopher Situation without being at least dismissed from his post, and probably proscribed from connection with any Aurora Dawn activity until the day of his death. Most of the present employees had been through several Alberts and a Boris or two, but the Christopher Situation was a natural catastrophe that only a few of the grayer heads in the office had witnessed until this day and, with the passage of the warning word, a nervous, grim hilarity gripped the office as it might the passengers in an airplane lost amid crashing thunderclouds.

When the elevator door opened at the Aurora Dawn floor and Messrs. Grovill and Leach stepped out, they knew immediately that matters stood very ill. Marquis's noise had subsided, to be followed by an abnormal hush throughout the usually thrumming offices; and standing by the receptionist's desk which faced the elevators was one Martin Rousseau, a pink-cheeked, neat young blade, newly minted into manhood by Princeton University, and

184

clinging to the job of personal secretary to Mr. Marquis like a caterpillar to a violently shaking stalk. His presence in this unsanctified outer space, and the superfluous heartiness with which he ushered them toward his master, disclosed clearly what he strove to hide: that a hot eruption was in progress, and that he was remaining, as well as he could, far outside the path of lava flow.

Through the big main office with its silent typewriters and averted faces walked the two advertising men; through the inner executives' offices; through Rousseau's anteroom, and up to the polished ebony door behind which abode their lord; Rousseau all the while issuing a series of remarks about the weather, not more comforting than the squeals of the wheels of a tumbrel. At the last door he assured them that they were expected and left with a hasty muttering about some important files. Grovill and Leach exchanged wan glances. "Let's go, Walter," said Leach, and opened the door, his ring rotating jerkily on his left hand.

Marquis sat slumped at his desk, confronting them. All the color was out of his usually red face, leaving it bluish-gray. One hand clutched a paper cutter; the other lay loosely on the desk, with the fingers shaking. He looked at them from under his brows without lifting his head.

"Gentlemen," he said in a strained high voice, "be good enough to inform me whether you are familiar with the contents of this envelope which has just been sent to me from your office, and which both of you have initialed." He indicated a thin brown packet which they both instantly recognized with sickness of heart; it contained the advance copy of Father Stanfield's forthcoming sermon, which, after many weeks of innocuousness following the blast against New York women, they had recently ceased troubling themselves to read. Although they had signified on the outside, as a matter of routine, that the envelope had passed through their hands, they knew no more of its contents than if it had been Aristotle's lost book on comedy. With some stammering, and a trembling giggle from Grovill, they conveyed as much to their interrogator.

The author hastily drops an opaque, soundproof curtain, to spare his audience the five tedious minutes that follow. Once at a military camp I heard a pallid young chaplain preaching against Harshness to Inferiors. He grew very warm and shouted that on the Day of Judgment bullies would be counted with murderers, for, he declared, "Humiliation is murder reversed—the spirit is killed, but the body must live on in pain." This oversensitive reverend would have found the present proceedings behind our curtain dreadful instead of merely repetitious and noisy, and he might even have fallen into the error of pitying the two advertisers instead of Marquis, who was surely much the worst off of the three, suffering so very acutely as he was at this time from an absence of Being where Being should be. In our era of scanty philosophy such sentimental mistakes are inevitable. At any rate, the curtain rises again. The soap man must have concluded his reproof.

The ivory paper cutter lay snapped into fragments on the desk. Grovill was muddy-faced and shivering, and Leach was staring straight ahead out of sunken eyes, his lips drawn so tightly as to be invisible. Marquis was picking up his telephone.

"Get me Father Stanfield," he shouted, and hung up. The telephone rang at once, and he snatched it up with an oath. Evidently the puzzled operator asked him to repeat his order, for he ground his teeth audibly, slammed down the receiver and turned the key on his little interoffice talking box. "Rousseau!" he said, and, after waiting three seconds without receiving an answer, he picked the box off the desk, smashed it on the floor, ran to the door, opened it and shrieked, "Rousseau!" The pink Princeton boy seemed to spring up through the floor. Marquis desired the presence of the telephone operator in his office. Rousseau scurried off to obey, and Marquis, going back to his desk, threw the envelope toward the advertising men and suggested that they do what they were paid to do and had pretended to do. Leach picked up the packet silently and examined the contents, Grovill reading over his shoulder. Meanwhile, Rousseau reappeared, followed by a white-faced, skinny girl with a set of headphones clutched in two rigid hands. Marquis began a vivid lecture on the uselessness of stupidity in the business world, which should have improved the young lady's character; but his colorful diction unluckily persuaded her into a fit of hysterics, so that the moral point was obscured, and she was led off from the interview by Rousseau, very little edified, in tears, and unemployed. While this interesting incident was going forward, the advertising men finished reading the fatal manuscript, with drawn faces. The weeping operator on her way out stumbled into Van Wirt, who entered with a cheery briskness that congealed into gloom under the chill greetings of Grovill and Leach. Marquis slouched silently, not looking at anyone for perhaps two minutes, then snapped over his shoulder at the fidgeting Van Wirt, "Where's young Reale?" To this propitious cue, our hero himself walked bravely upon the scene.

At his appearance Marquis brightened so visibly that the Situation promised to lapse into an Albert. He asked everybody to sit down so that they might work out the crisis calmly (for the three men had been standing like aged schoolboys since their arrival) and then he proceeded to tell Andrew of the dreadful thing that had happened.

Father Stanfield, it developed, proposed to deliver as his weekly radio address, in his own version, nothing else than Michael Wilde's libelous Oration Against Advertising! Every word of that tirade had evidently gone down into the crucible of the preacher's mind, there to be rendered molten by indignation and recast in his own mold—so Andrew surmised as he leafed rapidly through the manuscript. There, couched in Stanfield's shrewdly affected bumpkin style, were all the heterodox impertinences which the painter had inflicted on Marquis's dinner guests, simmered down to a ten-minute sermon and entitled "The Hog in the House."

The stoutest champions know discouraged moments: Hercules must have felt, when he saw the Hydra merrily grow two heads where he had just sliced off one, much as Andy Reale did when his eye first fell on "The Hog in the House."

"Now then," exclaimed Mr. Marquis, glancing imperiously at his four partisans, "I want action, and I want plenty of it and I want it now." He emphasized the word "now" by slamming down his palm as though time were a beetle scuttling across the desk which he meant to squash in its tracks. His hearers at once assumed the appearance of men planning plenty of instantaneous action. Grovill voiced a suggestion which came swiftly, whatever its defects. "I'm sure," he said with a hopeful rising giggle, "that Father Stanfield can be persuaded to tone down his remarks. I'll be happy to make the necessary representations—"

"Tone down?" bawled Marquis, breaking in half a cigar he was preparing to light. "Am I entirely surrounded by stupid idiots? Do you suppose I will permit a word of that communistic subversion to be uttered on my program? Do you suppose that the Republic Broadcasting Company will permit it to go out over their facilities? Hey, Van Wirt?" he demanded, turning on the network's man, "Would your company countenance such a thing?"

Mr. Van Wirt replied, with the exploring hesitancy of a man on fresh ice, that he was reasonably certain that in view of established company policies which he did not make but which he fully endorsed, his personal opinion was that he could not see how Chet could be made to see it. All present knew that by "Chet" Mr. Van Wirt referred to Chester Legrand, the remote and ultimate luminary of the RBC galaxy of executives. The sales manager, being of the correct pay grade to do so, referred to him by his first name with pious scrupulousness. If Chet could not be made to see a thing, it ceased to exist for all the souls in the Republic Broadcasting Company; in much the same way, most educated men will reject the existence of what the highest scientific authorities declare they cannot observe.

"— — - —," cried Mr. Marquis (no matter how the veracity of this scene is lessened, the author will not expose his readers to the rigors of the Marquis vocabulary; even though the United States Supreme Court has ruled that impolite words under certain conditions may become Art). "— — - —, do I have to wait for Chet Legrand to tell me how to run my programs?" He plunged at the telephone. "Get me Father Stanfield—Father Stanfield!" he blasted into the instrument, and hung it up.

"Mr. Marquis." The voice was the voice of Andrew Reale, dulcet as the hum of heavy honey bees amid orange blossoms. "I should like to make a suggestion, if a youngster may." Marquis consented with something like graciousness. "I have often wished," proceeded our hero, "that I had your forcefulness of manner and your direct way of speaking. It's the mark of an executive. It gets things done. What a pity that we're dealing with a religious fanatic who doesn't understand or appreciate a business man who talks business! I hate to say it, but I really think that an easygoing underling like myself is the best kind of person to approach Stanfield, because I have the patience to put up with enough of his nonsense to get my point across, while a real man of business tends to break off a conversation if it isn't conducted a certain way. I can be the velvet glove, conveying but concealing the iron hand of your policy. It's merely a suggestion. I may be all wrong."

"You're much too modest, Reale," spoke up Leach, his face twitching. "T.M., I urge you to do as he says. He did a brilliant job of selling Stanfield originally. He can handle him." The other men made vague approving noises. Marquis grumbled that as long as he got action, plenty of it, and now, he did not care how it was gotten, and if Reale wanted to talk to Stanfield he would not object, as it was certainly no pleasure to his taste. The telephone rang. Andrew Reale looked at Marquis, who nodded at him, whereupon he slid his chair to the desk and picked up the receiver.

"Good afternoon, Father Stanfield, this is Andrew Reale," he said. "I'm calling from Mr. Marquis's office. Mr. Grovill, Mr. Leach and Mr. Van Wirt are here. We're just talking about the sermon you sent us. . . . Yes, we certainly did enjoy it. All of us agree it's the wittiest thing we've read in ages. It's only a pity that it's too good. I mean, too good for radio. Oh, there's nothing we'd enjoy more than to put it over the air, but some things are impossible. You see, Mr. Marquis doesn't own the microphones, the broadcasting people do, and they're awfully humorless about criticism of advertising. They'd simply withdraw their facilities from Mr. Marquis's use, even if he were to insist on the sermon. . . . Oh, I assure you he thinks it's amusing and charming—"

The telephone was snatched out of his hand by Marquis, whose face was now the color of ripe grapes. "Hello, Stanfield," he said. "This is Marquis. That so-called sermon is impossible. I'd appreciate seeing another one on my desk at this time tomorrow. I'll send young Reale down to get it. Any further discussion is ill advised. No new sermon, no Faithful Shepherd hour Sunday night. I'm a busy man, forgive me. Reale will handle the details. Good-by."

In the silent room, the jar of the receiver in its cradle sounded like the breaking of an expensive vase. Marquis looked around at his followers, his lips tight in a smile of self-appreciation. "Only way for me to get the kind of action I want, when I want it and how I want it is to get it myself," he declared. "This meeting is over. Reale, you may have to charter a plane. Submit your expense account to Grovill and Leach. Bring the new sermon here at three P.M. tomorrow. I'd like you others here, too, at that time. Good day."

The four men availed themselves of their dismissal quickly and without words. As they went out, the pink Mr. Rousseau went in with a sheaf of papers, passing them with a very white smile. He was much too young to be palsied, and the agitated rustling of his papers could only have been part of a general similitude of briskness which Mr. Marquis exacted of all his inferiors on pain of thunderbolt dismissal.

Seldom had Andrew Reale looked with heavier heart out of the window of his high, handsome apartment on Central Park South than when he was hastily packing for this airplane trip to West Virginia. The green oblong of the park seemed filmed over with dust, and the air currents twenty-five stories above the streets brought no relief from the choking heat. New York was a stone oven, slowly baking its inhabitants. The one pleasant aspect of this dispiriting errand, it seemed to him, was that he was leaving the city.

He had hardly closed the door of his apartment, valise in hand, when he heard the telephone; but, having not a moment to spare, he stepped into the elevator and was gone. The bell jingled, and jingled, and jingled, and became discouraged and stopped. A few minutes later a page boy hung the operator's message on the doorknob, as the custom was, and departed. Andrew had done well not to wait, for it was an unimportant message, requiring no briskness and promising neither advantage nor pleasure. The note read, "Laura Beaton called."

CHAPTER 19

In which the reader will begin to suspect
that the author is not quite so artless as he seems,
and that the most minor characters in the history,
such as Milton Jaeckel, are indispensable to it.

CERVANTES, in his preface to the book of books (this side of Holy Writ, of course) heaps red coals of satire on pedantry that should scorch, to this day, the skins of some writers. Lest anyone think I have neither read nor taken to heart that lesson, I say here (being minded of it by the reference, in the last chapter, to Aristotle) that I do not expect the kindest critic to mistake such scraps of learning for scholarship. Every author is entitled to take his hobby-horse for a brief canter now and then; mine is a partiality toward the ancients among whose useless works I like to wander like an ignorant tourist in the Acropolis. My quotations are snapshots of ruins among which I have idled away too many hours. Excepting scholars, for whom it is a matter of bread and butter, no practical man should concern himself with a word written on any subject prior to seven years ago: or whatever date is prescribed in the statute of limitations on money agreements: and I mention this to warn away from the practice any young readers who may regard as an accomplishment what is nothing but a moony eccentricity.

To correct such a tendency, let us dutifully observe the life and ways of Mr. Milton Jaeckel, whose devotion to matters of the present moment to the exclusion of anything spoken, written, or done in the previous six thousand years of recorded time was above reproach.

The chartered plane that was bearing Andrew Reale southwestward flew across the setting sun and cast a flickering shadow for an instant across the face of Jaeckel, who had just risen from sleep and was glancing out of his window to see what sort of weather he would have for his night's work. Not for him blushed the rosy-fingered dawn; each day he was awakened by the scarlet claw of the sunset. He had no interest in the orderly, logical business which men did by day, dreary stuff drearily chronicled by clerks and adding machines. He knew that people said and did what was necessary and proper (and therefore boring) in the light of the sun, but that wit and amorousness, his literary harvest, were night-blooming plants, and he had accordingly adjusted his life so that he slept away the empty daylight. To him the world was always lit with an electric glare, and the glowing red ball which was this moment sinking behind the palisades and crimsoning the surfaces of the Hudson River and himself was an astronomic fact which he accepted but hardly expected to play an important part in his lifetime: more or less like Halley's comet.

A family man, Jaeckel breakfasted with his wife and two children, kissed the sleepy young ones good night and ventured forth to greet the evening. In his breast pocket were notebook and pencil, his tools. The routine of his work was as repetitious as a postman's, for wit and amorousness, too, fall into narrow patterns and ruts; Le Boeuf Gras, the Club Ferrara, the Krypton Room,

Oppenheim's, the Two Two Two, the Griffin; round and round the small bright area carved by fashion out of the wide gloom of the city; so many stops, so many paragraphs; the good restaurants for jests, the exclusive dancing rooms for new, significant victims of Cupid; four pages of notes to a column. Like all true workmen Jaeckel found unending variation and novelty within a task which to a duller eye might have appeared stale unto weariness. It is with the lubricant of such love of labor that the world's business moves forward.

But all good workmen have times when things go badly, and this evening was Milton Jaeckel's worst. Two complete circuits of "the town" (as he called the five streets among which he moved) had filled a scant page and a half in the notebook. The celebrated wits were borrowing from each other at such speed that this night he had encountered the same new quip at seven different places. Husbands were adhering to wives with obdurate fidelity, for without exception the pairings he had seen were either unimportant or legitimate. In short, nothing worth a journalist's attention was happening. His deadline an hour away, Jaeckel was hunched over a cup of coffee at the Two Two Two, his white visage drooping at the end of his thin frame like a dried flower. He was moodily planning to fill his column with political opinions and predictions when Michael Wilde walked in. The newspaper man was at his side immediately, for between the two there was the sort of natural understanding that subsists between the Nile crocodile and the bird *Aegyptius Pluvius;* as the reader knows, the greater beast gapes and suspends the natural motion of his jaws to permit the lesser one to find what nourishment it can, lodged in the fangs. The painter valued popularity sufficiently to interrupt any business in order to allow the columnist to pick over the shreds of his talk.

Wilde was alone, and the two men sat down at Jaeckel's table. See how the persistent, undismayed workman is at last rewarded! They had not been conversing five minutes when the artist brought out of his pocket a document which Jaeckel fell upon with grateful joy and commenced copying furiously into his notebook. It filled the four pages and overflowed—five, six, seven pages; the notebook became a Joseph's granary, with surplus for lean times to come. Here was a single item, hot and juicy, to fill a whole column and crowd all other jottings into the future!

The treasure, dear reader, was nothing but the very copy of "The Hog in the House" which we have recently seen creating such a turmoil in the office and breast of Talmadge Marquis. Logic requires an explanation of how it came into Michael Wilde's hands; Art requires the postponement of that explanation to a more appropriate time. Enough, for the moment, that Milton Jaeckel has the forbidden sermon and the whole tittletattle surrounding it. Trust the storyteller, and come along to see how Andrew Reale is faring on his second mission to the Fold of the Faithful Shepherd.

The true satirist of our time, who played such a hugely successful joke on us that his works are still taught in our schools as economic treatises—a procedure as sensible as using *Gulliver* for a textbook in geography—said with his usual penetration that inventions like the airplane, far from easing the burden of living, work to increase it because, while such devices do greatly help the process of concluding business, they also multiply the occasions for starting it, and since man's tendency to create confusion has, since the beginning of time, slightly outrun his capacity to cope with it, these toys of a new age simply project the old losing race on a gigantic scale, with man yielding ground by the increased drain on his nervous system.

Had Andrew Reale been concerned with such sociological chopping of hairs, he would probably have admitted the point after his bulletlike visit to Father Stanfield, for he was whisked through space to meet with mortification no less inevitably, if more quickly, than if he had gone on foot. Received by the preacher with courtesy, but with sternness marking an abrupt change from rustic joviality, Andrew suspected within ten minutes after entering the Old House that the case was beyond his talents, which were really limited to blandishment, easy language, and a nice sense of the favoring moment. In a silence that contrasted disagreeably with his first dinner at the Old House, Andrew ate with the Father and Aaron Pennington, whose face had assumed the texture and animation of an old leather bag; and even the innocent Esther, who served them as of yore, handled Andrew's plates with a cold roughness implying that, although she might not understand what he was up to, she was against it. When, pressed by duty, he at last opened the subject, the Shepherd's broad upraised hand cut short his first sentence.

"Jest fergit what you come here fer and we kin pass the evenin' sociable," he said gravely. "I ain't got nothin' against you, son. Yer a young colt fallin' all over yerself tryin' ter git runnin', and any kicks you give a body don't count; although if you was an old hoss like Mr. Marquis you would have a whalin' with a barrel stave comin', too."

"He ain't so young but what he can talk some old heads into doin' some pup tricks," murmured Pennington, evidently addressing a jelly bun, which he forthwith devoured.

"I won't attempt to apologize for Mr. Marquis," said Andrew suavely. "Men with power who have no brains also have no manners—that's an old story, even to a young fellow like me. But there are more important things involved. The Faithful Shepherd hour is the most potent religious force in radio, and to cut it short now—"

"Cut it short?" said Stanfield.

"I know Marquis," cried Andrew. "When he makes up his mind, it's like a December freeze. He owns that radio time. He'll cancel the program if you don't write a new sermon. Believe me," went on our hero, thoroughly believing himself for the moment, "all I want now is to keep the Fold on the air. It's beautiful, it's deep, it's American, it justifies the whole existence of radio—"

"Save yer talk, son," said the Faithful Shepherd. "I'm a-goin' on the air Sunday night, and my sermon's gonna be 'The Hog in the House.' Jest fly back and tell that to Mr. Marquis, and so let's talk about somethin' else. We got a square dance in the Social Hall tonight—"

"I'm afraid it takes someone like you, not like me, to talk that way to Mr. Marquis," said Andrew. "Of course, I don't blame you for letting me do it. It's an unpleasant chore."

Father Stanfield looked at him long and quietly. Aaron Pennington, remarking, "This table's crowded," put down a half-finished cup of coffee and left the room.

"Reale," said the Father at last, "you got room in yer airplane fer two more?" Andrew uneasily replied that he had. "Pennington and I will go with you to the city in the mornin'," the preacher said. "Excuse me, and good night." He hauled his black-clad bulk out of the armchair and ambled away without a backward glance. Andrew was conducted by Esther to his room. There he had leisure to congratulate himself on the quick thinking with which he had evaded the horrible responsibility of reporting the Shepherd's answer to Marquis who, as he knew well, often took vengeance on the innocent bearer of bad news, like a mad king out of Shakespeare.

This sort of adroit trick had been a large element in his success since college days, but tonight the attendant sensations were new. Everything in his world seemed to be turning topsy-turvy since the night of the fatal dinner party; for, in place of the self-congratulatory warmth that usually followed such a coup, he had nothing but a sense of shame. Examining his conduct from the very start of his relationship with Father Stanfield, he could discover no act that he had not done or seen done often in the radio circle to the applause of everybody; and he could only decide that as a result of association with a zealot like Stanfield he was losing his grip on reality. This intelligent conclusion not only enabled him to fall tranquilly asleep, but on the following day sustained him throughout the dismal airplane journey to New York.

Plunging down out of the brilliant noonday blue into the steamy haze under which New York lay with only peaks of skyscrapers poking through the dimness, the airplane flitted to the surface of the planet, touched its wheels to the earth, rolled to a stop and disgorged the pilot and the three passengers.—Critic, stop to consider that from the time the world began, up until forty years ago, such a sentence would have placed this history squarely among the fairy tales. You and I are living a fantasy that would have cost Scheherazade her head on the second night for the narrator's crime of implausibility; and have you strained to swallow a curious incident or two in this veracious account? I look about me, and blush at the commonplaceness of my tale.—Andrew brought his guests to his own hotel where his company maintained a suite for important visitors. Having provided for their accommodation, he was about to go to his own rooms when a headline in a newspaper on the clerk's desk shattered his newly-glazed serenity. "Soap Czar Throttles Faithful Shepherd's Sermon," read the big black type introducing Milton Jaeckel's column which, evidently because of the scandalousness of its contents, had been inducted into the dignity of the front page.

Like one that hath been stunned, Andrew bought the paper and scanned the story while going up in the elevator. All was there in astonishing exactness of detail—the origin of the sermon in "the internationally renowned painter" Michael Wilde's remarks at the Marquis dinner party, Marquis's demand for another sermon, Andrew's own airplane trip to West Virginia, and copious faithful quotations from "The Hog in the House" itself. As he read the ruinous exposure, Andrew grew panicky under the insistent reflection that Jaeckel's column was reprinted daily by mechanical magic in several hundred journals throughout the land which passed before the eyes of twenty-five million citizens, most of them presumably addicted to the use of soap and the radio.

The doorknob of Andrew's apartment was festooned with telephone messages: "Call Mr. Van Wirt immediately when you come in"; "Call Mr. Grovill—urgent"; "Call Miss Marquis around noon"; and last because oldest, "Laura Beaton called." Glancing through these, our hero became singularly animated, opened his door hurriedly and rushed to the telephone without troubling to take off his hat. It is a plain fact, though a startling one, that he proceeded to call, not his superiors, not the raven-haired goddess of his choice, but only his rejected sweetheart, Laura. Surely a young man in whom the pure motive of courtesy could so triumph over both interest and love, is not unworthy of being the subject of a history.

The quality of telephoned speech resists capture by that obsolescent device, a narrator's pen. The future of Homer's craft, in a time of machinery, probably lies with the mechanical storytellers such as the cinema and the colored-cartoon booklet, which may soon render all imaginative prose superfluous. Meantime, in this last gasp of the old method, let us use the poor resource of italics, intended here to convey not emphasis, but the far-off, disembodied and pathetic quality which a human personality acquires upon being reduced to electric pulses and recreated as the vibrations of a little iron disc.

Andrew Reale listened with a thumping heart while the call bell rhythmically rang once, twice, three times; then came the click as the phone was answered.

"Hello?" said a clear young voice.

Andrew had not heard Laura speak since her utterance of the words, "I think that what you are doing is contemptible." It seemed strangely pleasant to hear her now, as though they were communicating after a prolonged separation, although the actual interval had been four days. "Honey, this is Andy," he said.

"*Oh.*" A slight catch of breath, and a pause. "*How are you, Andy?*" The voice was hesitant.

"Very well, Honey. I'm sorry I was out when you called."

"*It was nothing important.*" Long pause. "*I see in the paper that you're having trouble with Aurora Dawn. I'm sorry.*"

"We'll be all right," said Andrew. "I'd like to know how on earth Jaeckel got that story." He stopped, and there ensued the silence which on the telephone is so freighted with tension because the demon of electricity waits to leap miles from one face to the other with more words and frets at delay. Andrew finally said awkwardly, "Did you want to tell me something, Laura?"

"*Only to apologize,*" said the faltering voice, "*for Mother's rudeness yesterday and to—to ask you what it was you wanted to say to me.*"

To alter the whole course of this tale was now within the power of our hero, but not of the historian, who is a helpless bystander, writing down what happened. Andrew Reale stammered, and stuttered, and began again, and stammered some more, and said at last that he had only wanted to congratulate her on her forthcoming marriage, and find out when it was taking place.

"*Oh. Thank you . . . it's tomorrow afternoon, at the Episcopal Church. . . . And when will you be married, Andy?*"

Replying that his plans were not yet definite, Andrew somehow felt himself shrinking all over, as though he had eaten the wrong side of Alice's mushroom.

"*One more thing, Andy.*" The voice was crystalline and sweet. "*I behaved badly Saturday evening. If I said anything bitter, I no longer mean it. You have my wishes and my prayers for your true happiness.*"

Andrew acknowledged these pleasant sentiments with uncouth phrases of gratitude.

"*Good-by, Andy.*"

A click cut short the vibrations of human sentiment, and the instrument was as dead as Old Marley.

So Andrew Reale disposed of less important business and went on to telephone, in rapid succession, the immediate Mr. Van Wirt, the urgent Mr. Grovill and the beloved Carol Marquis, in that order. He quickly learned that the tide in the affairs of Aurora Dawn had gone past flood and was spilling over the disaster bulwarks, as the next chapter will graphically describe.

CHAPTER 20

*Containing an account of the great battle
between the soap potentate and
the Faithful Shepherd.*

*T*HE IRRESISTIBLE FORCE of Talmadge Marquis's money had
run into the immovable object of Father Calvin Stanfield's principles.

This was the phrase buzzing through the halls of Radio as the
big battle loomed. Like many catchy phrases, it was philosophi-
cally unsound, implying the existence at the same time of the two
contradictory categories, "irresistible" and "immovable." The truth
of one of the words implies *per se* the falsity of the other, or, to
put it another way, only *one* of these two statements can possibly
be correct:

      1. An irresistible force exists.
      2. An immovable object exists.

Readers of high-school age will find this analysis useful when
next confronted with the sage inquiry, "What happens when an
irresistible force meets an immovable object?" For the mature audience, it is adduced to indicate what the outcome of the struggle
had to be: either Marquis must prove resistible, or Father Stanfield movable. Few wagers were made on the issue, widespread

though interest was. The movability of Stanfield was widely assumed to be the only likely outcome, failing that kind of intervention from Above, which economists, politicians, and even priests count on not to happen in these graceless times.

The structure housing the Republic Broadcasting Company was a vast cubic stone tomb, soundproof and lightproof, built to protect its treasure of wireless entertainment, like the frail mummy of a Theban princess, from the corrosive outer world. It was built in tiers, honeycombed with studios, filled with complicated electrical machines, transfixed with elevator shafts, and lighted and decorated with a subdued mathematical balance of solid colors and soft materials which made human beings in these austere spaces feel and look as intrusive as large monkeys. Whether this bleak emphasis on the animal aspect of our race was in itself depressing, or whether the combined effects of artificial light and pumped-in air were deleterious to good cheer, there were few happy faces to be seen in this prosperous and useful hive, most of its inhabitants looking either as though they were pursuing someone, or (in the greater number of cases) being pursued. Since they were almost all making large amounts of money, it is hard to understand why this should have been so. Possibly their preoccupation with time—for all happenings here were regulated to the second—kept the image of mortality constantly before them, placing them in the predicament of the guests of the legendary Baron Rothschild whose clock was supposed to boom out every hour, in the midst of the revelries in his castle, the words, *"One Hour Nearer Death!"*

These same faces were happier today than usual, as though festivity had brightened the air. From the moment shortly before noon when the newspaper containing Jaeckel's story had appeared on newsstands, this holiday feeling had invaded the building and had been fed by jests and rumors. It was told that Chester Legrand had asked Mr. Marquis to meet with him; soon afterward it was known that Mr. Marquis had agreed to come to Mr. Legrand's office at three o'clock; then it was happily bruited about that the chief of the corporation's lawyers, Mr. Morphee, would be present at the encounter; and, biggest sensation of all, the word passed shortly before three o'clock that Andy Reale (who was well known among the inhabitants of the great cube) had brought Father Stanfield back with him from the West Virginia hills, and that the preacher was coming to the meeting. For once, Rumor spoke with no idle tongue. At five minutes to three, Talmadge Marquis strode grimly through the swinging glass portals, flanked by Grovill and Leach; two minutes later, there arrived Father Stanfield, Pennington, Van Wirt, and our hero; both antagonists proceeded to the top floor where, solitary in the luxuries of sunlight and ordinary air, lay the offices of Chester Legrand; and the door had scarcely closed on Van Wirt, the last to enter the sacred space, before everybody in the building knew that the Miltonic trial of strength had begun.

Like most truly heroic conflicts of the twentieth century (setting aside the duels of machines in war), this fight took place around a table—a long, beautifully-stained mahogany piece, set in a surrounding of wood-paneled walls, thick blue carpets and drapes, wide windows and appropriate minor pieces of wood, leather, and chromium, all disposed to give the impression that here was a place for great decisions arrived at with good manners by powerful gentlemen. Legrand was at the head of the table. On one side sat the lawyer Morphee, Marquis, Grovill, and Leach, while arrayed opposite them were Stanfield, Pennington, Van Wirt, and Reale. Legrand opened a cigar box and passed it to the Faithful Shepherd, and while the tobacco went around he spoke.

"Gentlemen," he said, in a frank, mellow voice, "I have to thank both Mr. Marquis and Father Stanfield for the favor they have done me by meeting here in my office. Having started our business in this conciliatory way, I shall be very much surprised if we don't compose the matter to everyone's satisfaction in a very short time." This mild utterance soothed like music, and Andrew Reale, in whose hierarchy Legrand was approximately the Pope, felt his forebodings melt away. He was consumed with admiration for this good-humored, dignified, handsome personage whose very name was a synonym for Policy, whose abundant graying hair, sturdy frame, and nice dress gave him a presence that matched his position, and whose decent charm pervaded the room like autumn sunlight. To such a man, thought Andrew, nothing was impossible. All would yet be well.

"Let's talk," went on Legrand, "with complete honesty. Let's have the baby on the table and decide what to do with it. Shall I talk first? Mr. Morphee and I read with considerable surprise—"

"Legrand, this doesn't call for much discussion," broke in Marquis, glowering at his clasped hands before him. "Father Stanfield, for reasons best known to himself, has proposed to deliver a sermon on my hour Sunday evening which I find unacceptable. I have always given him the utmost latitude, involving my company in serious difficulties on a previous occasion, but he has overstepped the mark this time. What he wants to say is scurrilous and subversive, I might say communistic, and casts reflections on the radio industry, on the advertising profession, and on my products. I have requested that he provide another sermon in its place, and I have come to this meeting with the full expectation that he will produce the same and end the matter at once."

Legrand looked inquiringly at the Faithful Shepherd.

"I don't want to waste nobody's time," said the cleric, "and my answer is what I told young Reale last night down in Pleasantville, only he thought I'd better say it to Mr. Marquis myself, which maybe he was right. I figger to go on the air same as usual Sunday night. My sermon will be 'The Hog in the House.'"

In the silence that followed, the blue wreaths of cigar smoke curled slowly through the room undisturbed by the speech or motion of any of the sitters at the table.

"Well," spoke Legrand at last, seriously, "that's how we stand.

Not quite in accord, at the moment. Before we go ahead, may Mr. Morphee and I read the disputed sermon? We have only Milton Jaeckel's story for information."

"That is remarkably accurate," said Marquis. "I'm sure Father Stanfield can give you a copy of the full text, since he evidently had several made for distribution to the press."

"I got to correct you," said the preacher. "Someone in your outfit give the story to the papers, bein' as how that copy I sent you is the only copy they is. I keep my sermons in my head. I cain't hardly figger why any of you done it, but it don't matter none."

"I regret to have to accuse you of bad faith," cried Marquis, growing red in the face as he drew folded papers from his breast pocket and slapped them on the table, "but this copy has not left my possession since the moment I received it, and I have guarded it for the express purpose of keeping its contents from the eyes of reporters. You obviously wanted to force my hand by giving out the story, but I think you will find me a pretty stubborn cuss all the same. Pretty stubborn!"

Father Stanfield regarded him gravely. "I ain't often been called a liar," he said. "The last time was long afore I took to preachin'. I cain't hardly break a feller's jaw fer him now, so I dunno what to do 'ceptin' assure you that I fear God too much to tell lies."

Pouring into the bellicose atmosphere came Legrand's deep, pleasant voice again. "May I say that the conversation is taking a wrong turn for no useful reason? How Milton Jaeckel got the story is beside the point, for the moment. He got it and printed it. Now we must minimize the damage. Allow me." He picked up the sermon and read it, holding it so that the lawyer could see it. The other men indulged in their favored modes of fidgeting, all except the preacher, who had acquired the repose of a watching animal. Marquis puffed his cigar and scowled; Grovill looked hopefully from one face to another, ready to giggle at any encouragement; Pennington pulled out a large pocketknife and pared his nails; Andy and Van Wirt drummed their fingers in unconscious duet; while Leach's ring rotated at a smoking speed.

Legrand let fall the last page and glanced curiously at the Faithful Shepherd. "This is strong," he said. Stanfield nodded and replied, "I reckon you-all will survive it," at which everybody except Marquis laughed.

"I'd like to make a suggestion." A strange, hoarse voice from the lower end of the table said this. All attention turned toward Tom Leach who sat forward tensely with one forefinger upraised, his face white, his ring halted in its rotation.

"Yes, Mr. Leach?" said Legrand, puzzled.

The lips of the advertising man worked silently for a moment; then he said, with a slight stammer, "Mr. Marquis, I believe we should permit Father Stanfield to go on with the sermon as it stands. We have much more to gain than to lose."

Talmadge Marquis looked as astounded as if one of his legs had suddenly vanished into air, but he recovered quickly and said, "I was under the impression you were working for me."

"I am, sir," said Leach, "and it is my opinion that the best interests of Aurora Dawn require—"

"Keep your G——n opinions to yourself when they flatly contradict my stated policies," said Marquis.

Leach wavered in his chair as though he had received a blow, and glanced around appealingly at the other men. Then he stood up in an unsteady way, and walked out of the room. There ensued dead quiet for long seconds.

"Father Stanfield," said Legrand finally, "I'd like to make the position of our network clear to you. We pass no judgments and take no sides. The use of our microphones and sending stations belongs to Mr. Marquis on a certain hour each Sunday night. What is broadcast then, within the limits of decency, of course, is in his power, and nobody else's, to decide."

"Folks figger on hearin' me," said the Shepherd, "and I reckon they got a right, bein' as how I'm the unworthy bearer of the

Lord's word to them. I hate contention, friend, but I got to preach my sermon Sunday night."

"I hope you understand," said Legrand, with unvarying calm seriousness, "that for all purposes Mr. Marquis is master of the network at that time."

"He ain't master of the radio sets tuned to listen to me," said Stanfield. "It ain't yer station that makes radio a business, it's them sets. Mr. Marquis aims to reach into a powerful lot of homes and turn off the radios on Sunday night. That don't set good on my stomach. I'll part company with him gladly after this program, but I'm a-goin' to preach 'The Hog in the House.'"

"Not on my time," ground out Marquis, whose thin smile had made its appearance during Legrand's explanation. Mr. Morphee, the lawyer, a silvery-haired, somber-mannered tall man, leaned forward and said to the Shepherd, "You see, Reverend, it's a simple matter of contract under law; Mr. Marquis owns that time."

"They ain't *nobody* owns Time," exclaimed the Faithful Shepherd, "except the Lord God by whose word Time was created and by whose mercy Time don't come to a stop in chaos at every second. I don't know nothin' about contracts or laws. The contract that says I cain't preach ain't no contract, and the law that says I cain't preach ain't no law. What I am or what I ain't fer good or fer bad don't signify. I carry the Word of the Holy One, and they ain't no man made from the dust of the ground can stop me—"

Now Marquis came to his feet with an oath loud enough to drown out Stanfield's next words. "I don't propose to listen to this rustic faker sermonize for my benefit," he shouted, and, leaving the table, he snatched up his wide tan hat and jammed it on his head. "Legrand, we'll have a dance orchestra this Sunday night, and I will arrange thereafter—" Having his back to the table, he did not see the preacher lumber toward him with surprising swiftness. Stanfield reached him, spun him around and seized him by the shoulders.

"It ain't fer me to strike a man," he said, "but yer a spoiled child in a man's hide, and they's scripture fer takin' a rod to you. If you say another disrespectful word about my callin', as you live and as I live I'll pull down yer breeches and shame you before these gentlemen." Stanfield was a very large man, but Marquis was large also, and it is to be recorded to the latter's credit that he did not stir a hair while Stanfield was holding him, thus avoiding further unbecoming conflict. It is also to be recorded to his credit that when Stanfield released him with the words, "Now jump, if you still feel froggy," he did not take up what might have forgivably been interpreted as a challenge, but confined himself to an indistinct murmur to the lawyer, Morphee, about the laws against assault and battery.

The Faithful Shepherd picked up his black hat and turned toward the men at the table who had observed the brief scene in frozen dumbness; as he did so, Aaron Pennington rose and walked to his side. "Mr. Legrand," said Stanfield, "I beg yer pardon fer raisin' my voice in yer office. I ain't no shinin' example of a gentleman. Unless we got further business to transact now, I reckon I'll see you Sunday night." He surveyed the table from end to end, but there was no comment from anybody. "Good afternoon, and God bless you," he said, and went out, followed by Pennington whose tough gray face presented as close a counterfeit of pure delight as it would ever do in this world.

"The man is obviously cracked, and probably dangerous," said Marquis after the door had closed. "Reale, you did me no favor by involving me with him." He glanced with distinct ill-feeling at our hero, who decided against reminding the soap king, at the moment, that the Faithful Shepherd had been procured for Aurora Dawn at Marquis's urgent demand.

"That was a painful and thoroughly unsatisfactory episode," remarked Legrand gloomily.

"The matter is closed," said Marquis. "Grovill will arrange to have a first-class dance band with an outstanding girl singer at the studio Sunday night."

"Yes, sir, the scripts will be ready late tomorrow," hastily put in the faithful remainder of the Grovill-Leach partnership.

"The network's part, as I see it," went on Marquis, "is simply to have enough studio police available to prevent that fanatic from disturbing the new Aurora Dawn show."

Legrand turned to the lawyer, who shrugged his shoulders, saying, "That's it." Thereupon the network executive stood up to shake hands with Marquis. "We will do what we have to do," said he in the traditional business tone of conclusion.

The walls, doors, and floors of the room in which these great events occurred were extremely well made. It would take a wiser head than the historian's to determine how it was that even before all the participants had departed from the scene, an accurate account was spreading through the corridors of the Republic Broadcasting Company, complete down to bits of dialogue, stimulating a rude community hilarity that could be likened to nothing so much as the *Festum Asinorum*, the Feast of Fools: the one day in the medieval year when all the solemnities of fealty were grossly burlesqued, and the ruling powers were personified for the day in a crowned and robed live jackass.

CHAPTER 21

In which our hero learns that amputation is not necessarily, in amorous afflictions, an easy cure.

LADIES, my next paragraph is for the gentlemen readers; do me the grace to stand aside. And you young men, the age of my hero, Andrew Reale, or greener yet, stand you aside, too, for I speak to others—but listen.

Now then, my jolly boys who were young and are old; who were foolish and are sensible; who gutted the years recklessly and now number the days in wisdom; who desperately clasped girls and now fondly pat wives; open the closed books, wake the memories, sniff the dried roses of regret, and then let us fill a cup, and drink with love to that most noble, ridiculous, laughable, sublime departed figure in all our lives—the Young Man That Was. Let us drink to his dreams, for they were rainbow-colored; to his appetites, for they were strong; to his blunders, for they were huge; to his beloved, for she was sweet; to his pain, for it was sharp; to his time, for it was brief; and to his end, for it was—to become one of us. In the land where the bright sunlight fades not, where the flowers are spring flowers and the grass is an April green forever, he still walks his jaunty, infinitely mistaken way. God pity us all—with what precious coins have we bought our philosophy, eh, my boys? Drink up, drink up, and let us return to our tale. The candles are burning down, the hour is late, and not too much is left to tell.

Andrew Reale stood irresolutely outside the church on Fifth Avenue where Laura Beaton and Stephen English were about to be married.

For half an hour he had loitered on the corner across the street from the house of worship, watching the members of the wedding party arrive. Andrew was aware of the bucolic figure he must be cutting as he stood and stared while streams of people hurried past him northward and southward, but he could not help himself. Back in the Republic Building, his desk was piled with emergency work due to the sudden drastic change in the Aurora Dawn program; yet suddenly, forty minutes before the appointed time of the marriage, he had risen, put on his hat, and strode out of his office like a sleepwalker. Without volition, it appeared, he had walked to this corner and begun his senseless vigil.

He hardly thought about the wedding. As the time wore on, all manner of disordered fancies took hold in his brain; for instance, with face after face after face rushing past him, it struck him all at once that the universal presence of ears on human heads was the most remarkable fact he had ever observed. Of all these hundreds of people flowing by, not one of them but had a pair stuck in the skull in about the same place, with about the same shape, just as though everyone had emerged from a factory making a standard model with slight variations; and when he reflected that all these ears had simply *grown*, without mold or control, his head swam, and he trembled on the brink of superstitious awe of the Power that could cause such a wonder. He found himself scanning the crowd in the tense hope that someone without ears would appear; it seemed to him that such an advent would be reassuringly natural, a commonsense note amid this fantastic inexorability of two ears, two ears, two ears . . . The emergence of the white-clad Laura from a limousine snapped him out of this absurd preoccupation. As she vanished into the church with her companions, he wandered across the street and stood outside the solemn door, not knowing what to do next.

Andrew felt as much out of place, standing on the threshold of the church, as the church itself looked, surrounded by the stone sides of high office buildings and the immense windows of department stores, a pathetic remembrance of the lost days when this area of earth had been green fields, dotted here and there with houses from which the first worshipers had come. Commerce had lapped around it, but still it stood, a quiet island of unprofitable sanctity amid the flooding tides of business. Our hero had passed the place a thousand times without noticing it. Churches, to him, were natural facts of existence, like fire plugs; they were to be seen in civilized communities, and surely were of use, but warranted no narrow inquiry into their origins. His religious outlook was as simple as the figure O: he would have conceded a God, because atheism was a difficult, not quite respectable flight of the imagination, but in practical life he forgot about such abstractions. There was for him this difference between the extinct god Jupiter and the current Christian deity, that the name of the latter made a more forceful oath. He had not prayed since he had prayed in vain at the age of twelve that his father might not die, and he had not been inside a church, save for weddings, in ten years. He was, in short, a thoroughly modern and enlightened young man.

As he wavered outside the sanctified portal, a strong hand gripped his elbow. "Hullo, you here, too? We're almost late. Let's go in," said the voice of Michael Wilde, and before the bemused Andrew could greet the painter, he had been propelled out of the hot white sunshine into the peaceful dimness of the church. Still holding Reale's arm, the artist sidled into one of the rear pews and sat down with him. "Reale, your presence is a reassuring note," he said in subdued tones. "It argues a flicker of good conscience in you, whereas I have been thinking that you had died down to a complete advertising man. You have come, I trust, to halt this horrid mummery?" Andrew glanced at the painter to see whether he was joking, but Wilde's face was pale and serious. The young executive stammered in a whisper that, on the contrary, he wished the couple all happiness, and saw no reason to interrupt.

"Damn! Spare me those lies," growled the painter. "You love Beaton from the bottom of your soul, and she loves you. I have seen you together; you move like one person. Her marriage to English is an offense against Heaven, Reale, and it is your duty to stop it, because you are the cause of it."

There was a murmur among the small knot of guests clustered in the forward pews around the center aisle, as the organist, a tiny man with a large head and wisps of silvery hair, took his place at his instrument and touched it, drawing forth sonorous chords.

"I came here today," went on the painter in a soft but urgent voice, "not knowing whether I myself might not rise to protest. Believe me, there are reasons. Wake up, boy! Your wife, the love of your life, is in that dressing room twenty feet behind you, about to be taken away from you by an old man. Go in there. Throw yourself at her feet. Get her to pardon you—it will take about twenty seconds—and then carry her out to another church and marry her!"

The worn harmonies of the Lohengrin Wedding March commenced vibrating in the air, the organist using so little effort that it seemed the organ would play on by itself if he were to take away his hands. Now, with grave step and slow, the minister entered and walked to his place before the altar. Andrew felt strangely dizzy as he heard the music, and the painter's insistent whispering seemed to increase his vertigo. But he stared ahead, and said nothing.

"Listen, Reale," pursued the painter, gently shaking his arm, "English wanted me to be best man, do you know that? And I refused because he told me he knew Beaton doesn't love him. She's not getting married, she's becoming a sister in the nunnery of money. Stop her."

—A pathetic remembrance of the lost days—

Andrew found breath to mutter, "Laura must know what she's doing," and lapsed into silence again.

The music grew louder, and the bridegroom entered from a side door with a stout, gray-haired best man, the general manager of his bank. It was an interesting touch to the picture because English's portly companion shed a quality of reliable sedateness that enveloped both of them; so that even the rapturous Mrs. Beaton, watching from the front pew as the two men proceeded to their stations before the minister, thought with a twinge in her heart that it would not have hurt had the millionaire been just a *little* younger. Such fond might-have-beens are natural last qualms in a bride's mother, as pointless as her tears.

"What a blind bungler you are!" whispered the irrepressible artist to Reale. "Do you think it isn't evident to me that you're giving up Beaton in the hope of marrying Carol Marquis? Why? That little beast has no heart. She'll never give herself to you; what do you offer her? She'll marry some fop of a rich man's son. Maybe she'll fall into the hands of an adventurer who'll take her little mind and witch's body for the sake of the seven million dollars which she'll have after her father's last apoplexy. You're a rotten dub of a fortune hunter. You have no title and no notoriety, and you're awkwardly simple."

"It's none of your business, Wilde," retorted Andrew, stung at last, "but as it happens Carol Marquis loves me and I love her. Drop the subject."

The music changed to the Mendelssohn March, the tear-starting, heart-cutting bride's melody, and Laura Beaton appeared at the rear of the center aisle, and commenced to move toward the altar with small, hesitant steps.

She was alone. There was no male relative within a thousand miles of New York to give her away: her uncle in Albuquerque was too ill to fly to the ceremony: and she had insisted on walking unescorted rather than on the arm of a stranger. Admiring murmurs arose from the guests as the solitary white figure emerged from the gloom at the back of the church and stepped into a glory of colored light slanting down from a high stained window. Since this weary world was fresh and new, no daughter of man ever found more favor in the eyes of those who saw her than did the famed Honey Beaton on this wedding day. Her well-advertised figure swayed with a sweet grace that agitated every man who beheld it; her face had the pensive mournfulness of a seraph in an old sad painting. Our hero, who had risen to his feet at her appearance, found it necessary to steady himself on the back of the pew as he looked at these charms which he had recently discarded, for his dizziness became unaccountably much worse. Now she was pacing so close to him that he could smell the perfume which she had worn ever since he had given her the first bottle of it; and now, to his confusion, the blue eyes that had been fixed ahead moved, looked straight into his own without altering expression, and then returned to a rigid forward gaze. She passed him—passed him as silently and irrecoverably as an hour of happiness passes you, reader. Michael Wilde muttered fiercely in his ear, "Grab her around the waist and run like the wind! She'll still go with you."

Andrew flung himself away from the painter with a despairing exclamation and placed himself in a pew across the aisle. All eyes being on the bride, his violent movement was unnoticed. Laura reached Stephen English's side, and the ceremony began.

> *"And as one sees most fearful things*
> *In the crystal of a dream,"*

the ambitious young radio executive saw his first love formally united to a rich and pleasant gentleman. The words were said, the ring went on her finger, and the proceeding was ratified with a brief and genteel kiss. Soul and body, Laura Beaton belonged to Stephen English.

A sort of temperate jubilation ensued. Guests came forward to salute the happy couple, and surrounded them with a discreet murmur of congratulations. Nobody seemed sufficiently ill-bred to shout or laugh or even cry; Mrs. Beaton herself, out of a feeling for tradition, pressed a handkerchief repeatedly to her eyes, but it was innocent of moisture. In the same fine moderation of spirit the couple was followed up the aisle and out the door by the little crowd, without jostling or jokes. Andrew, left sitting alone in the church (for the painter mingled with the departing guests), heard a very mild cheer arise, while the roar of an automobile motor told of the departure of the newly-knit one flesh. The burden of Honey had been finally lifted from his shoulders, and the road to success, as he had logically planned it all out, now lay broad and open. This polite wedding had already fulfilled one of his clear-headed prophecies of the night in the yellow taxicab.

Do not press, reader, for an explanation of our hero's failure to display gaiety at this desired unfolding of events. It must be obvious by now that he behaves with a jerky inconsistency which makes it impossible to pass him off as an author's invention; for the figures in novels dance to a most logical fugue of motives and counter-motives, while Andrew Reale repeatedly violates the rules, and behaves much as your wife, your brother, your enemy, and you are constantly doing in that least probable of all stories, your own life. Who can explain why this clever young man sat in a gloomy pew in a deserted church staring at the altar as though he saw a ghost there? Perhaps the everlasting note of mystery in marriage had sounded through his muffling layers of worldliness and set up an echo in his heart. A very strange thing had just happened, after all. A few sentences had been uttered, a trinket passed, and a woman had yielded up her identity and her person to a man. What mightiness lay in the words, or in the place where they were spoken, or in the bland little man who spoke them, to effect such an earthquake in three—that is, in two lives? These are suggested as possible processes in the mind of our hero to cause his curious petrifaction in the empty church. His stream of consciousness at the moment not having been recorded, it is unavailable to illuminate this obscure passage of the story.

At last he rose, and, in the somnambulistic manner in which he had come, left the church and plodded his way back toward the Republic Building. So sunk was he in his peculiar abstraction that he walked unheeding by a large circle of people, gathered in the street at a corner a few blocks from the church in sufficient numbers to halt automobile traffic, pushing, staring, and chattering in the immemorial manner of simians or humans observing a curiosity. Unfortunately for the proponents of premonition, warning, second-sight, or associated psychic phenomena, it must be recorded that Andrew Reale thus passed within ten yards of a spot where Stephen English and his bride lay senseless, and had not an inkling that this was the case, but returned to his work glumly sure that the Englishes were enjoying the sweets of wedlock in perfect health and bliss.

The fact is, however, that inside the ring of onlookers which he passed, a delivery truck stood smoking in the middle of the intersection, its front end smashed; lying on its side in front of the truck lay a long blue limousine, surrounded by shattered glass; and even as Andrew trudged obliviously by the sad scene, two policemen pried the twisted door of the automobile upward like a trap door and gently lifted out the white-clad, bloodstained, and apparently lifeless figure of Mrs. Stephen English.

It is supposed by many readers, most critics, and all publishers that an author has unlimited power over his characters and can guide events in his tale at will, and from these there should be vigorous protests at this accident. Critics may say that it is too opportune, readers that it is too cruel, publishers that only Russian novelists can afford to injure their heroines. Good friends, you may all be right, but this accident is, unhappily, what occurred at this point in the astonishing history of Aurora Dawn. The author humbly submits that, since the tale is a true one, Fate and not he must apologize, if apology be necessary; and perhaps the Hooded One would not lack for arguments, pointing out to you that your own meeting with your wife (or husband) must in retrospect seem so opportune that you can almost see the glint of puppet wires against the dark backdrop, also that the deaths of children are senselessly unfair, and so forth, and so forth, and finally offering to show you within the next thirty seconds just how cruel and arbitrary she can be, if she chooses—at which moment you would doubtless abandon the discussion with some haste. At any rate, the historian cordially begs you to turn the page, inasmuch as the best part of these extravagant events begins in the next chapter.

CHAPTER 22

In which the great Aurora Dawn scandal
reaches its climax, and our hero acts drastically
to protect an investment.

W̶E̶ ARE BLESSED above the other nations in the number of our
inhabitants who understand and easily explain anything that happens in our land; most of them write in daily or weekly news
publications. This recorder, however, cannot grasp the wonder of
our free, sweet, strong country no matter how hard he ponders
over it and is even more at a loss to account for single occurrences
such as the one about to be narrated. It is a fact that our populace,
with large good nature, permits the men of power to have their
way so long as the days are rubbing along without too much stress,
but occasionally rises like a wakened lion to roar mighty displeas-
ure over what seems a trifle. A president may change the whole
money system; let him beware of changing the date of Inde-
pendence Day. A senator may nefariously acquire ten million
dollars, and then fall to infamy for giving his daughter an expensive coming-out party. Perhaps a deep-running native wisdom
sees, in these tiny events which burgeon into national alarums, a
significance which escapes the owl eyes of historians.

   At any rate, this plain work will make no effort to interpret the phenomenon that was commonly called "the Aurora Dawn riot," but will simply state what everyone who was reading newspapers in the year 1937 knows anyhow, namely, that it happened; and since for most of the audience it will be a twice-told tale, will give only the briefest possible sketch of it.

The huge modern wall clock in the lobby of the Republic Broadcasting Building was slowly ticking off some of the most expensive time of the week, Sunday afternoon and evening. Once every minute the long steel wand of the second hand made the circuit of twelve jet balls, disposed around the face where numerals are in old-fashioned timepieces, as though to indicate that for the radio people who lived under the duress of Time the angle between the clock's hands was information enough, and the vulgar obviousness of numbers could be abandoned. Five-thirty, said a narrow angle in the lower right quadrant, and the time belonged to the Argonaut Cheese Corporation. Six, said the long vertical line of the two hands, and a small parcel of eternity was doled to the Oakleaf Beer Company. Six-thirty, said the downward congruence of the hands, and the inheritance passed to Warwick Cigarettes. Only two hours remained before the appointed rendezvous of the Fold of the Faithful Shepherd with the American people, and Time was rolling toward the moment as it had rolled toward the death of David and the birth of Shakespeare, at the same rate, with the same inflexibility; and nobody in the living world knew as yet whether or not Father Stanfield would go on the air.

Outside the Pennsylvania Railroad Station a turbulent mass of people, perhaps thirty or forty thousand souls, had gathered to cheer the Faithful Shepherd's expected arrival in New York. In the explicable way in which a dog trapped on a steeple or a woman with her stomach where her heart should be can suddenly become the center of the burning attention of a hundred million Americans, the case of Father Stanfield had grown in three days into a celebrated cause about which no citizen in the hills or in the plains, by the great river valleys or along the coasts, had failed to form an aggressive opinion. The spark of interest struck by Jaeckel's monstrously popular column had been fanned by spontaneous editorial comment into a spreading blaze of indignation. Jaeckel's—that is to say, Wilde's—one-sided view of the story: the throttling of a courageous pastor by a money-bagged tyrant: had been swallowed everywhere in default of any reply from Talmadge Marquis, who had driven all reporters from his doors. Letters and telegrams, ranging in style from the elegant prose of college presidents to obscene threats of guttersnipes, started to pile up in the offices of Marquis and the Republic Broadcasting Company. Ministers called special church meetings and urged their flocks to cry out against the injustice; amateur crusaders talked on street corners; Congressmen ventured bravely to add their august voices to the clamor. Chester Legrand, scared by the threat of an avalanche of public disfavor, had gone to Marquis and urged him to reconsider, but the soap manufacturer was not to be moved. The only man with the power to bend his will, Stephen English, lay enfeebled in a hospital, and nobody had dared further to mention the disasters looming for the sales of Aurora Dawn soap, after pink little Martin Rousseau had been dismissed and kicked head first out of Marquis's inner chamber for bringing up the subject. Since most of the soap man's unyielding reactions found their way at second hand into the press, which was devoting as much space to the episode as it usually reserved for crimes of passion, the general prejudice against him was more violently confirmed with each edition. He was universally excoriated as the type of irresponsible money-autocracy, and it is safe to say that throughout the length and breadth of the land not a voice was lifted to plead that he was merely suffering from an absence of Being where Being should be.

To all newspaper queries, Father Stanfield had given only one genial answer, "I'll be there Sunday night"; and this widely publicized utterance had called into existence the good-humored throng that now pressed around the railroad station waiting to accompany him to the studio. Nobody could accurately state the composition of this mob. There were college clubs, young people's church groups, women's leagues, veterans' posts, fraternal lodges and the like in definite little clumps, but they were submerged in a horde of undifferentiated human beings, many of them probably on hand mainly to watch the fun. It was an unorganized demonstration. One inspired editor later called it "an exercise of the people's sacred and seldom-invoked right peaceably to assemble for the redress of a grievance." The college boys had brought red torch flares with them, and a small number of communists, overcoming their repugnance to Stanfield's religion in their affinity for public commotion, had provided big banners proclaiming Mr. Marquis's shortcomings in satiric terms.

Into the streets had also come a large number of blue-coated patrolmen, who, with a sensible intuition of what was afoot, confined their watchfulness to the thwarting of vandalism and fistfighting; and they had so little to do that most of them caught the hilarious air of the crowd and wore broad smiles as they moved to and fro. What with blazing red lights, swaying banners, plenty of police, and a restless crowd of high-spirited people, the whole scene outside the Pennsylvania Station on this fateful Sunday evening was as picturesque and stirring as any the usually cold city had ever provided.

In one corner of this pleasing panorama of spontaneity there was an inharmonious detail of planning. Directly in front of the station stood three busses, evidently waiting to take the people of the Fold to the studio. This transportation had always been furnished by the Marquis Company in special busses festooned with Aurora Dawn slogans, as these machines clearly were not; and the one clue to the identity of the thoughtful provider of them was the presence in front of them of a small sound-truck displaying the trademark of Republic's bitter rival, the United States Broadcasting System. The reader will gain special insight into the mystery on learning that there sat beside the driver of this truck a little, pale, sour-visaged man who surveyed the mob with satisfaction while he flicked a ring round and round the third finger of his left hand.

Round and round went Tom Leach's ring; and round and round the circle of twelve jet balls went the second hand of the Republic Broadcasting Company's clock. Quarter past seven, proclaimed the generous angle of the hands. The tall masts atop the building silently poured into the void a series of electric waves that were translated by receiving sets into the Lily Maid Cold Cream Serenade. Now there were left only the Claridge Balloon Tire Circus and Aurora Dawn's own Bob Steele Frolic in the crumbling barrier of time between the present moment and Father Stanfield's scheduled appearance; and in Chester Legrand's offices directly under the great masts, an eleventh-hour council grimly sat. The *dramatis personae* were those of Thursday, less the Messrs. Stanfield, Pennington, and Leach, who were elsewhere engaged. Andrew Reale, hurriedly called from the last rehearsal of Marquis's substitute musical program, sat in his shirt sleeves, looking young, overfatigued and miserable; having learned through the newspapers of the startling misfortune of the Englishes, he had been making regular, useless efforts to ascertain their condition, and had, indeed, been at a telephone vainly trying to reach Mrs. Beaton when the page boy came with the instruction to conduct him to Legrand's office. Seldom had Andrew responded to a summons and sat down to a crucial task with less heart. Beside him the loyal Grovill slouched in his chair, head in hands, clothes drooping around his bulk as though he had lost twenty pounds. Van Wirt and the lawyer, Morphee, sat stiffly and silently opposite them. At either end of the table, Legrand and Marquis confronted each other. Legrand's face was drawn into sharp business lines, and his gray hair was unkempt. Marquis had clasped his hands before him to still a trembling, and he was glowering out from under his eyebrows. The air of the room was heavy with the staleness of cigars and smoke.

"I will not retreat one inch," the soap maker was saying in a voice muffled with passion and raised almost to soprano pitch. "I am the master of Aurora Dawn's policy and I have to apologize to nobody for what I have done. Furthermore, I consider that I have made no mistakes and done nothing unjust or ill-considered, and if I had it to do over again I would proceed exactly as I have done up to the present. My decision regarding Stanfield stands."

"At the risk of repeating myself let me point out to you," said Legrand, running his fingers through his hair, "that your decision involves not only your own policy but that of the Republic Broadcasting Company. We, as well as you, will have to answer to the public for barring the preacher from the air. You are forcing on us the necessity of deciding whether to back you or back him—"

"I don't agree that any such choice exists for you," Marquis interrupted. "Under a legal contract I have paid you your stated price for this radio time and it is mine to do with as I will. Your action is limited to carrying out my desires with your technical facilities. If the public is stupid enough to blame you for what I do, well, that's a risk you run in the broadcasting business."

Legrand drew out of his breast pocket a rumpled yellow envelope. "Immediately before I called you," he said, "I received among the thousands of protests that have been jamming our office activities, this wire from Bill Wing, chairman of the Federal Communications Commission. Let me read it to you." He smoothed the message reverently before him on the table and read aloud: "*Receiving demands from high officials to take action in Stanfield case. Urge you persuade Marquis allow him broadcast as only way to quell newspaper talk. If he is barred we may be compelled conduct inquiry. Wing.*"

Marquis emitted a sound like that of a seal clearing its nostrils upon emerging from water. "Naturally," he added in elaboration of the sound, "the radicals in the government want this radical

Stanfield to be given a chance to spread his propaganda. That radical mob at Penn Station has the same idea. I'm not impressed by anything that radicals in or out of the government may care to say about my business."

"It would be a happy day for the radicals," said Legrand, "if you were correct in enrolling under their banner everyone who disagrees with you. Bill Wing, however, is state treasurer of the New Jersey Republican Committee."

"It wouldn't matter to me," shouted Marquis, waving a shaking hand at Legrand, "if he were Herbert Hoover. Neither he nor anybody else but myself can dictate policy to the company of which I am president."

(The reader is reminded that all quotations of Mr. Marquis's conversation are inaccurate in so far as they have been pruned of certain interjections which ladies and children could not possibly understand. Color and emphasis are lessened thereby. On the other hand, this volume may be safely left in parlors frequented by youngsters who have learned to read but not to discriminate— a recommendation not lightly made for all modern novels. But to go on:)

"Public opinion dictates to all of us who are in business," said Legrand. "Our firms exist by public favor. Public opinion can force this company to act against the wishes of a client."

"Grovill!" said Marquis sharply. The fat man started as though coming out of slumber and turned a white, sagging face to his employer, who proceeded, "Please go to your office now and prepare the necessary papers to transfer the three Aurora Dawn shows with Republic to the United States Broadcasting System."

"Yes, sir," said Grovill, looking around in bewilderment and not moving.

"One moment," interposed Morphee, the tall old lawyer, in church-organ tones. "I'm quite certain that Mr. Legrand was not suggesting that his company would fail to meet its contractual obligations. He was merely advising a client, as I'm sure you will agree he should, what he considers the wisest course to be followed in a situation which is, I'm sure you will confess, both unprecedented and delicate—"

The telephone beside Legrand interrupted this memorable dialogue. Legrand picked up the receiver. As he listened, his eyes widened, and he stared fearfully at his desk clock, which showed seven-thirty-five. Properly to convey to the reader the shocking news he was hearing, we must shift scenes again in mid-chapter, and return to the Pennsylvania Station; grant the writer the latitude of the moving pictures and come along.

Some ten minutes before this instant (it is impossible, almost, to tell a tale of radio without the aid of a chronometer, such is the terrible urgency of Time in that queer new trade), Father Stanfield and his Fold had arrived by train and had emerged into the tumultuous, torch-lit, good-natured riot on Seventh Avenue. At once Tom Leach leaped to the roof of his sound truck with a portable microphone, and shouted in a voice amplified to the strength of thunder, "He's here, folks!" at which the host sent up a shout that tore the concave of the night. While the farm people were filing through the crowd to the busses, Leach danced around on top of the truck howling, "Your attention, *please!*" As the jubilation subsided, he spoke thus, every syllable booming out in a Niagara of sound:

"Ladies and gentlemen, I am speaking for the United States Broadcasting System. In order to prove that American free-enterprise radio does not endorse the suppression of freedom of speech and religion, USBS proudly announces that if Father Stanfield is still barred from the Aurora Dawn hour at 8:30, he can broadcast his sermon through this very microphone over our nationwide facilities, by courtesy of Lustro-Dent Toothpaste, which has gladly yielded its time!"

The outburst of joy which followed this announcement has never been forgotten by those who saw it. The college boys snake-danced, the women wept, the men cheered, the children ran about screaming, the communists tore their banners to shreds, cascades of paper poured down from the windows of the surrounding hotels, and a small brass band (which Leach had judiciously provided) blared out a blood-curdling martial tune. Father Stanfield climbed to the top of the truck and clasped hands with the pale little man, setting off fresh paroxysms of happiness in the throng.

What must have been the sensations of Tom Leach as he stood atop the shaking truck, stared at by eighty thousand eyes, hearing roars of applause for himself from forty thousand throats? Did he thank any deity for having granted him the strength to challenge Marquis at last? Did he congratulate himself for having gone to the president of USBS on the day that Marquis had humbled him, to tell him the story, offer his services and propose the daring scheme which was now bursting into bloom so brilliantly? Did he regret cutting at a blow his twenty-year partnership with Grovill? Did he see the road, lying straight and dusty before him to the grave, which he must trudge yoked to a wife who would not forgive him his costly excursion into moral principle? A historian limited to external facts can answer none of these questions; he can only relate that as Tom Leach looked around at the swarm of happy faces and felt the grip of Father Stanfield's great hand, he gave his ring one mighty flick which thrust it off his finger and sent it spinning and glittering through the air to everlasting loss in the black street; whereupon he looked around wildly, and then burst into the first whole-souled laugh he had uttered since his young days.

And so it was that the triumphal procession of Father Stanfield and his Fold set forth toward the Republic Building ten blocks away, the sound truck and busses rolling slowly in the van, the brass band and the gay mob following behind in a continuing display of merriment and satisfaction, while the police, in obedience to an order from the mayor (who was a great admirer of the Faithful Shepherd) cleared the streets before the oncoming mass and kept order while it passed. It was at this moment that an assistant of Legrand, posted at the scene, telephoned to transmit these developments in a shaky voice, taking care to explain very plainly the ingenious move that USBS had made to turn the crisis to its advantage.

So much less time did it take him to tell the news than it does a painstaking author, that when Legrand hung up the receiver and drew his eyes away from his desk clock, that honest timepiece read only seven-thirty-seven. He swiftly repeated the tidings, to the consternation of his hearers; then he went on with some sternness, "It must be clear even to you, Mr. Marquis, that we now have no alternative. Reale," he added, turning to our hero, "the Faithful Shepherd program will be broadcast as originally scheduled. Please go down to the studio and make the necessary arrangements quickly."

"Reale, stay where you are," said Marquis in an extremely high voice. "Legrand, I will deal in my own way with USBS for stabbing me in the back when they have nine and a half million dollars of my business, and I assure you that you will profit greatly by the steps I will take against them, if you stand by me now. I still want Stanfield kept off my hour."

Legrand and his lawyer exchanged a brief glance, and the radio man thrust his fingers once quickly through his hanging gray hair. "It's no use, Mr. Marquis," he said. "Permitting USBS to pose as the only free-speech network would damage Republic far beyond your ability to repay us. Go ahead, Reale."

"Hold on!" shouted Marquis. "I serve you notice that I will at once withdraw all Aurora Dawn accounts from you and sue you for deliberate breach of contract."

"I anticipate both actions," said Legrand.

"You will thank Mr. Legrand in a cooler moment," interjected the lawyer, "for overriding what is, and I'm certain you will some day say so, obviously an emotional and irrational decision on your part. He is taking the only step that can save both Republic and Aurora Dawn from the most serious damage in the sphere of public relations. I say again, and I am sure you will eventually agree, you owe him gratitude for his—"

Marquis interrupted to reply at some length to this observation, but his answer, due to the stated limitations of the historian, must go entirely unrecorded. He was concluding his retort for want of breath when Legrand said to Reale impatiently, "Please go ahead, my boy. We've very little time."

Our hero had sat dully during the debate, confident that the result would be, as always, submission to Marquis. Only half-listening, he had given himself up to painful reflections on the subject of his erstwhile sweetheart, Laura. He had been startled out of this reverie by the news about USBS. Rapidly calculating his position, he realized that if Marquis broke with Republic all would be over for his clever plans; he, a Republic man, would be received as a leper in the soap man's household thereafter. Since the abruptly broken meeting with Carol, he had been prevented by the turmoil of events from seeing her for more than a few minutes at a time, and nothing was decided between them. To be cut off from the shallow, heedless youngster would be to lose his hold over her in a month, he reasoned, thus missing the gamble after an alarming investment of self-respect and personal felicity. In this wise, if not in these words, did the gallant Andrew hastily judge his footing, whereupon he rose and spoke thus:

"Mr. Legrand, although it is scarcely my place to do so, permit me to urge you to reconsider, before it is too late. It seems to me we are breaking faith with Mr. Marquis, and no business can long survive that breaks faith."

"Andy!" wailed Van Wirt. "Be quiet and do as you're told. Discuss it another time." The others seemed too amazed to react.

"By your leave, Mr. Van Wirt," went on the brave young man, "I feel too strongly about this to be silent. I am a very small fish, but I have my scruples. Mr. Legrand," he said appealingly, "if your orders to me are still to break our contract with Mr. Marquis and arrange to let Father Stanfield broadcast, please be kind enough to release me from those orders or accept my resignation. I cannot comply."

Marquis, who had listened with an open mouth, now cleared his throat and violently swore it was wonderful to see that there was still a man's man in the Republic organization. Legrand immediately said, "I'm sorry, Reale, because I understand you worked well. Your resignation is accepted." He turned to Van Wirt. "Bill, see to the broadcast, will you? It's extremely late." With a sorrowful glance at Andy, and many rueful sighs and shakes of the head, the bereaved sales manager proceeded to comply.

Marquis walked to Andrew Reale and put his arm around his shoulder. "You'll never regret it," he said. "Come, get your jacket and we'll listen to"—he threw an ill-wishing look at Legrand— "*our* broadcast in the sponsor's booth. Carol will be there to meet us." He started out, leading our hero, while Grovill pulled himself to his feet and dogged his employer wearily. Marquis, with his hand on the doorknob, remarked over his shoulder, "Walter, I want you to work with the legal staff all night tonight if it is necessary so that Mr. Legrand may have his notice of cancellation of our contracts at eight o'clock Monday morning." Grovill said, "Yes, sir," in an empty tone, as he followed his defeated lord out and closed the door.

These are the true events that underlay the great Aurora Dawn riot, and its ending in complete victory for free speech, free religion, and every other description of freedom which, on the following day, the newspapers said had been vindicated. Accompanied by a thousand mob antics of exultation, Father Stanfield and his Fold came to the Republic Building, were welcomed graciously by the staff and went on the air in due course of time, exactly as though the tempestuous occurrences narrated here had never happened; had, indeed, been no more than a dream, dreamed by Laura English, as she lay in drugged sleep in the Mercy Hospital, a few blocks away. This history would like to pause and watch by her bedside, but it must move on faithfully to recount what was actually contained in the cataclysmic sermon, "The Hog in the House," and what happened to the universe when it was uttered.

CHAPTER 23

"The Hog in the House."

*N*OBODY CAN EXPLAIN THE FACT that radio works. Turn your dial and cause sounds; you are performing as improbable a deed as the stopping of the sun by Joshua or the splitting of the sea by Moses.

Hold, before you throw this book into the wastebasket, and ask any scientist whether action at a distance is possible, that is, exerting force in one place and causing effects in another place without an intervening medium to transmit the force. Then, when he has told you (quoting Newton) no, of course it isn't possible, ask him what the medium is that transmits radio waves. He will either answer that nobody can say yet, thus confirming the first sentence of this chapter, or, if he regards you as an easy mark, he will reply "Ether," and quickly change the subject. Let us not use space here to jeer at ether, the most flogged of all whipping-boy hypotheses ever brought into the court of science in the absence of His Royal Highness, Truth. If you happen not to be familiar with the subject, glance at the disheartened discussion of ether in a current encyclopedia. Ether, if it exists, is apparently an even less digestible miracle than the plague of frogs or the perpetually oxidizing Burning Bush.

This moral history has no quarrel with miracles, either of radio or the Bible; let other pens maintain scientific and religious heresies. It is merely sought here to point out how peculiarly fitting it was that Father Calvin Stanfield, a believer in the old miracles which people will not recognize for lack of evidence, should make use of the new miracle of radio, which people will not recognize because there is too much evidence. Probably this mysterious device was never more appropriately employed than when it spread forth, from the little metal box in front of the Shepherd's mouth into every inhabited corner of the continent, the address called, "The Hog in the House."

"Let a hog in yer house, and he'll crawl on yer table."

Father Stanfield spoke these opening words, halted, and looked around at the crowded studio. It was an oblong cavern of a room, walled with a rough substance that eliminated echoes by absorbing sound and abolished cheer by being the coldest shade of green in the spectrum. In the middle of one of the long walls was a wide platform, and here the preacher stood, flanked by the penitential stools for the sinners and the golden pews for the redeemed —also by several queerly shaped pieces of radio equipment. Overhead there arched, in pink cardboard letters four feet high nailed to a wood frame, the legend, "AURORA DAWN PRESENTS," forlorn as a campaign poster after elections. In the seats directly before the stage the folk of the Fold were grouped, and the rest of the studio, seats, aisles, and doorways alike, overflowed with human beings. This was against the company's rules, but the usual controls for herding audiences had proved too flimsy to contain the mob which had glutted every foot of space. The glassed-in sponsor's box to the right of the stage, where there were seats for sixteen persons, provided a contrast by holding only three: Andrew Reale, Talmadge Marquis, and Carol. In place of the train of attendants usually to be seen with Marquis on such occasions of state, were thirteen superbly upholstered empty armchairs.

"That's my text for tonight," went on the Shepherd. "It ain't from the Good Book, but it'll serve. It's a sayin' of my father, who was a God-fearin' man and lived long enough to know a few things and put 'em in words.

"I'm gonna talk to you folks about this business we call advertisin'."

His eyes rested on Marquis, who shifted his gaze to the ash of his cigar and stared at it as though it were the most remarkable object on earth. Carol moved her hand so that it touched Andrew's wrist and clung there like a kitten's paw. Our hero glanced gratefully at her and returned his attention to the preacher.

"They is a punchin' bag in our land that every highbrow and scribbler swings at sooner er later—and that's advertisin'. Seems nobody with a college education has got any more use fer advertisin' than they got fer a dead polecat on a hot night—'ceptin' the fellers who make a livin' advertisin', and even they get sorta bristly, like it's a humpbacked kid o' theirs and they'll fight you if you speak mean about it. Now if I use five-and-ten-cent words and disappoint the perfessers and reformers who expect me to rip up the business with hacksaws, I'm sorry. I don't think advertisin' is no dead polecat and no humpbacked kid, neither. I ain't even agin' it.

"When my pop he said, 'Let a hog in the house and he'll crawl on yer table,' he wasn't agin' hogs, neither. Fact, we was all pretty near raised on pork. Pop was jest statin' a plain fact about hogs. All I aim to do tonight is state plain facts.

"Feller come out our way one winter when I was thirteen, and set up shop on the main street of town. Name was Slade, and he was a shoemaker. He hung up a little wood sign outside his shop, 'Slade's Shoes.' Seems like he didn't git enough trade to suit him, 'cause pretty soon up goes a big red and yaller sign, 'Slade's Special Superb Shoes.' First time anyone put up such a big bright sign on Main Street. Plenty of folks stopped to gawk, and a few bought shoes, I reckon. Well, maybe Slade figgered he'd hit on a smart idee, er maybe he took a trip to a big city. Anyhow, one mornin' in May I'm comin' in town fer some kerosene to burn out caterpillars, and in front of Slade's shop is a crowd, and on his roof is a sign bigger'n the whole shop. It's a picture of a naked gal a-winkin', and across her middle is a sash, and on it it says, 'How Kin I Help Lovin' A Feller With Slade's Shoes On?' But the crowd ain't lookin' at the sign, they're lookin' at Slade, who is quite a sight, all tar and feathers and astraddle of a fence rail. Some hooligans carry him to the town limits and come back and burn up the sign, and nobody never sees Slade no more, and we got a right quiet lot o' signs along the main street to this day.

"Signs is like hogs: nobody claims they's pretty, but everybody knows you gotta have 'em. But Slade's signs got to be like a hog in the house. God give folks power to see red and yaller so's they could praise His glory in robins and dandelions, in the sunrise and the autumn, not so's their attention could be yanked sharp by any yahoo with enough paint or 'lectric bulbs. God give man Woman to sweeten his way through the vale of tears, not to set him hankerin' after nobody's shoes. Slade's sign invaded folks' lives so's they got mad and booted it out hard, which is what gen'rally happens sooner er later to a hog in the house.

"They is some wild-eyed folks likes to holler, 'Abolish advertisin'.' Shucks, tryin' to stop advertisin' in this land is like tryin' to stop freckles with a rubber eraser. Maybe in these here countries where the gov'ment makes everythin' and hands out everythin' and runs everythin' they don't have no such problem, but as long as you got different fellers makin' and sellin' the same thing and tryin' to beat each other at it yer gonna have 'em hangin' out signs. That's all advertisin' is, in radio, magazines, it don't matter none where, it's the same thing—hangin' out signs.

"Me, I had three years of life with the gov'ment handin' out everythin' and runnin' everythin', in the army. I'll take the old way, signs and all. Only thing is, I look around our land and right now I say we ain't got signs; by and large, we got a hog in the house.

"Big hollerin' displays all over the landscape, like them corkers

238

—*That's hog*—

you folks all seen across the Hudson, blottin' out the sunset, blindin' you to God's wonders so's they kin tell you about autos and salad oil—that's hog.

"Promisin' yer poor little homely daughter she'll marry the star halfback if she'll jest wash out her mouth with Reuben's medicine or bathe herself with Simon's Soap; promisin' yer puny son he'll be a champeen if he eats their bran mush; promisin' any sad people to make 'em happy when they cain't—that's hog.

"Bawlin' slogans at you like you was dogs to train you to buy stuff—that's hog. When some folks git mad enough to object they say, 'It *sells,* don't it?' They reckon that's as good an answer as sayin', 'It glorifies the Lord, don't it?'

"Takin' Heaven's newest gift to a undeservin' world—pleasure sent through the air by radio—and readin' their signs in yer parlor until it's all signs and no pleasure—that's hog.

"Leadin' yer prettiest daughters out o' yer homes into big cities, undressin' 'em and printin' pictures of 'em to sweeten up their products with the sweetness of Eve and Mary—that's a hog right in our laps. We all got so used to it none of us don't even see it fer what it is.

"All I've stated is plain facts that anybody knows. Here in America the Lord has spread the richest feast that a body of citizens has ever sat down to: fields, mines, forests, rivers, schools, industries, people—what have we got that ain't the most and the best? But the banquet is kinder spoiled now, by a hog in the house. Jest like my pop said, he's crawled up on the table and put one foot in the mash potatoes and the other in the cranberry sauce. They ain't many Americans will object to a feller hangin' out a sign when he got somethin' to sell; but they ain't many Americans either, I don't think, will go on livin' fer ever with a hog in the house."

This was the fateful utterance of Father Calvin Stanfield, word for word. Only because this history might seem incomplete without it, has it been recorded, for it is a mild paraphrase of Michael Wilde's Oration, and nothing else. We who have lived nine years since that night are inclined to give the sermon somewhat less importance than the newspapers, the Shepherd, and even Marquis attached to it. Spoken or not spoken, what difference did it really make? The sun rose next day, the insects ate the leaves, the birds ate the insects, the cats chased the birds, and all the wheels of the world rolled on as before, with scarcely a wobble to bear witness to the shattering event that had exploded on the little rock of Manhattan. If all mankind were to give a single horrid shout and expire in a mass, the face of the planet would be marvelously little changed. Most happenings called epoch-making are smaller in effect than that, but we are endowed, possibly for our preservation, with the abiding illusion that what is about to take place this week overshadows all that has passed since Light was created.

In these nine years much has occurred, including a war, but nothing has happened to the harmless profession of advertising except that its prosperity has increased. Our citizens in the happiness of their lot ignored Stanfield, and to this day still ignore the whole matter, even as dancing picnickers disregard the gnats on a fine summer's day.

Return we to the epoch-making moment, however, when the Faithful Shepherd spoke the last words. Observe the great things that ensued.

CHAPTER 24

*Wherein the plot thickens, as all plots should do
near the end of the volume.*

*M*ANY AMERICANS EITHER, I don't think," said the voice from
about twenty million loudspeakers, "will go on livin' fer ever
with a hog in the house.

"Brothers and sisters, let us sing, 'Tramp, Tramp, Tramp, the
Souls Are Marching,' written by our own Elder Bryce."

In the burst of song which followed, Stephen English reached
a pallid hand out from under stiff hospital sheets and turned off
the little radio on the white table beside his bed. "Lloyd," he said
to a fat, bald young man in a dark gray suit and bright red bow
tie, who sat near the foot of the bed watching the banker's face
anxiously, "please call Mr. Marquis immediately—he must be at
the studio or his home—and tell him that I would like him to
arrange an emergency meeting of the board of directors of the
Marquis Company for nine o'clock Tuesday morning."

The secretary said, "Steve, you won't be out of here by Tuesday," but the banker shook his head patiently. "I can walk on
that ankle with a cane, it's only sprained," he said, "and the cuts
are nothing. Look at those newspapers." He pointed to a pile of the
day's gazettes which the secretary had brought, lying in disorder

on the bed. "Aurora Dawn has suffered damage which must be repaired swiftly. I'm to blame for allowing Marquis such authority in public relations; sooner or later this had to happen." He leaned back on the propped pillows and closed his eyes. "See how it is with Laura, Lloyd," he murmured. The secretary left, and found the banker in the same position when he returned two minutes láter. "She's awake now," he reported, "but the doctor is with her. I couldn't go in. The nurse says she was cheerful when she woke up."

"God help the poor girl," said Stephen English.

Two thousand seven hundred miles away, three miles above earth, in a metal machine moving westward, Flame Anders sat, smoking a cigarette and talking gaily to an extremely handsome man with long, curly black hair. You must know, reader, that she had run away two days earlier from Walter Grovill, reducing him to the piteous condition in which we have recently observed him. Her paramour was a models' agent who had jilted her, just before her marriage to the advertising man, and had recently decided to win her back, this feat being accomplished by the expedient of telephoning her one afternoon. As garrulous now as she had been silent for two years, the red-haired beauty chattered continually through Stanfield's sermon—which traversed the continent, mounted into the sky, overtook the airplane, and emerged through Mrs. Grovill's radio effortlessly, doing this in less time than it took the preacher to voice a single syllable. Quoth the happy Flame, when the sermon was over, "Oh, my, isn't poor Walter in for it now! That Mike Wilde sure started something. Honest, Dan, I wish you had been there last Saturday night and heard him. He was out of this world." A thought struck her, and her matchless face assumed the old pensive expression for a moment. "Last Saturday," she repeated. "It was only last Saturday. Gosh, Dan, how much can happen in a week!" The fortunate, well-favored Dan answered nothing, being engaged in shuffling playing cards for a game of chance called gin rummy, and thus became the only person in this history to enter it and vanish beyond its scope without uttering a sound.

In the sponsor's booth in the big studio where the historic speech had just been delivered, Talmadge Marquis sat hunched, his arms extended along the sides of the deep soft chair, the cigar in his mouth growing cold, his face as gray as the cigar's ash. When the Fold lifted their voices in song he sighed heavily, dropped the cigar into a chromium tray, and looked at Andrew and Carol with his lower jaw hanging open, a suffering glance.

"It wasn't so bad, Dad," said Carol. "It'll all be forgotten tomorrow."

Marquis said, "I have a fearful headache." But when his daughter suggested that they go home he declared that he did not intend to slink away, and settled back morosely into his chair.

Our hero, with Carol Marquis's hand firmly and intimately clasped over his, felt the sensations of a weary marathon runner who sees the finish line in the distance and knows that the race is his. With the sense of assured triumph was tiredness of the bones, and a pang of doubt as to whether the trophy was worth the toil, a depressed view which he dismissed as a mood of fatigue. It was warm and comfortable, despite misgivings, to feel success. Carol's display of affection, starting with an impulsive kiss when her father told her of Reale's loyal stand for him, was extravagant, particularly in the number of times she loaded him with the terms "dearest" and "darling." As he accepted her endearments and caresses with the passive dignity of a spent champion, Andy reflected that no young man, probably, ever realizes how very calm he can feel in the great moment when at last he attains what he has wanted all his days.

The Fold had not yet ended its song when an attendant in the livery of the broadcasting company entered the glass booth with many expressions of respect, attached a telephone to a cord hanging from the back wall and handed it to Marquis, saying, "Call from Mr. Stephen English's secretary." Marquis seized the telephone. The conversation was brief, and consisted on his part of several affirmative noises and a dry "Good-by," after which he handed the instrument to the uniformed bearer, who backed politely out of the door. The soap man turned a stricken face to his companions and told them what English's secretary had said. His fingers shook, but he made no effort to control them.

"Once again," he said in a quivering soprano voice, "once again I have to suffer for the incompetent stupidity of my subordinates and the treachery of everybody I trust. Except you, Reale," he added, "and even you I must hold responsible for the ill-advised notion of bringing Stanfield on the air."

"Andy has been wonderful and you know it, Dad," said Carol quickly.

"I said that of all the people around me he alone hasn't utterly failed me," grumbled Marquis.

"Possibly," said Andrew with great charm, "Mr. English's meeting may prove pleasant."

"The last emergency meeting did not," said Marquis, biting at his lower lip. "It was when everyone betrayed me on the change of the soap's color, which to this day I know was a good idea." He pulled himself up out of the deep armchair. "Serf and the others have been hoping for fifteen years that I would antagonize Steve English again. Well, I'll face them. My policies in radio have made Aurora Dawn what it is. I have been absolutely right in this Stanfield business from start to finish, and if Leach and Legrand hadn't stabbed me—" he broke off, with his hand on the slender aluminum rod that served as a doorknob. "I'll be with the lawyers at Grovill's office for a couple of hours, Carol. See you at home. 'Night, Reale." Pale and stooped, the soap magnate walked out heavily.

Now the packed-in audience began to fill the studio with laughter as Father Stanfield interviewed the first penitent sinner. Andrew reached over to the loudspeaker and snapped the button, and suddenly there was silence in the glass box as profound as that of an underground cave. Before the eyes of the young couple the people continued to go through the motions of mirth, but without the sound to make their antics intelligible they looked like badly worked marionettes. Andrew had no eye for this interesting contrast. He turned to Carol and asked her how it was that her mighty parent could fear the opinion of Stephen English or anyone else in matters pertaining to his own company.

Readily the girl confided to him what the reader will remember from the early sketch of the soap magnate: that the Marquis Company was not truly her father's since his inspiration regarding the "Snow White, Snow Pure" campaign, when English's bank had taken a controlling interest as the price of rescuing the tottering finances, and had also compelled Marquis to give sizable portions of voting stock to his managers; that part of the bargain had been retention by Marquis of the presidency; but that English could topple him, and the managers devoutly wished for such a consummation. Carol outlined this state of things rapidly and nervously, with mounting disturbance of spirit. Her tense little hands made a thousand quick flutterings as she talked, and her eyes wandered about distractedly, shifting often to the large studio clock which was nearing the hour of nine. Suddenly she jumped up, pressed the button which turned off the soft indirect lights of the booth, and pulled Andrew by the hand to the darkest corner, out of sight of the studio audience.

"Oh, Andy darling," she cried softly, pressing him in her arms, "I do appreciate everything you've done and tried to do for me. I wish things didn't look so hopelessly messed."

Our hero felt singularly puissant at this moment. "Give me a little time, Carol, dear," he said, "and I may pull your dad out of this. Don't despair."

The girl hid her face against his chest for a moment; then she drew away from him and said, "I must go. Call me tomorrow at noon. Good-by."

"If you're going to join your dad, let me come with you," said

247

Andrew, but Carol shook her black locks vehemently, gave him a swift kiss on the mouth, and slipped out through the door, leaving him alone in the gloomy, hushed, glass booth.

Graveled by the new shadows on his fortune, Andrew Reale dropped into an armchair and considered the situation. Was the fruit of scheme and sacrifice, he wondered, to prove a Dead Sea apple, crumbling to an ash when he touched it? Deposed, Marquis was hardly an advantageous father-in-law; on the contrary, to be linked to a fallen tyrant meant to acquire the odor of his disrepute, and who could say how rich or poor the unstable soap man might prove to be, once deprived of his shaky power as the head of a large corporation? His handsome city and country homes, his lavish style of living; might these not be the shell of a rotted credit? Andrew decided dourly that in his present plight, shorn of his job and his beloved—his former beloved—only one role remained to him, the least tasteful he had ever acted: that of bellows to the dimming fire of Marquis. His hopes turned on the preservation of the sponsor's authority. Let his friends in radio, artists, technicians, and executives alike, rejoice at the nearing downfall! Andrew Reale must whip his brains for a way to rescue his future father-in-law.

As he sat in the darkness and thought over the pass he was at, our hero suddenly felt as though a bulwark in his mind had given way, and through the breach came pouring a turbid torrent of thoughts, memories, scents, sounds, images, and sensations relating wholly to his old sweetheart, Honey Beaton—a flood which clogged his brain and halted all rational traffic through it. In vain did he try to stem the intrusion, and focus his faculties again on the ugly problem at hand. Motions of her hands and head, forgotten dresses she had worn but once long ago, strange dishes they had tasted together, little phrases of hers which when uttered had seemed to disappear into the air like light smoke—such things presented themselves to him in a luridly colored vividness and in dizzying succession. He groaned and pressed his hand to his forehead, and, looking out through the glass, he saw the studio audience with their heads bent in the customary thirty seconds of silent prayer before Father Stanfield's benediction.

"Oh, Lord," said Andrew Reale aloud in the gloom, "You don't owe me a thing, and I suppose I don't really believe in You, but I'm in this business deep and I'm in it for good, and I need help. If ever I'm to get a favor from You, this is the time. Send me a way to save Marquis from his just punishment! That's all Andy Reale has left to pray for."

He felt ashamed of the outburst as soon as it was uttered, for a strict upbringing had given him a sense of decorum, if nothing more positive, in the presence of the Unknown. All at once it appeared to him that he could not put off for another ten minutes his visit to Laura's bedside—for no other purpose, of course, than to express his sympathy and give her his good wishes for recovery. Jumping up from his armchair, he strode out of the sponsor's booth and stood in the brightly illuminated green hallway, somewhat dazed by the light.

An old proverb says, "Beware of what you ask of Heaven, lest it be granted," but readers who incline to see more in what follows than a remarkable coincidence, are warned that they will incur the odium of being regarded as superstitious. Your own minister will tell you that requests for temporal aid are a misuse of prayer and that only spiritual gifts can properly be asked for. When Andrew Reale told these things to the historian many years later, he remembered this curious twist of sequence, the prayer and the accidental meeting with Mrs. Smollett immediately thereafter; and as he narrated it, so is it faithfully set down; by no means as a proof, however, of what a well-known agnostic coldly terms, "the animistic idea of an extra-causal propensity in events."

There came walking up to Andrew, at any rate, as he stood outside the door of the sponsor's box, a plump little brown-haired lady, bright of eye and nimble of gait, wearing an elaborately

249

made brown silk-and-velvet dress several inches too long to pass as fashionable, a queerly shaped feather-topped hat, rings and bracelets with big stones, and a double string of coral beads which hung to her waist. More than anything she resembled a fortyish female servant dressed up for a family holiday, except that she had an erect, merry bearing that did not argue a lifetime of drudgery. Her first words did much to explain the outlandish picture, for her accent was British, indeed not unlike the standard comic Cockney which Andrew had heard to weariness at auditions of hopeful actors.

"There's a good lad," she said as she approached, "and could you tell me if I might see Father Stanfield back 'ere somewhere after the shaow? I don't want to get lost in the mob again like I did before. 'E knaows I'm comin'—'E's expectin' me."

The workers in radio studios are numb to surprise at the nature of visitors, no matter how strange; it will soon be acknowledged by geographers that the lobbies of American broadcasting companies have replaced the streets of Constantinople as the world's crossroads. Said Andrew politely, "Madam, the public is not permitted to use this hallway, and I'm afraid there may be trouble—"

"I'm *not* the public," said the little lady firmly, taking an envelope from her pocket. "I've a naote from Cal right 'ere askin' me to meet 'im tonight 'ere at the shaow. 'E wraote it three weeks agao. I'm a very special friend, I am. Look 'ere, you can read it."

Andrew took the letter and glanced at it. The writing was Stanfield's, the salutation was "Dearest Gracie," the signature was, "Faithfully always, Cal"; it consisted of affectionate greetings and brief directions telling "Gracie" to meet Stanfield at the studio on this night, before the program. Andrew perceived that Stanfield had planned the appointment before the tempest over the advertising sermon; small wonder that the rendezvous had failed. He glanced sharply at the British lady, who returned the look with a beam of pride at the contents of the note. A thrill of interest shot through Andrew Reale.

"Did you say that you were a *special* friend of Father Stanfield's?" he asked, handing back the envelope.

"A *very* special friend," said the Englishwoman with an expression almost roguish enough to be a wink. "I'm Gracie Smollett—Mrs. Gracie Smollett. When Cal knew me, I was Gracie Kenny. I 'aven't seen nor written to 'im for nineteen years, but, as you can see, 'e's glad to 'ear from me. I tried to meet 'im by the revolving door, like it says in the naote, but dear me, what a mob! I couldn't do it."

"My dear Mrs. Smollett," said Andy, taking her arm and beginning to talk rapidly and easily, "I'm happy to be of service to you. My name is Andrew Reale, and I am in charge of Father Stanfield's radio arrangements. I'm afraid you won't be able to see him now, because the crowd will overwhelm him after the show; but if you'll let me take charge of you, I promise to arrange for you to meet him later tonight, or first thing in the morning."

"Why, that's lovely of you, I'm sure," said Mrs. Smollett, following docilely as Andrew led her to a small private elevator. "I knaow 'e'll be lookin' for me."

"Meantime," said Andrew, "a guest of the Faithful Shepherd deserves the best of everything. It's a hot night. Permit me to buy you a drink."

"I am *saow* warm with standin' and pushin'," said the little lady gratefully, stepping with Reale into the car, "I'll be aowbliged."

The door closed, and the elevator whined softly toward the street.

It is not necessary to follow our hero in his descent; all too soon will we see what use he made of Mrs. Smollett. The reader is again cautioned, however, against getting down on his knees, on the basis of evidence in this chapter, and praying for some material good which he desperately needs. This life is evidently not arranged to operate that way, and nearly all theologians agree that it is better so. For my part, friend, would that each of us could have his heart's desire tomorrow, and try the result for himself, without having to take the word of theologians.

CHAPTER 25

In which our hero believes he has reached bottom.

THE MIDDLE-AGED BACHELOR of your acquaintance will tell you that one particular lost maiden of his youth dominates his dreams, and appears over and over during his lonely slumbers to comfort him with the bright ghost of love. It must have been such a celibate thinker, in the early days of psychological theory, who advanced the dogma that we sleep not because we need rest but because we require the psychic fulfillment that comes from dreaming. This majestic proposition has now fallen into neglect, while others of its sort have gained such wide currency as to pass for plain fact even among the educated; which only shows that fashion is not absent from the chaste field of science; but the idea will yet have its day, and its handiest empirical proof will be found in the dreams of middle-aged bachelors.

The fact that Father Stanfield dreamed about Gracie Kenny was no distinguished compliment to the lady, inasmuch as their three-week romance in London in 1918 had been the solitary love-interlude in the Faithful Shepherd's life. His efforts to trace her after the war had been to no avail, and the years had insensibly stretched into decades, bringing him no warmer solace than the persistence of a winsome young British phantom in the illusions of the night. Spectral sweethearts have this advantage over too, too solidly fleshed wives, that they do not age; and for what it was worth, Calvin Stanfield in long, cold years had earned the consolation so sweetly addressed to the swain on the urn: "For ever wilt thou love, and she be fair."

On the morning after his triumph over Marquis, the preacher lay asleep in a bedroom in his favorite mid-Manhattan hotel. Refreshed by eight hours of deep sleep, Stanfield tossed now in the last moments of light dozing before waking, and dreamed of Gracie, who had been more than ever in his thoughts since the brief, amazing telephone call from her three weeks before. As always, he clasped her in his arms, but this time she did not dissolve in air, but turned into a big unfriendly white dog that squirmed in his grasp and snarled and snarled at him with a snarl remarkably like the ring of a telephone . . . the Shepherd opened his eyes, raised himself on an elbow and picked up the telephone by his bedside in a hand that made the instrument look toy-like. "Hello," he said. "Who? Andrew Reale? Where are you, son? Why, I reckon so, seein' it's urgent. Come right up."

When our hero arrived at Stanfield's suite of rooms a few moments later he found the outer door ajar and, stepping inside hesitantly, he saw the Shepherd, dressed in trousers and a bathrobe, sitting in an armchair with his hand over his eyes. Andrew stood silent, waiting. After a minute or two the preacher looked up, smiled apologetically, motioned Andrew to a chair, and resumed his abstracted meditation for what seemed a tormentingly long time to the tense radio executive. Finally he sat back and said cheerfully, "I like to git in a prayer or two afore startin' the day's business. Want some breakfast, son? You look like you ain't been sleepin' or eatin' a whole lot."

Andrew declined the invitation nervously.

"Well," said the Shepherd, "then let's git the urgent business a-rollin'."

The young man dug into his breast pocket and brought out a

254

folded sheet of white paper which he opened and passed to the clergyman. There were several typed paragraphs on it.

"I assure you the matter *is* urgent," he said. "Will you be good enough to sign this?"

As Stanfield glanced over the paper, Andrew drummed his fingers on the side of his leg, pressed his lips tightly together and stared with tired, reddened eyes.

This was what the preacher read:

"For the purpose of clarifying recent unfortunate incidents in connection with my broadcasts under the sponsorship of the Marquis Company, makers of Aurora Dawn products, and to correct unfair and misleading impressions now current, I, Father Calvin Stanfield, wish to make the following statements:

"First, that throughout my association with Mr. Talmadge Marquis I have found him always courteous, tolerant, understanding and liberal, and that he displayed all these qualities unfailingly in his attitude toward my sermon, 'The Hog in the House';

"Second, that wild and irresponsible newspaper gossip, not Mr. Marquis, was solely responsible for the deplorable turmoil regarding that sermon;

"Third, that I freely extend to the Marquis Company permission to use these statements in newspaper advertisements or in any way they choose, for the express purpose of preventing further injustice to Mr. Marquis, whom I regard with the highest respect and esteem.

"Calvin Stanfield."

"Whew!" exclaimed the Shepherd, and let the paper fall to his lap. He looked inquiringly at Andrew, who returned the look with an impassive expression. "I don't rightly know what yer game is, son," said the clergyman at last. "You know I ain't gonna sign this. You knowed it when you come here."

"I think you will sign," said the hero of this history, "after I explain a few things to you."

"Nothin's impossible, I reckon," said Stanfield, "but that'll be some blue-ribbon explainin'."

"You may not know," said Andy, "that Marquis is in very diffi-

255

cult circumstances as a result of your sermon. He has to face an inquiry by his board of directors, and they have the power to throw him out. You won the fight. Be generous. Sign that paper, so that he can produce it at the meeting. It will save him. Otherwise he will probably be ruined."

Stanfield regarded him soberly. "I'm sorry fer Marquis, but they is more hope fer a fool than fer a man wise in his own wisdom. I ain't ruinin' him; he ruined hisself. It ain't fer me to save him, 'specially with no outrageous lie."

Andrew, paler and more haggard than ever, said, "I regret you feel that way." With this he reached into the breast pocket again and handed to the cleric his letter to Gracie Smollett, saying, "I have some information about Mrs. Smollett for you."

The preacher's eyes widened as he took the note; then he smiled. "You seen her afore I did, eh? I figgered I'd lose her in the crowd. What's she like?"

"A little British lady—very sweet," said Andrew. "Quite pretty. Hair just has a touch of gray. She's at the Buchanan Hotel now."

A tender, wistful and melancholy light was in the Faithful Shepherd's eyes. "A touch of gray, eh?" he repeated softly. "A touch of gray."

Andrew picked his hat off the table where he had laid it, and turned it rapidly round and round in his hands. "I'm genuinely sorry, believe me, Father Stanfield," he said in a low voice, looking at the moving hat, "that Mrs. Smollett stumbled into me and inadvertently disclosed as much of your private affairs as she did. She's very simple, and not discreet."

"Shucks, it don't signify none what she told you," said the Shepherd gently and absently. "It all belongs in the long ago."

"Not quite," said the dauntless lover of Carol Marquis. "It's not right for me to tell you first, I suppose, but the fact is, sir, you have a son who was adopted by the man Smollett, and brought up as his own child. Father Stanfield," he hurried on, as the preacher registered dumb amazement, "this interview is becoming more and more painful to me, and I must get to the point. Please believe that for reasons it would be useless to dwell upon, my situation is fully as desperate as Mr. Marquis's because of what happened with 'The Hog in the House.' I must ask you again to sign that paper, or I will not keep the information about your past to myself. I will," said our hero, keeping his eyes steadily away from the preacher's face, "give it to Milton Jaeckel, with consequences to your reputation and the prosperity of your Fold which you can readily imagine."

The preacher sat without sound or motion for a while, then said thoughtfully, "This boy—where's he at?"

"Cape Town," said Andrew. "The Smolletts went to South Africa to live in 1921. Mrs. Smollett became a widow last January. She came here for an operation on her eyes. But you probably know all that."

"I didn't know nuthin'," said Stanfield, "'ceptin' that Gracie was in Boston. Buchanan Hotel, eh? Reckon I'll talk to her."

As he reached for the telephone Andy said hastily, "I'm sure you don't want me intruding any longer. If you'll just be good enough to sign that paper and let me have it—"

"Oh, yes. The paper." The Shepherd looked at the document in his lap as though it were a strange cat that had crept there. "You comin' at me with too many things at once, son. How was all that about Milton Jaeckel? Guess I wasn't payin' no mind."

Feeling as though he were making a second effort to ignite a sodden firework, Andrew repeated his proposal. The preacher regarded him with an increasingly quizzical, disturbing gaze.

"Son," said Father Stanfield when he ended lamely in the middle of a sentence, "what is it in this world that you want so very bad?"

Our hero suddenly wished that he had slept and eaten before coming to this critical scene. Clearly, he was weak; Stanfield's simple question affected him like a surprise blow to the stomach. Actually trembling in all limbs, he mustered language to say,

"That's beside the point. But if you must know, my whole happiness depends on this matter. That's why I'll seize any weapon."

"Yer right in what you say," answered the preacher, "but not the way you think. Yer whole happiness depends on lookin' into yer soul and figgerin' out what wrong notions got you crawlin' so low. The first night you sat alongside o' me at the Old House, eatin' soup, Reale, I liked you. I ain't never felt no different, spite o' all the hocus-pocus I seen you mixed up in, but yer sick, boy, you got the sickest spirit I seen in a long time. This is one rotten big snowball of a sin you come rollin' into my presence this mornin'. I reckon you been tumblebuggin' her along fer quite a spell. She's growed big, she's jest about ready to take charge an' roll away downhill with you thrashin' around in the middle."

Andrew murmured, "That may all be, but I'd still like you to sign that paper, if you please."

"Or else we git this here big turrible exposure of me and my iniquity, eh? Why, go to it, son," said the preacher. "I intend to make public confession before the Fold, but if yer newspaper friend will git extra good outta the story, why, give it to him. What I got to bear fer my sin I got to bear, but somehow I think I done my penance in twenty years of loneliness and they ain't no harm gonna come of this turn. When the Lord hits, he hits like a hammer, and when he blesses, it's a pleasant harvest time with no rain. He sends me Gracie, and he gives me a son. All will be well. Praise Him!" Father Stanfield looked out of the window and turned his face to the sky. Andrew Reale experienced a desire to slide under the carpet unperceived.

At last the Shepherd turned and looked at him, a serene, searching look. "They ain't much I kin do fer yer spirit, though I'd sure like to. Yer a bearer of good tidin's, and under that choke of weeds in yer heart I think mebbe it ain't all bad ground." He paused for a long moment, then picked up a pen on the table beside him and signed the paper clearing Marquis. "This is the first lie I've told since I was younger'n you," he said, holding the sheet out to

Andrew. "Whatever yer after, I reckon you gotta git it afore you'll smell the sulphur and brimstone in it. God help you, son, and give you what you really need—a understandin' heart."

An observer might have deduced, seeing the strange contortions of face and body that Andrew Reale hereupon underwent, that it cost him an effort of will to reach out and grasp the paper not less than it might have required had the object been a live coal; but he took it, and fairly bolted from the Faithful Shepherd's presence.

As he closed the outer door he could not help throwing a quick glance over his shoulder; so that he carried with him down the elevator, and out of the lobby, and into the hot, noisy street, and for a longer time than the ordinary persistence of vision could possibly explain, the picture of Father Stanfield, his face aglow with happiness such as Andrew had not seen on the faces of the richest, most powerful executives of radio and advertising, sinking to his knees by the window in the streaming sunlight.

CHAPTER 26

In which our hero really reaches bottom
—and learns, like Dante, that beyond the Nadir
there lies the climb to Hope.

*B*IG WITH A PROJECT for the use of the trophy he had in-
geniously garnered, Andrew Reale rushed up to the clerk's desk in
his hotel and snatched his key and several letters; but before he
could examine the correspondence his attention was arrested by a
hand on his elbow and a sad voice saying, "Hello, Andy." He
turned to see the eminent Walter Grovill at his side, dejected and
deflated as only a jolly fat man can look who has lost much flesh.
"Didn't expect to see me this early in the morning, did you?" said
the advertiser, and added a thin sound such as a ghost might make,
giggling by itself in a haunted house. "I've been up all night with
T.M."

Andrew politely declared his delight and invited Grovill to accompany him upstairs, directing the clerk, as he left the desk, to
summon a messenger boy for him. In his suite, the ambitious
Andrew begged Grovill to forgive him while he attended to pressing business. The peaked guest dropped wearily on a couch. Andrew threw the handful of letters on his desk unread, sat down
and speedily penned the following note:

Dear Mr. Marquis:

I obtained the enclosed document from Father Stanfield this morning; not without some difficulty, as you may imagine, but here it is, and it speaks for itself. I believe you will find it useful at your directors' meeting.

If I can be of further service to you please call on me. I will remain in my rooms all day.

Respectfully,
Andrew Reale.

He sealed this message in a long envelope together with the paper Stanfield had signed, laid the packet aside, and picked up the conversation with Grovill by solicitiously observing that he did not appear in good health.

Venting many moans, the fat man recounted a number of woes with which the reader is familiar: the flight of his wife, the loss of his business partner, and the extended harrying by Marquis, for whom Grovill, one of the last of his faithful adherents, had become a beast of all burdens: adding this new information, that on the day Flame Anders had abandoned him he had succumbed to a fit later diagnosed as a mild heart attack. Regarding this lengthy catalogue of misery Andrew was sympathetic, reserving a proper curiosity as to what it all meant, here and now. The advertiser put a period to the roll-call of his afflictions at last, and proceeded thus:

"Andy, T.M. likes you. We both think you're the most promising young fellow we've seen in the radio and advertising field since—well, since Tom Leach started in my office fifteen years ago. Tom didn't do badly with me. When he walked out so stupidly, so pointlessly, he was making fifty thousand. He would have gone to fifty-five next year.

"I'm old and sick, Andy, and I need a partner like Tom. There are people in my office that I could jump up, but they're all hacks. No flair, no zip, no depth."

Andrew's heart seemed to be beating somewhere up in his throat, interfering with his respiration.

"You've got what I need, and I'm willing to pay for it—youth, knowledge, imagination, and spirit. I've come to offer you Tom Leach's job, Andy—junior partner in my firm, which will become Grovill and Reale—and I'll start you at twenty-five thousand a year."

So simply, so baldly, like a hot red sun rising out of a tropic sea, did the great ambition of Andrew Reale appear at last over his horizon as a reality. Before he could get his mouth open to frame a speech of thanks, the doorbell rang. It was a messenger boy, to whom Andrew entrusted the precious envelope for Marquis with a generous gratuity to speed the delivery. When he returned to his sitting room he found Walter Grovill pushing himself to his feet, ready to depart.

"Don't give me your answer right this minute, Andy," he said. "Think it over. None of us knows where we're at right now. T.M. has postponed cancellation of the Republic programs, at least until this directors' meeting blows over. We'd just better pray that he pulls through. Our office runs on Aurora Dawn money, Andy; all the other accounts wouldn't pay the salaries. The managers don't like us, so if anything happens to Marquis we just shut up shop, and I retire. Maybe I ought to do it anyway."

Andrew issued a stream of polite reassurances on Grovill's health which seemed to cheer the wilted fat man no little. While Andy's tongue was thus occupied with routine work, his mind weighed the advisability of telling Grovill about the Stanfield statement, but found sufficient reason to break silence wanting.

"Well, thanks, Andy," replied Grovill to the words of comfort, "but I'm not as young as I look, and heart trouble isn't like a cold in the head, you know. You might find yourself—" he interjected a giggle in a sufficiently minor mode, almost, to pass as a sob— "Andrew Reale, Incorporated, sooner than both of us think."

Scoffing away the lugubrious suggestion, Andrew accompanied

the plump dignitary to the elevator door with repeated phrases of gratitude, and promised an early answer to the flattering offer. His guest safely off, he returned to his rooms and sank giddily into the chair at his desk.

Now was the glorious summer of his content at mid-June, according to all his schemes and dreams. Carol was won; Marquis would surely remain in power; and rule of an advertising agency was his for the asking. The climb was over. Andrew Reale stood at the summit of life.

To what must we compare the vista before him? Reach into childhood memory, reader, and blow the dust off the picture of Jack, having climbed up through the very clouds to the top of the Beanstalk, looking around at the strange Giants' land into which he had come: a flat new landscape having no relation at all to the world below, and conveying no impression of altitude attained. Andrew seemed now to find himself in a swampy vastness under a sky of gray, facing a long road which lost itself far off among bleak hills. There appeared no way to turn, left or right or backward, that offered surprise, interest or pleasure, and it was evident that he must simply plod along this road until, somewhere in the distance, he died. Nothing in his life seemed green, nothing purposeful. His imagination painted in a new detail to the dismal picture: Marquis, springing like the Old Man of the Sea from the back of the tottering Grovill on to this new Sinbad, himself: a burden to be carried along the road for ever.

And now, in the exaltation brought on by the thin atmosphere of the peak of success, a tremendous event took place in Andrew Reale's life. He philosophized.

The things that Michael Wilde and Father Stanfield had said about his way of life rose in his consciousness with the regality of wisdom, except that he somehow forgot he had heard them before, and they seemed profound new perceptions of his aroused intellect. "Why," he concluded to himself, "what are we but a crowd of well-kept slaves in golden chains, wearing out our lives in a devil-dance of lying, throat-cutting, sensuality, luxury, cheating, conniving, and fooling the public?" He loathed himself and his life. He felt a desperate urge to write a book. The many pleasant and comfortable years he had known, the agreeable times that the career had given him, the boon of care-lightening amusement that he had helped to bring his countrymen by taxing his nerves in the tasks of radio: all these were erased from his memory. In this great awakening of conscience (which the moral reader may ascribe to the influence of Father Stanfield, and the practical reader to lack of sleep: here only the facts are given), he felt only the single quickening urge of the reforming enthusiast: Destroy! O for two pillars to tug down, and bring the Philistine temple of radio and advertising tumbling to ruin!

"Why," he sneered, "no wonder we are paid so much. We do the dirtiest work in the land. What self-respecting street sweeper would change places with me if he knew what I had to do for my pay?"

Bent under this admirable self-scourging, he threw his head on his hands and leaned his elbows forward upon the desk in an attitude of despair. Thus directed downward, his eyes fell on the letters he had not yet read—and on top of these he now noticed a thick envelope addressed in the hand of Carol Marquis. He picked it up, turned it over and was startled to read the following message on the sealed flap: *"Take a deep breath, Teeth dear."*

This document requires to be reproduced in full, and the historian himself is impatient as our hero fumbles with the envelope in his anxiety to tear it open, and finally strips it off the letter like a fruit peeling to read—what you will now peruse:

Darling Teeth:

I don't know how to tell you this, but straight is good enuf, I guess. By the time you read this I will probably be married to Mike Wilde. We're taking the midnite plane to Mexico . . . I know I owe you all kinds of apologies, specially for last nite . . . Honestly, I'm sorry. . . .

You'll surely think I'm the worst female alive, and you may be rite, but really, Andy dear, I do like you a terrific lot. If Mike hadn't happened, who knows what mite have been . . . but what's the use . . . I hope I won't lose your friendship, because I admire you and I know you have a splendid future in the advertising business. All your dreams you told me about will come true soon enuf, I feel sure . . . I wish I deserved to be the one to share them with you, but that's out, I suppose. I'll always be proud of you, tho. . . .

Teeth, I'm writing this in an awful hurry and I'm also trying not to hurt you but I want you to know the truth. . . . I was just a silly kid when we met. I played up to you because I wanted to see whether I could get you away from Honey Beaton. But I was really beginning to be terribly, terribly fond of you, and then . . . Mike happened. You mean a whole lot to me, Andy, tho, don't think you don't. You sort of woke me up. After knowing you I was able to really appreciate Mike—that isn't exactly what I mean . . . You understand, tho . . .

Mike says he's marrying me for my money . . . he's a beast, and I wish I weren't so absolutely mad over him . . . but he says that that's all you were trying to do, too, and so I shouldn't feel bad about you. I'm too conceited to believe that about either of you . . . anyway, I know you liked me . . . and I want to thank you for your loyalty to my Dad. You won't be sorry for that, tho . . .

There's something on my conscience that you must know, but don't ever, ever tell Dad. Teeth, I'm responsible for the whole Aurora Dawn riot . . . Mike's been coming up to the house to see me every nite, usually very late, for the past few weeks. Well, the day Stanfield's sermon came in the mail—you know, the day you left me at lunch and flew down to West Virginia—Dad came home roaring mad and showed the sermon to me at dinner, and then stuck it into his inside pocket. He was fast asleep when Mike came . . . I told Mike the story and he rolled around laughing and insisted that I get him the sermon. I know it wasn't rite, but I sneaked into Dad's room, got the envelope out of his pocket and brought it to Mike. He read it over and said it was too rich, he'd have to show it to Milton Jaeckel . . . I can't stop him from doing anything, Andy . . . he rushed out and came back with it an hour later, and I stuck it back in Dad's coat. Now what do you think of little Carol? You're probably glad you're not marrying such a friteful

265

little fool. I mean well, tho . . . and I really like me at heart . . . I know me best. . . .

Forgive me for everything, Andy, and wish me luck. You'll come across another girl like Honey who's really rite for you, and then you'll be happy that this happened. . . . You still have the nicest smile I've ever seen or hope to see, and how I wish Mike could dance the rhumba like you . . . I guess we can't have everything, tho . . . you see, I'm growing up already. Good-by now. We're honeymooning in Taxco, and then . . . whatever Mike says . . .

Always,
Carol.

P.S.—*I'll never forget the snowstorm and the rose garden.*

C.

The author must intervene, before permitting the hero to react to this vital document, to state that, although it is extremely unlikely that any description of posterity will read this account, the remotest risk must not be taken at this point; and it must here be declared plainly in defense of the American educational system of the first part of the twentieth century that young ladies like Carol Marquis were all very well versed in spelling, grammar and punctuation; and that the departures from good usage in the above epistle were deliberate misdemeanors. The reader will please consider the plight of a young lady compelled to transfer her fascination to the baldness of ink on paper in a time when the literature on which she is fed boasts emaciation of vocabulary and either flippant or burly attitudes toward romance, thus excluding her from a knowledge of the graceful ways of language suitable to her purpose. One does not expect a young lady to spend her winged days rooting in libraries. As a consequence, striving for some measure of femininity at any cost, she may be driven to bizarre violation of the rules of composition, causing the male correspondent to puzzle his head over her reasons for mutilating the mother tongue. Mystery, at least, is thereby achieved, and mystery is no small element of feminine charm, they say. All this is no explanation, but a humble guess, put forth with the utmost lack of confidence, for we are here contemplating a black riddle from which we shrank in the opening chapter, the workings of a young lady's mind.

Andrew Reale's new philosophic detachment from the vanities of radio disappeared like a dream under the rude shaking of this letter, and his first clear thought through the blood-mist of agony brought on by the thrust to the quick of his ego was, "How do I stand now?" Even as he groaned and writhed, he calculated, and the result was not unfavorable. In no way did it seem that Carol's jilting of him could disturb his advantageous position with Marquis and Grovill, which depended on his demonstrated cleverness alone; indeed, mutual chagrin might bring the soap man and himself closer, for he could not but believe that Marquis would regard askance the alliance with Bohemia. All was not lost. Only Carol was lost. Speedily reaching this view of things, our hero found it easier to breathe.

As, when the dentist, having firmly clasped his cruel forceps on the aching bicuspid, with a mighty pull wrenches it out of the mouth, the moment of unendurable pain is the moment that cures, and the exhilaration of convalescence floods in on the weary sufferer, rendering the after-pangs of the extraction a fading discomfort easily borne; so did Carol Marquis's letter bring to Andrew Reale's spirit the sharpest anguish that young men are given to know, followed soon by a curious sense of undefined relief and gladness. His first calculating thoughts had been reflexive, the cat tumbling through space and twisting to land on its feet; now, sore but upright, he surveyed his situation with brightening eyes. He was glad to see that the single misfortune had hardly damaged the pattern of his success, for, philosopher or no, he retained a workman's pride in the smooth clicking together of a plan, and a young man's horror of being dumped into confusion by a faithless girl. The question rose again: did he want what he had won?

As he paced around his room digesting these thoughts, an

electric shock of remembrance coursed through his nerves. He suddenly recalled the paper which Father Stanfield had signed, now either in Marquis's hands or on its way to them. His meditation went no further. Upon the instant his hat was on his head and the front door was closing on him with a vigorous slam.

CHAPTER 27

In which this true tale comes to an end
—whether happily or not,
the reader can best determine.

EVERY NOVEL NOWADAYS is supposed to have a purpose, not
the purpose of instructive entertainment which was the sole aim
of literature for several thousand years until it suddenly obsolesced
a few decades ago, but the purpose of correcting a specific social
disorder such as capitalism, deforestation, inadequate city planning, war or (as some authors view it) religion. All this began, it
is said, when a great French realist, Zola, discovered at the start
of the century that "Truth is on the march." It is evidently still
marching, and will continue to march as far into the future as
anyone can peer, and so it behooves literature to get into step
and move to the regulated cadence of Purpose, if it is not to be
damned for dawdling by the wayside while Truth marches away
over the horizon. Truly, we live in a gay parading epoch, do we
not? Time marches; Truth marches; Man marches; it is hardly to
be doubted that the very March hares march. Critics will justly
scan this history with the question in their minds, what is its
purpose? Sifting the light stuff of which it is made, they may
legitimately conclude that they have found the tiny gritty nugget

of a message in Michael Wilde's strictures against the trade of modeling—therefore the author begs leave to point out that this cannot possibly be the case.

Laura English lies injured in a hospital bed, true enough, but surely no one believes that every model, bruised of heart, who marries a rich man, is forthwith struck down by a delivery truck. On the contrary, to develop the aforesaid Purpose artistically, the historian would have first falsified the events so that Laura remained unharmed; he would then have portrayed her at a moment when she was swimming in the luxuries bestowed on her by her opulent husband: an exquisite gown, a rich fur wrap, gleaming silver, lush furniture, glowing jewels, rare perfumes, long, low, sleek, purring roadsters (see the fiction in any current ladies' magazine for the rest of the details); and then, by ironic touches, would have conveyed that all these treasures were as dross to her and brought no true warmth to her frostbitten heart. The very acuteness of Honey Beaton's misfortune makes her atypical. Let it be taken as understood, then, that neither the brief scene that follows nor anything else in the book is aimed to discredit the glamorous profession, modeling, or the honest agencies that buy and sell young ladies' charms. What the Purpose is comes out at the end of the chapter, and it is disappointingly simple.

Despite Stephen English's insistence that he could walk with a cane, the hospital doctor ruled that he must be trundled to Laura's bedside in a wheelchair for his first visit to her following their accident. This happy reunion took place at approximately the time that Andrew Reale slammed his door in the last chapter. It is hard to say whether Laura was more moved by the sight of her proud spouse being wheeled into her room, or English by the melancholy case in which he found her; for, though her greeting was jolly, her voice clear, if weak, and her eyes bright, she was far from being a suitable subject for fashion photography. One side of her face was bandaged, and a thickness under the coverlet in the lower part of the bed indicated plaster around a broken limb. They exchanged quiet inquiries about each other's condition until the attendant left them, when English abruptly changed his tone.

"Laura, I'm desperately sorry about what has happened," he said, "and I wish I could rid myself of a feeling that it's my fault."

His wife cast a puzzled, half-smiling glance at him. "That's a strange notion," she said. "It was just a piece of bad luck, and we'll both recover from it soon enough."

The millionaire shook his head. "I'm afraid I challenged my destiny when I asked you to marry me," he said, "and the challenge evidently has been thrown back into my face—which I can bear—but the demonstration seems to have been mainly at your expense."

"Stephen," said Laura, "the smells of a hospital depress me, too. I'm quite sure you'll forget these thoughts when we're back again in the sunshine. Everything will turn out well."

English regarded her uncertainly for several moments. "I have a very astonishing piece of news," he said. "Mike Wilde is married. He eloped last night. He telephoned me just before the event."

"Well!" exclaimed Laura, animation evident in her voice despite its lack of strength. "Who is the lady?"

"Carol Marquis," said the millionaire.

Laura started up from her pillow, and sank back immediately. She did not speak for a while, and her voice was faint when she said at last, "They're wide apart in many ways, but I think they can be happy."

"Have you no other comment?" said English.

"I think not," said Laura, her eyes on the window opposite her.

"This will make a great difference, I should imagine," said the banker, "in Andrew's plans, as you described them to me."

"But Andrew's plans can make no difference to me," said his wife.

"In this matter, Laura," said English in gentle tones, "the frankest self-searching offers the best chance of happiness."

Laura turned her head and looked into his eyes. "Dear Stephen," she said, "we are married." She held out her hand, and he reached to take it, with a hopeful smile. Their palms met. Their fingers clasped.

*　*　*

Why did Andrew Reale rush out of his room upon thinking of the Stanfield statement?

In military life, where it is maintained that men act logically, in order that committers of errors may always be compelled to explain "why they did so" ("Because I made a stupid mistake" being insufficient), it is customary for generals or admirals, in justifying a decision, to say, "Having considered factors Alpha, Beta, and Omicron and having weighed the choice between courses One, Two, and Seven, it was determined to close with the enemy and open fire"; when the admiral knows that, in truth, a dispatch was thrust in his hand, a diagram held before his eyes; his soul leaped at the prospect of the lifelong-awaited battle; and he gave the order, which everyone knew he must give. This pleasant myth of logical behavior, which lends form and ritual to martial life, is not in place in a serious history. Perhaps in the afterglow of life Andrew's wiser mind, wandering through the corridors of memory, will come upon this episode, framed and varnished by time, and, surveying it with a wry smile, will determine how the picture fits together, motive to action. But you know, good reader, that under pressure of This Minute your logical mind is usually no better than a horseman carried away by a runaway nag, worrying more about staying in the saddle than directing the course. With no tally of our hero's motives, then, let us rejoin him as he jumps from a taxicab one block from Marquis's house and proceeds cautiously up the street, keeping himself out of the angle of vision of the Marquis windows.

It was exactly an hour since he had entrusted the packet to the messenger boy. An alert, conscientious lad could have delivered it and returned to his post thirty minutes ago. Andrew remembered, however, that the courier, a tall starveling of spotty complexion, had looked glittering gratitude when he received the dollar bill intended to encourage haste. There seemed some chance that he had improvised a detour in his route by way of the nearest ice-cream store. For once, Andrew hoped for weak character in a messenger boy, and posted himself in a shadowed doorway to wait.

And soon, springing into sight around the corner, welcome to Andrew's eyes as the ace of spades to a gambler, the messenger boy came on at a trot, salving his professional conscience for the purloined half-hour with a few saved seconds. Andrew fell out of ambush on the astounded Mercury as he was mounting the Marquis steps. A few words of explanation, another dollar bill, the envelope was his, and the bony runner was fading down the street in the direction of a cafeteria. Your reader of the dialectical materialist persuasion will call this a last-minute but excellent touch of social irony: Marquis, the capitalist, deprived of the means to save his skin, because of the appetite of a boy insufficiently nourished under capitalism. This work needs every shred of praise it can earn, but it can accept none through false pretense; and the historian must confess that, though merit may lie in current ideas for remaking the social fabric, he believes that boys will be voracious and dilatory under any economic system whatever.

It is certainly true, all the same, that on so slender a pivot as the conscience of a messenger boy did the destinies of Andrew Reale and Talmadge Marquis turn. In this way was our hero enabled to halt the Moving Finger, and lure it back to cancel half a line regarding his conduct in the affair of Father Stanfield. Could we take down the Recording Angel's ledger for 1937 and see the account of this matter, it might read so:

"Sent Mr. Marquis the statement, thus assuring himself a fortune.
"For reasons not specified, reconsidered, tore the statement to fragments on the very steps of Mr. Marquis's home, and scattered them

to the winds. Did this while sound in mind, knowing that he was probably destroying Mr. Marquis's power and with it his own excellent chances for becoming very rich very quickly.

"Here ends the tale of Andrew Reale in radio."

If the Recording Angel wrote it so, he is much more kindly than the poets would have him, for in calling Andy "sound in mind" he generously overlooked a fact that must be told here. The incomprehensible Andrew Reale, having ripped to pieces and thrown away a golden future with his own hands, capered off down the street, shouting, loud enough to bring wondering old ladies to their windows, "Free! Free!"

*　*　*

Softly, friend; tread softly, pray. A hospital corridor echoes to careless footfalls. We follow Andrew, who no longer capers, just a little farther: to the bedside of Laura English. Here is the room with the clean little card over it bearing that strange new name. Andrew has permission to draw aside the white curtain and visit for a few minutes. Let us stop at the door.

Advised by telephone who her visitor is, Laura is still making pathetic efforts to improve her appearance when he comes in. She has brushed her beautiful hair out over her shoulders, straightened her negligée and even put on lipstick with a shaky hand that has left an inartistic red smudge in one corner of her mouth. Her hands are smoothing her hair as Andrew enters; hurriedly she drops them and folds them on the coverlet before her. Not looking around, she attempts a cordial expression of welcome when she hears the curtain drawn aside, but the words catch in her throat, and she has to turn her face to him silently. Her eyes are bright and tearful, and she smiles—but not such a smile as she wore in church, nor such a one as she displayed last April on the cover of *Frivol* Magazine; the kind of smile, in fact, that no human being has ever seen on her face except Andrew. Our hero, however, observes only the bandages and the evidence of a broken bone; he wavers, and falls on his knees beside the bed, and buries his head in her arms, and weeps aloud. Laura hesitates for just a moment, then presses his head to her bosom, quite as though they were young lovers still. "Oh, don't, Andy, dearest, don't," she says. "The doctor tells me it will only leave a little scar—and my leg will be well so soon! Don't cry, my darling, I can't bear it. It's so awful to see a man cry!"

Our heroine speaks to the point. Need we spy further on Andrew in his weakness? Draw the curtain.

What history except a true one could come to a climax with the hero on his knees and in tears? A hundred years ago the author might have capped the scene with Scripture: "The Lord is nigh unto the broken-hearted, and will save those of a contrite spirit," but this work is addressed to a generation for whom the Lord has been satisfactorily explained away as a cosmic projection of the father-urge. As for the Absolute Unknowable Life Force, what does it care about broken hearts and contrite spirits? It runs the universe unknowably and evolves new life-forms through natural selection, and there an end.

This is the place to state the Purpose, and now the historian is in for it, for he has to admit that he has no genuine message, but only a moral, to offer. What a shoddy substitution! Your literary message throws an arc light into the far future, whereas a moral casts a candle-glow on a small area of the present. A message boldly claims for the novelist fields heretofore usurped by politicians, economists, scientists, social philosophers, and theorizers of every description; a moral bashfully remains within the old limits of common human experience. The author bows to all the rebukes he is going to get for his moral, and wishes it were not too late to rebuild the tale around some new, inspired communication.

However, here it is, for I mean to be as plain as Aesop's compilers were. You will recognize it; it is only the Pardoner's Latin platitude, threadbare half a thousand years ago:

Radix malorum est cupiditas,

or, to revert to the plain English of the first sentence of this book,

The road to happiness does not necessarily lie in becoming very rich very quickly.

Stating the Purpose thus in black-and-white instead of implying it subtly is another offense, but the author has to risk it. Otherwise, in these days when the Muse is supposed to incite Iliads instead of recording them, readers might have believed that it was, "Radio and advertising are the curse of our age." Friends, the old punch-and-judy show of Folly has been played against a thousand backgrounds, and the curtain will yet rise and fall on a thousand more. There are good people and bad people scattered through all the paths of the living. I should not care to debate out the proposition, "Resolved: that authors are better men than advertisers." The author has but one excuse for writing about other people's follies, the classic apology of the selfsame Pardoner:

"For though myself be a ful vicious man,
A moral tale yet I yowe telle can."

EPILOGUE

In which the author takes discreet cognizance
of the maxim, "The tale may have a moral,
but plain folks follow the story."

THE PLAY is played out, but see, there is an afterpiece. The curtain is going up once more.

Stephen English sits in the spacious, high-ceilinged library of his apartment, reading a letter. The room looks out on the wide East River with its inglorious traffic of ferries, barges, tugs, dredges, and the small craft that swarm in an inland waterway. Such as it is, the view is costly to apartment dwellers, containing as it does a genuine, if jagged horizon and almost a quarter-sphere of hazy sky. The dark wooden walls of the room are filled with books, most of which are beautiful enough to grace shelves for the effect on the eye rather than on the brain. Irregularity of placing and traces of wear in the bindings indicate that this is an unusual rich man's library in which ink and paper, as well as calfskin and buckram, come under scrutiny.

The banker is one of those lucky people whom advancing age changes by a gradual, not unsightly lessening of substance, going first to leanness and at the last to boniness, rather than by the sag and spread of all the lines of his physique. The date-line of the letter he is reading shows the year 1945, but, except for a somewhat spare appearance and a more general gray in his hair, he scarcely looks different from the bridegroom who was joined to Laura Beaton eight eventful years ago. The letter is from that same paragon among human females, and the last page, to which he is even now turning, runs so:

The doctor says it will be in mid-September. Andrew, junior, has worn me to a shadow already. How I will cope with two children I can't tell, and that brings me to the point. If the child had your character and sweetness he'd be no trouble—and just on the chance that naming him after you might help, I'd like your permission to call him Stephen English Reale. Don't ask me how I know it will be a boy. Andy's family never have girls, it seems, or so he maintains.

Dear Stephen, I'm being flippant about something that means very much to me. I have never known anyone as decent and as generous as you, and I expect I never shall. Even the man in Bleak House, *which you read to me in the hospital (was the appropriateness a complete accident?) only released a girl who was engaged to him—and I thought he was impossibly good! Whenever the war depresses me too much about human beings, I remember you and instantly feel better. —Please write soon, telling me that you consent. I will love the baby more if I can call him Stephen.*

Andy is out with the animals, as usual, but he asked me to greet you for him. He's very well, and I pray that this letter finds you so. When will you come to stay with us?

Affectionately,
Laura.

The millionaire dropped the letter on a small table beside his armchair, and stared with visionary eyes at a high-backed old chair on the opposite side of the room, in which his wife had sat on that important night, their delayed wedding night, the first night after her release from the hospital. The dimness which Time casts over most scenes of the past it had somehow neglected to supply in this instance, for the amount of imaginative effort necessary to enable English to see his former wife still sitting there was astonishingly small—a little less, in fact, and the memory could properly be called a hallucination. There she was, in a plain black gown which emphasized her pale charm as a black velvet case does that of a pearl, erect and prim in the chair, her hands firmly gripping the ornamental knobs of the arm rests, her face impassive as it had been in the church, her eyes following his movements like the eyes of a dog watching a stranger. The cinema of memory reviewed, with painful accuracy, the desultory, unmeaning conversation that had preceded his sudden, determined statement: "Laura, I wish to have our marriage annulled." Then came the stormy part, the long protests from her, the brief rejoinders by himself, while (how clearly!) he saw a wild rising hope wrestle with a sense of duty in his maiden wife's spirit. Once again he felt his own hopes flag and perish under the reiterated vehemence of her objections, obviously the product of determination to do right, and nothing more. Once again he brought himself to mention the freedom of Andrew Reale, and to inquire whether she did not wish her marriage vows unsaid as they were unconsummated. The wraith in the high-backed chair responded as always: with a weak unfinished sentence, with shamed silence, and with a flood of wretched tears, her yellow hair falling about her bowed head, the new red scar vivid on her cheek and neck.

Stephen English sighed and shook his head. The scene ran out. All the incidents that followed belonged in the Ever-after which the storytellers never record, his memory being no better. He picked up a leather writing-portfolio and a pen from the table and commenced to write:

Dear Laura,

By now I am almost an old man, and many things are plain to me that were once obscure, but I have yet to find out just what virtue there abides in giving, when it is the only possible course for a man to follow. It seems to me that I have never been charitable, for charity is the privilege of those with limited means, or kind, for kindness is admirable only when unkindness exists as a profitable alternative. I cannot accept the honor of being Stephen English Reale's godfather

279

as though it were my due for any act of mine. If you and Andrew
wish to be so gracious out of friendship, I will accept the favor with
gratitude. The Roman, Marcus Aurelius, whose ideas seem increas-
ingly sensible to me as I grow up, says, "It is possible to be happy—"

here the banker broke off, crossed out the reference to the philosopher, and then crumpled the whole page quickly and started
a new one:

Dear Laura,
How good it is to hear from you! Of course, call him Stephen
English if he arrives a He, and I'll come to stand godfather, if you'll
have me. All goes well. I am immersed in trivial business, as always—

the millionaire stopped again, gazed out of the window for several
minutes, and then absently put the writing materials aside. His
right hand reached to the shelf beside him and took down a worn
copy of Marcus Aurelius's *Meditations*. As he placed the book on
his lap it fell open to a much-thumbed page, in the middle of
which a sentence was underlined in ink: *"It is possible to be*
happy, even in a palace." English took up his pen and wrote in
the broad margin beside it, "5/27/45. Perhaps. Time appears to
be running short."

*   *   *

It is a literary custom today to leave one's characters on the last
page still breathing hard from the climactic action, with no hint
of what becomes of them thereafter, the reader being free to fill
in the aftermath on the principle of aesthetic inevitability; but
since the author has already talked along into an epilogue, he may
as well tell exactly what has happened to the people of his story,
giving it the merit of completeness to atone a little for its deficiencies.

Talmadge Marquis emerged from the directors' meeting chas-
tened and humbled, but not deposed. By the time the soap man
faced the fire of criticism the situation had a tone of anticlimax,
for celebrated causes evaporate quickly in our land; and, after un-

dergoing the disagreeable experience of having all his personal policies discussed in his presence as though they were the vicious habits of an animal that might have to be destroyed, he escaped with no more serious damage than the appointment of one of the managers as supervisor of advertising policy, with the understanding that Marquis was never more to exercise authority in such matters. The burden was given to the oldest manager, who died within a year, whereupon Marquis quietly restored himself into his old ways, unopposed by English, who was preoccupied with a crisis of another corporation. To this day, therefore, the many Aurora Dawn programs enjoy his unique administration, and those who observe him with scholastic detachment have despaired of his acquiring, at least in this incarnation, sufficient Being to overcome the phenomenal deficiency with which he began.

As for Father Stanfield, after "The Hog in the House" he desired to give up radio broadcasting, but Chester Legrand induced him to continue without commercial sponsorship as a matter of public service. The Shepherd's popularity soon brought on a number of imitators, who were not finicky about merchandising the gospel; none of them, in fact, was far above the level of coarse fraud. In their efforts to gain his audience they all had recourse to synthetic confessions spiced with sensational sins, because the radio production experts had eventually analyzed Stanfield's success in the formula, "Sex, sugar-coated with religion." The breaches of good taste began to border on the scandalous. Stanfield left the air in disgust, and the Federal Communications Commission finally issued a ban on "confession" programs, to the general relief, but causing anguished concern for the future of free speech in America on the part of several advertising executives. Stanfield, united with Gracie and a strapping Cockney-speaking son, lives on at the Fold in great peace, in an Indian Summer of life that brings increasing abundance about him each year.

To the author's knowledge, Mr. and Mrs. Michael Wilde abide

in wedded harmony, although Milton Jaeckel and other gentlemen of his trade have lately reported their appearance in different places, each with a partner other than the one contracted for by ritual. Mrs. Wilde's name in particular is linked, with a frequency almost passing coincidence, to that of the leader of an eminent jazz band; but if gossip were truth, whose marriage could be called happy? The Wildes are an up-to-date couple, and have surely extended latitude of companionship to each other in the enlightened manner of our better levels of society.

No such tales are told about Andrew and Laura, possibly because they have disappeared into the obscurity of ordinary people, beyond the focus of Mr. Jaeckel's art. Shortly after their marriage, Laura's ailing uncle, Tom Wilson, passed on, leaving his prosperous ranch to his niece. The blissful couple, holding their happiness more dear because they had so nearly lost it through their errors, went to New Mexico with Mrs. Beaton for a holiday on the ranch, in the common impulse to withdrawal from the world that animates the first months of a true union. They stayed on as Andrew, with all his radio plans temporarily at a standstill, turned his attention to the finances of the ranch, an enterprise mainly devoted to the raising of the Hereford variety of cattle. A year passed in this way, then another, and the return to New York became less and less an imminent reality, and finally ceased to be even a project; country existence proving increasingly satisfying and comfortable to the Reales as well as to the repatriated Mrs. Beaton.

The pacific way of life into which they settled suited Laura, who gradually acquired a charming roundness, quite different from the modish angularity into which she had disciplined herself during her photographic career. Her face was slightly furrowed in a few years by the care of an exceptionally spirited son, but her scar became hardly visible, and she soon ceased to limp at all. No observer of this blooming woman today can fail to notice a fullness of figure auguring the nativity of Stephen English

Reale, and certainly the connoisseurs of salable beauty in the Pandar Model Agency would be horrified to see her in such a decline.

Andrew Reale has reformed less than one might hope, considering the change in his way of life. The advertisements of his prize bulls in the *Hereford Journal* still disturb orthodox cattlemen. He was the first client to order and pay for a back cover in four colors on that staid publication. He also confronts Laura, once every half year or so, with a scheme for raising a new kind of crop, or a new breed of beasts, which will make them millionaires in a few years. Laura's quiet good sense has outweighed these explosive enthusiasms ever since an early disastrous venture into melons, and Andrew himself has acquired a sort of wry self-knowledge which enables him to wait a week for the fulmination of a new idea to die down before he regards it seriously. Nature, he finds, cannot be cajoled like a soap manufacturer. He has had the good sense, in the main, to leave the actual working of the ranch to Tom Wilson's old overseers, confining himself to the work of sales, purchases and administration; thus, things go well. His first moral revulsion against his early career has passed away, and he sometimes even thinks nostalgically of the adventurous tension of his broadcasting work, although he could not be persuaded to leave the ranch. Literature has suffered a blow, in that he never wrote his book exposing radio, after all; in the process of gaining Laura, he mislaid the reforming urge. Of making such books, however, there is no end, and literature may be consoled with the reflection that it might have suffered a greater blow had he written it.

Into such domesticity do the heroes and heroines of comedy settle after the curtain falls. Shorn of the shining plumes with which they soared and swooped through their high adventures long ago, earthbound and undistinguishable among the mass of quiet folk, they move placidly through the chores of their days.— Are you disappointed, good friend? Would you have had the boy and girl of our fading fable preserved forever in the bright amber of a first nuptial kiss? Come, I will be faithless to the conspiracy of my craft long enough to tell you a tremendous secret: the sweet of life comes when the couple emerges from the church door into a true marriage, with its small troubles and joys, a thousand years of which would not yield enough stuff for one page of the storyteller. May you and I be granted no worse portion while we walk under the sun.

And Aurora Dawn? Why, reader, you know as well as I that the images of the pink, half-naked goddess decorate our land more prominently than ever at this writing. It is a pity, really, that they are all wrought in perishable paper or paint, and that sculpture is not useful in advertising; for it is amusing to consider that men of after-ages, digging up these multitudinous images among our ruins, might engage in a hundred-years' controversy to decide what manner of deity this was that we worshiped.

O11